The
Guru Next Door

What Readers Say About
The Guru Next Door

"This charming and thought-provoking book tells the story of a young girl named Annie and her journey to adulthood, independence and happiness. It also provides a glimpse into the world of Bruce Di Marsico, creator of the Option Method for undoing the beliefs that lie beneath our unhappy feelings. A worthy and worthwhile read." — Michael Neill, author of *You Can Have What You Want* and *Feel Happy Now!*

"When I first began to read *The Guru Next Door: A Teacher's Legacy*, it quite literally brought me to tears. Wendy Dolber has truly captured the essence of the experience of knowing Bruce Di Marsico, my late husband, through this intimate story. I was enchanted by Annie, a young girl, through whose eyes and heart the reader travels; discovering that she *is* loved and that she *can* be happy no matter what is happening around her. Unconditional love can come to us in many unexpected forms. For Annie, as it was for many who knew Bruce Di Marsico, it was the unlikely guru next door. Thank you, Wendy, for giving more people an opportunity to be touched by his sweet wisdom through this warm and powerful story." — Deborah Mendel, author of *Be Happier Now — Your Personal Roadmap to a Life of Joy and Happiness: The Option Method Workbook*

"*The Guru Next Door: A Teacher's Legacy* is a fascinating study of personal tragedy and personal empowerment. Wendy Dolber paints believable pictures of life's circumstantial difficulties and uses the teachings of Bruce Di Marsico, the creator of the Option Method, to disarm them one by one. Option is not a method of convincing yourself that 'everything will work out for the best' and maintaining a positive attitude. Instead, Wendy shows how you can choose happiness in any situation by questioning the fundamental beliefs behind unhappiness and ultimately deciding to be happy. She shows how such questions as 'Why are you unhappy?' when asked without judgment or assumption can lead to powerful life-changing self-knowledge." — Wah!, author of *Dedicating Your Life to Spirit*

"Since I first encountered the Option Method a couple of years ago, I have often wished I could have had a chance to talk with Bruce Di Marsico. Reading *The Guru Next Door: A Teacher's Legacy* was the next best thing. In it, Wendy Dolber brings Bruce's ideas to life, weaving his words into a narrative that illustrates in action the principles behind the Option Method. The book illustrates beautifully the powerful idea that happiness is the freedom to always tell the truth to yourself, without judgment or regret, and that this freedom is possible for everyone." — Robert Holliday, Option Method student

". . . a real gift . . . You captured the man, his zest, his verve, his precious unique intensity . . . a terrific way for people to become acquainted with Option. Your exploration of his religious feelings and his extraordinary conception of God and happiness will bring further clarity to this dimension of his work." — Frank Mosca, Ph.D., Option Method practitioner and author of *Joywords: An Introduction to the Option Method*

"This inspiring story of Annie and her enlightened mentor Bruce projects a powerful message for all of us that we can learn to be happy regardless of the situation in which we find ourselves, and that this happiness is available to us by our own choice. You will think about the characters of this spellbinding book for a long time after you finish reading it and every time you do, it will bring a smile to your face!" — Jana Bodorova, New Jersey

"It is now almost thirty years since I had the pleasure of sitting in at a handful of group Option Sessions with Bruce Di Marsico. When I heard word that Wendy Dolber was writing a story that promised to resurrect the spirit of a man who I consider to be one of the wisest spirits to appear in the West since the Renaissance, I was naturally skeptical. What manner of alchemy would it take to bring such a bright light back to life? Through a labor of great imagination all I can say is — damn, she did it!" — Ken Stateman, former publisher: *The Mind's Eye*

"I was fortunate to be a member of the last two-year class taught (just before his death) by Bruce Di Marsico, creator of the Option Method. But now, thanks to Wendy Dolber and her book, *The Guru Next Door: A Teacher's Legacy*, readers will be able to follow along as Bruce teaches and unravels the deceptively simple Option Method principles, to the great joy and benefit of Annie, the young 'heroine' of the book. I have long been convinced that Wendy Dolber would be a major force in carrying on Bruce's Option legacy, and *The Guru Next Door* . . . is a wonderfully effective confirmation of that early conviction. The setting of a young girl first 'listening through the fence' then later sitting with Bruce as he questions her through her fears and frustrations, perfectly patterns the method Bruce used in his classes. Under Bruce's compassionate questioning, the Option Method emerges, seemingly with no effort. You'll discover, along with Annie, a powerful, life-affirming Method that is so simple, even a child can do it! So if you've been racing around, clutching for 'something' to calm your fear and anxiety, *The Guru Next Door* . . . is a must read!" — Raymond Gombach, Option Practitioner and Workshop Leader

"Based on the life and writings of a real person whose work has inspired millions of people to be happier, *The Guru Next Door: A Teacher's Legacy* provides a unique perspective on the teachings of Bruce Di Marsico from one of the people who knew him best." — Mandy Evans, author of *Emotional Options and Traveling Free: How to Recover from the Past*

"Wendy Dolber has been striving to make the teachings of Bruce Di Marsico accessible to the general public for many years. In *The Guru Next Door: A Teacher's Legacy*, part self-help manual, part allegorical saga, she has lovingly presented the warm and vibrant life force that was Bruce, seen through the eyes of a lonely, scared child searching for happiness amid the chaos of her dysfunctional family unit. In this tumultuous and increasingly more uncertain world we live in, Bruce's legacy has never been more needed. Wendy has been a tireless proponent of his simple yet profound treatise that the vessel of happiness resides within each of us, just waiting to be uncorked. I feel a glowing pride in my sister who has unswervingly performed this yeoman's task of bringing the Guru to our doors." — Pamela S. Dolber

"Wendy Dolber has done a remarkable job of weaving Bruce Di Marsico's original teachings about the truth of happiness and unhappiness into a fictional life story about a young, troubled girl named Annie. In this story, Bruce, depicted as he was in real life, is a constant, supportive force for Annie as he loves and accepts her as she is. Bruce offers Annie the greatest gift of all: the truth that we always have the power to choose happiness, under any conditions, if we want to. Wendy, thank you for sharing more of Bruce with all of us, who never cease to benefit from his amazing creation of the Option Method." — Melissa Ford & Karen Taylor, Option Method teachers

"A fascinating, heart-opening book!" — Dr. Joe Vitale, author of *The Attractor Factor*

The
Guru Next Door
A Teacher's Legacy

Wendy Dolber

 Dialogues in Self Discovery LLC
Montclair, New Jersey

Excerpted writings of Bruce Di Marsico reprinted with permission. Excerpts from Raymond Gombach's eulogy copyright (1995), printed with permission.

First printing 2008

Printed and bound in the United States of America

ISBN: 978-1-934450-00-0

Library of Congress Control Number: 2007901394

Cover design by Jim Zaccaria Design

Cover photo by Della M. Huff

Author photo by David Eric Photography

Interior design by Williams Writing, Editing & Design

ATTENTION CORPORATIONS, UNIVERSITIES, COLLEGES, AND PROFESSIONAL ORGANIZATIONS: Quantity discounts are available on bulk purchases of this book for educational, gift purposes, or as premiums for increasing magazine subscriptions or renewals. Special books or book excerpts can also be created to fit specific needs. For information, please contact Dialogues in Self Discovery LLC, 41 Watchung Plaza, Suite 153, Montclair, New Jersey 07042, 973-714-2800.

*This book is dedicated to
the gurus all around us and the guru within us all:
always accessible, always truthful, always loving.*

Contents

Acknowledgements

Writing is a solitary experience, but I was never alone. Bruce Di Marsico, my teacher and friend who passed away in 1995, was always with me in spirit. Bruce's words fed the process from beginning to end. His elegant approach to helping others to be happy, his vision of the possibility of perfect happiness for everyone, his unconditional love created a rich backdrop for the story of a troubled girl and a gifted teacher. I thank you, Bruce, for sharing yourself with the world so fearlessly and effectively.

I never could have written this book without the support of friends, family, writers, editors, and my readers. First, Deborah Mendel, Bruce's wife: thank you for entrusting me with Bruce's writings and for reading the manuscript and confirming that I got it right (at least from our perspective). Raymond Gombach, you were my first reader and my stalwart supporter above all others all these years. I remember recently when I was questioning myself yet again about the approach, you said to me, "Just get it out there!" I love you for that and for permission to use your wonderful eulogy. Susan O'Brien, my fellow yogini: you were my first "civilian" reader who had never heard of Option Method. Susan and my friends Ariana Hoffman and Jana Bodorova, you all gave your time to critique my efforts, and I am completely grateful. A very special thanks to Dr. Lucy S. Tyler, who painstakingly corrected my typos and grammatical errors. To Christina Baker Kline, for your thoughtful editing advice. To the writer's club, for your open, honest feedback. To friends in the Option community: Marvin Beck and Roe Di Bona, for your thoughtful comments and rigorous upholding of Option principles; Mandy Evans, for your generous trust and sparkling encouragement; Frank Mosca, for reading the book so quickly and for your generous praise; Karen Gerritsen, for your generous editorial insights; Ken Stateman, Lydia Becker, Brady Bevis, for your support and passion for this project; John Salacan, for your love and support. A special thanks to my Option students, especially Rob Holliday — you are truly an inspiration. To my dear sisters, Pamela Dolber and Leslie Webster, for your unconditional love and respect and for always being there for me. And, of course, Charlee, the Boston terrier, who reminds me every day that the world is made for leaps and bounds.

Introduction

The Guru Next Door: A Teacher's Legacy is a fictional work based on the life and teachings of Bruce M. Di Marsico (1942-1995), my teacher and close friend. In the late 1960s, Bruce created the Option Method to help people to be happy. While Bruce held private sessions and trained Option Method practitioners for decades, he was not well-known to the general public. This anonymity was by design. Bruce wanted to spend his life helping people to be happier. He preferred to live a quiet life, with plenty of time for contemplation and writing. He wrote extensively on the philosophy and application of the Option Method for his students' use and taped many lectures and sessions. But until recently relatively few people have had access to his voice. Through this book, I wish to broadcast Bruce's voice to the world.

My intent is to share my experience of the essence of the man and the thinking behind his profound teachings. I have woven some of his writings and teachings into the fabric of this book, often using the actual events of his life and sometimes creating situations, such as conversations, lectures, and sessions. Bruce's actual writings float through the book in italics or in quotes. Otherwise, I have taken the liberty of putting words in his mouth as I imagine he would have spoken. I could have written this as a straight biography, but it would not have served my purpose. Nor would Bruce have liked it. He was never one to dwell on his own history.

Some people will read this book because they are interested in the Option Method and want to learn more about the thinking behind it. Some people have heard about Bruce Di Marsico and want to know more about him. This book can even be considered a manual for practicing the Method. But the book is also the story of a young girl's search for happiness and can be simply enjoyed on that basis.

Annie, the main character and narrator, is fictional, and the people in her life, except Bruce, are fictional. I loved using Annie to tell Bruce's story because he loved children so much and had a special relationship with them. I never saw anyone respect children as much as he did. In his presence, children seemed to become serene, wiser, perhaps knowing they were in the presence of someone who really listened to them and trusted them to understand. Bruce spoke to the child within us all. His words reached a place of trust and innocence, and they came from a place of unconditional love.

Annie's interactions with Bruce are fictional and not meant to reflect my life, except for three things. Option Method is the cornerstone of my worldview and continues to have a profound effect on my thinking and my happiness since the day I first heard Bruce's voice. I was the person who stood at Bruce's bedside at the moment of his death, with my hand over his heart as it took its last beats. And I am the person who received Bruce's writings from his wife, Debbie, my best friend. For safekeeping. I asked her if it would be all right if I did something with them. This is what I did, for one thing. This is for you, Debbie, and all the people whose lives were changed forever as a result of Bruce's teaching. I hope you like it.

Wendy Dolber
Montclair, New Jersey

The
Guru Next Door

Prologue
Cor Super Ratio —
Heart Above Logic

*A*nnie, December 8, 1995

People were waiting in line to get into the memorial service for Bruce Di Marsico. There were so many mourners that the funeral directors had opened the seldom-used "overflow" room across the hall from where the service would take place. I had been to the funeral home the night before helping to get things ready. I had seen the place where the black marble urn with his ashes would go — the urn his wife had picked out of the catalog. I had helped arrange the quickly collected pictures among vases of fresh flowers. There was one of him taken five years ago in Atlantic City, a stock hotel publicity photo taken with two leggy showgirls. Another showed him as a very young man sitting under a tree at the seminary, lost in thought but somehow still connected, as if at any moment he would suddenly look up and say, "So, how can I help you?" — a question he seemed to have invented.

Other photographs chronicled his life within the close circle of friends. There were shots of them together in Mexico, Jerusalem, Puerto Rico, New York City, and many more of him alone, camped out as he so often was in his backyard, cigarette in hand, with pen and notebook, and Pepsi with lots of ice. And there were shots of the later years, with new props — fanciful walking sticks supporting a still robust but fading man, followed by sleek oxygen tanks and aluminum

1

canes for the bad days, but always that expectant look, that willingness to stay up all night talking if it would help someone clear a path toward a happier life.

I had come late hoping to get lost in the crowd. I was content to be in the overflow room. This was going to be an emotional experience for me. I had known Bruce for most of my life and even though our relationship was unusual, it had been one of the most important in my life so far. I would be much more comfortable listening through the loudspeaker they had set up. How appropriate, considering how much time I had spent over the years eavesdropping on Bruce's conversations. We had lived in the house next door to Bruce and his wife from the time I was born — when my mother and father were still together, then afterwards, when Dad left for good and Nana moved in. Even as a young child, I found Bruce fascinating. My mother once told me that the first time I saw him, when I was just nine months old, I threw my arms wide open and smiled a huge gurgling smile. In nice weather, she used to sit with me in our backyard, she in her lawn chair, and me in my playpen. If I caught sight of Bruce in his yard or on his back porch, I'd bounce up and down until my mother picked me up and took me over to say hello.

When I was old enough to be allowed to play outside by myself, I would sneak over to Bruce's house and play in his yard. Often when he was sitting outside writing or puttering in the garden, I would go over and plop myself down beside him. His wife would bring out cookies and lemonade, and Bruce would read me little snippets of what he was writing, words I didn't really understand, but I loved the warm weightlessness of his tenor voice and the way he talked to me as if I were important. If my grandmother noticed me there, she would always come and get me. No matter how many times Bruce told her it was okay, she insisted I was bothering him. I think it probably would have been okay with Mom, but she was no match for Nana, who ruled the roost whenever Dad wasn't around.

So as a young child, I created more and more strategies for insinuating myself into Bruce's life in the most unobtrusive way possible, including hiding on his property. I watched him constantly. The window of my bedroom faced his house. The first thing I would do each morning was go to the window to see what was going on. Bruce often taught groups of students in his home, and in the warm months he would bring them out to the backyard to talk or sit on the porch. They always migrated to the kitchen later in the evening and talked long into the night around the kitchen table. If it was a quiet evening, as it often was on our secluded block, I could hear parts of the conversations. I loved falling asleep in my bed hearing the sound of Bruce's voice from across the way.

The minister's voice came over the loudspeaker, describing Bruce's life, how he had grown up in New Jersey and wanted to be a priest, how he had eventually left the seminary to pursue psychotherapy, how he had developed his own approach called the Option Method right around the time I was born, 1970. How he had eventually left the trappings of his doctorate behind and taught the Method to lay practitioners. How he had wanted to create a system where anyone could help themselves and others to be happier. "Some of you have given me your favorite of Bruce's writings. I'd like to read one from Annie," the minister said.

At the sound of my name, I sat up a little straighter and looked quickly from side to side to see if anyone was looking at me. No one was, but I did recognize some of the people in the room. I had seen them at Bruce's house for years. They probably would have drawn a blank if asked who Annie was. But I bet many would remember if someone said, "That's the little girl next door who always seemed to appear in Bruce's life from out of nowhere. She's all grown-up now."

The minister read, *"To enter into a new life, which is in our sense spiritual and miraculous, it is possible to do by choice."* I knew the words by heart. It was the first line of a kind of poem Bruce had written one summer thirteen years ago, when I was twelve. By that time, I had became more and more disobedient when it came to "bothering"

Bruce, which became easier as our household increasingly revolved around my mother's emotional ups and downs. *"We can choose to live a miraculous and spiritual life,"* he had written. None of the adults in my life talked this way. These were ideas that swirled around Bruce all the time, like a gentle whirlwind that from time to time would envelop me and transport me to a place where I could see myself and my life in a completely different light.

I learned later that that gentle whirlwind spun off into a breeze that made its way far into the world, that Bruce had many students who followed his Method and his teachings, that he wrote volumes about the possibility for personal happiness. That gentle breeze had blown through my troubled life — whispering an alternative view of the world where I could escape the burden of adult problems and be an innocent child again.

"To enter into a new life, which is in our sense spiritual and miraculous, it is possible to do so by choice." That summer he was there in his backyard every afternoon as I came home from babysitting or the pool or tutoring — one of my many excuses to get out of the house, to get away from the oppressive atmosphere of my depressed mother and overbearing grandmother. I would see him there under the huge oak as I careened up our driveway on my red Schwinn. If I caught his eye, I'd ask, "How's it going today?" He would look up and wave his yellow pad at me with a smile that went directly to my heart.

I'd go and sit by him, and he'd read me what he'd written:

To enter into a new life, which is in our sense spiritual and miraculous, it is possible to do by choice. One can choose a way of life and state of mind which makes it possible to receive the gifts and graces which are fruits of being in union with happiness.

Bruce's words were mind-boggling to me then, and I understood them in a completely different way than I understand them today. He made it sound as if happiness was something we could choose. I had never heard anyone say that before. In fact, the adults in my house never even spoke of happiness. That was something reserved for other people who didn't have failed marriages and bouts of sadness like the ones that settled over my mother like bad weather.

"How can we choose a state of mind?" I asked him.

"That doesn't sound like a real question," he said, smiling. "Are you really asking or are you saying it's not possible?"

I thought about that. I wasn't really asking. I had already decided it wasn't possible. I told him that.

"So how did you decide that?" he asked. "Was it a choice?"

"It doesn't feel like it," I said. "It feels like it's just the truth."

"How do you feel about that?" he asked me.

I had to stop and think about that. "I don't like it," I told him.

"So, what if," he asked, "what if you can question this so-called truth? Does that make it seem more like a choice?" I laughed. "What's so funny?" He smiled.

"I was just remembering how when I was little, I'd bend forward and grab my ankles, let my head hang down between my legs, and walk around like that so that the world was upside down and backwards," I said. "Talking to you makes me feel that way."

Then I'd go home and find my mother watching from an upstairs window. "Annie, how many times do I have to tell you, don't bother Bruce and slow down, Annie, please slow down. You don't have to ride your bike so fast." That summer, everything I did seemed like too much or not enough for my mother. I either talked too much or not enough. I hung around the house too much or spent too much time "gallivanting around the neighborhood." If I wasn't hungry, she'd accuse me of starving myself. If I cleaned my plate, she'd make a comment about overeating.

One night we had a huge fight about asparagus. She had made them every night for a week, and I was tired of them. I refused to eat one more asparagus and she refused to let me leave the table until I did. We were sitting on opposite sides of the table glaring at each other over the asparagus when I suddenly realized that nothing was holding me there. I could simply get up and walk out the door. So I did, and she locked me out of the house. I pounded on the door and rang the bell, but she wouldn't let me in. I was so frustrated that I sat down on the steps and cried for an hour.

As it got darker, I noticed the glow of Bruce's cigarette in his breezeway porch, which was directly in front of me, across our two driveways. I realized to my embarrassment that he could probably see and hear me. "Can I come over?" I said into the darkness. "Sure," he answered. I went over and sat next to him. We were silent for a while and then he asked me if I would like to hear what he was writing. He read:

"To enter into a new life, which is in our sense spiritual and miraculous, it is possible to do so by choice. One can choose a way of life and state of mind which makes it possible to receive the gifts and graces which are fruits of being in union with happiness. The essence of God is Happiness. Confess that no one has to be unhappy and do whatever you want."

"It's the upside down poem," I said.

He laughed. "I call it *Cor Super Ratio* — that's Latin for Heart Above Logic. But I like your description better." He tore the page from the yellow pad and handed it to me.

"The essence of God is Happiness," I read out loud. No one had ever spoken to me about God and happiness. I thought God belonged to other people. At my house, God was ignored or sneered at for his incompetence. What kind of God would allow concentration camps? What kind of God would allow cancer and earthquakes? And happiness? The idea that God and happiness were connected was an amazing thought. It made God so accessible — something I could understand and relate to.

But at that moment, I didn't really want to hear that no one had to be unhappy, especially me. I was the poor little girl from the broken home, whose mother was unbalanced and whose father was unavailable. Anyone would be unhappy, wouldn't they? I did like the part about doing what I wanted. In my anger, what I wanted most at the moment was to grab the nearest rock and smash it through our window. I wanted to break into my own house and sit there like a statue until my mother behaved herself. I told Bruce that. He asked me to just think about what I might want if I considered that I didn't have to be unhappy. I didn't want to consider such a thing. I wanted him to feel sorry for me, to tell me that my mother was mean.

"What if you weren't unhappy?" he asked again.

"I don't like the way she's acting," I said.

"And?"

"If I weren't unhappy, it would be like saying it's okay."

"Why would it mean that?"

"Because. If I'm not feeling bad, why should she change?"

"Why does she have to change?"

"So I don't feel bad."

"So does her behavior make you feel bad?"

"Yes, that's what I've been saying."

"And how does it do that?"

"Didn't we just go in a circle?"

He smiled. "It may seem like that when you're inside it. But it's really more of a spiral. At some point, the circle opens up, when you're ready to see the way out."

I couldn't disconnect my mother's unwanted behavior from my feeling bad, but I was beginning to imagine a possibility — that there might be another way to see things. Even at twelve, I could see that I wanted to blame her so that she would have to be the one to change. The problem was I hated the way it made me feel.

The minister continued reading:

Listen to your heart, for that is where knowledge acts.

Do only what attracts you.

Do what you feel like doing.

Cor Super Ratio . . . The Heart Above Logic.

For many years I had slept with the "upside down" poem under my pillow. For some reason it had always been my favorite piece amongst the many, many words that Bruce had shared with me over the years. I would find them in my secret hiding places around his property that he always pretended he didn't know about. He would give them to me when we spoke from time to time, and in later years I would write down things I heard him saying to others.

Look inward to see what you want to do and be glad to do it. Being obedient to your heart is not obedience — it is your life and your joy. Your whole reason for existence.

What was my reason for existence, I wondered. Here was a man who spent his life helping others to be happier. He had only lived to be fifty-three years old, and I knew the last ten years of his life had been filled with excruciating pain and serious illness. Yet he never seemed unhappy. In fact, he was often filled with joy and enthusiasm. His life seemed well-lived, complete. Where would I be when I was fifty-three? What was my reason for existence? How had my exposure to this remarkable man affected me? I realized that up until now, I had simply relied upon him to be there. I knew I could always go and ask Bruce; because he was there, there was always another way to look at things, a way out of unhappiness. Had I shortchanged myself by relying on him so much? Hadn't he always told me that I already knew everything? All he did was ask the questions, he always told me. I was the one who knew the answers and saw the possibilities.

For the next two hours, dozens of people shared their stories of how Bruce had helped them. What story would I tell? There were so many stories, so many times over so many years when he had asked me a question, or I had heard him say something or do something that turned my head around. There were so many times when in the midst of some confusion or problem, I would remember something he said. So many times when we would talk together and I would come away happier. So many times when I watched him live the lessons that he taught. So many times when he seemed to be writing about exactly what I needed to hear.

As I sat listening to the stories of Bruce's many students, friends, and family, I wondered what would happen to all the wonderful stories. What would happen, even, to Bruce's teachings, which were spread out among people's memories and within his unpublished writings. If I were to tell my story, I would want people to know Bruce as I knew him so that they could understand why I loved him so much. If I were to tell my story, I would have to go back to the beginning, to my first memory of Bruce. If I were to tell my story, it would start with the words of the child I once was, who knew a man who was happy.

Bruce, 1977

Happiness is in my heart. I can feel the glow.
Peace and love and joy complete are all I want to know.
Following the way to the sun that shines within my being —
brings me to a world of joy that forms beyond my seeing.

I like remembering my first real conversation with Bruce. If I close my eyes and concentrate, I can relive the whole scene. Any time I want to.

I'm seven and I may not live to be eight, I'm thinking. I'm supposed to be taking a nap, but I'm really hiding. Only babies need to sleep in the middle of the day. I'm not a baby. I can tie my shoes by myself, and I can dress myself too. I pick out my own clothes, even if Mommy and Nana lay out what I'm supposed to wear. They say I'm contrary and wrinkle up their noses at the sight of me in my favorite blue shorts and red-and-white-striped top. Again?

I go barefoot like any Indian princess too, and Mommy says my feet will be impossibly dirty, and Nana adds that I'll cut my foot on glass and have a big ugly scar that will ruin my chances to be a ballerina. Maybe they'll even have to cut my foot off. At the ankle. Daddy says stop scaring her and they start yelling and Daddy roars off in his car with the top down and his golf clubs in the passenger seat, like his best buddies. "He should have married them," Mom says. "Mr. and Mrs. Five Iron." It's supposed to be a joke but she doesn't laugh and when I do, she gives me that scary look and tells me, "Go take your nap," like I'm a bad girl. I have a gigantic lump in my throat, but I don't cry. We look at each other, holding our breath, our mouths all hard and mashed in. Mom takes one step toward me, and I'm up the stairs in a flash.

In bed, I squeeze my eyes shut pretending to be asleep. I even suck my thumb for a while. That's the only baby part of me left, and it's a secret. It makes me feel good, a real shot in the arm, Mommy would say. It makes the lump in my throat go away. I curl up like a shrimp with my thumb in my mouth and the cool end of the blanket under my lip until I hear a door slam. Mommy is taking a nap too. I try to go to sleep but my foot starts jiggling and my legs start going and pretty soon I'm over by the window that's right across from Bruce's house. It's begging me to come visit. I start to feel all sneaky, and the Indian princess in me takes me down the back stairs without a sound. I crouch down and hotfoot it into the bushes between our yard and Bruce's house, and wait. I'm really gonna get it now, I tell myself. I feel all tingly like that time the caterpillar went down my back.

I like sitting here in the bushes even if there are bugs. I could sit here all day and watch everyone coming and going. I could tell you stories about that. Daddy is always going somewhere, and Mommy hardly ever goes anywhere anymore. At our house, hardly anyone else comes and goes, except of course Nana, who is always here, Daddy says. Every time he turns around. That's because I'm a handful. Mommy had to quit her job just to take care of me. Even as a baby, I drove them all insane until they practically had a nervous breakdown, Nana says. Mom gave up all her chances for me.

At Bruce's house everyone is always coming and going. Bruce has oodles of friends and they're always hanging around. I can see them through their kitchen window, which is right across from our kitchen. Sometimes they stay up all night talking and eating and smoking cigarettes. At my house, we would never put up with that. Dad has all his fun away from home, Mom says. And Mom had all her fun before she had me. I'm the bane of her existence.

Just when I think the coast is clear, I can't believe my eyes. Here comes Nana. She's got shopping bags from D'Agostino's in New York City, as if we didn't have perfectly good food here in New Jersey. Now I really know my life is over. If Nana catches me outside, I'll be napping for the rest of my life. But I forgot. I am invisible. No one can see me when I'm in my secret places. I can hear Nana puttering around in our kitchen, getting lunch ready. Tuna salad on white bread and a cup of Campbell's tomato soup. And for breakfast tomorrow, she'll fix me cereal with bananas. It's Saturday so for dinner we're gonna have pork chops, potato latkes, applesauce, and spinach. Now that she's here, I know Daddy won't come home. He'll say he doesn't want pork chops for dinner, that he'll eat at the club. And Mom will sit at the table picking at her food, making Nana mad.

I think there's no one home at Bruce's so I sneak across the yard and down the concrete steps to the little room next to the cellar. The door is unlocked as usual, and the cool darkness feels good after the heat outside. I just sit there on a milk crate watching shreds of light and smelling the heated dust seep through the old wooden door. I'm surrounded by earth-caked tools and gardening supplies, dusty volleyball nets and damp concrete — familiar things. I breathe it all in and suck my thumb a little, listening.

Often when I come here I can hear things — conversations by the back door, vibrations of machinery in the workshop, the heavy sound of Bruce's car coming and going on the gravelly driveway. Today it's quiet. No one is running down the stairs, hauling in groceries from the car. There are no voices. No laughter. Just the soft whir of summer insects, pulling me to sleep. There's this big orange beanbag chair in the corner and I just have to go and try it out. I curl up in the middle of it, sinking into the crunchy sound, and before I know it I'm awakened by the worst sound I ever heard in my entire life.

I can hear my Nana calling to Bruce in her Queen Elizabeth voice.

"Hello! Sir!" she screeches from across the hedges. "May I have a word?"

The whole neighborhood must be listening and thinking, "Who is this woman?" Nana never says "Yeah" or "Hi" or "Howarya?" Nana says "Yes, hello, how are you?" in the same loud screech no matter how close or far away she is. Daddy says most people speak from their brain first, heart next and mouth last, but Nana speaks only from her mouth. I can hear Bruce answering, his voice getting softer as he crosses over to our property.

"We have lost Annie!" Nana announces from our back porch. "We are about to call the authorities, but we thought we would try to ask the neighbors. You haven't seen her by any chance? A little thing, seven years old, dark curly hair, brown eyes."

"Of course, Mrs. Rosen. We know Annie. Haven't seen much of her this summer," he tells her. He should only know.

"Well, if you see her, please let us know. Her father is off God knows where and her mother is quite beside herself." And then, to my endless shame and horror, she calls out for all the world to hear, "Annie, this is your Nana. If you can hear me, come home at once, young lady. You. Are. Making. Your. Mother. Ill."

That last part ricochets off the house and jet-propels itself throughout the entire neighborhood, into all my friends' houses, into my teacher's apartment by the YMCA, into the candy store where I always buy my peanut M&M's. I have made Mommy ill. My stomach does a complete flip-flop and my hands turn into large white clams. Fright is running up and down my spine until I am shivering, and I suddenly have to tinkle really badly. And then the most horrible thing of all happens. The door to my hideout opens. My stomach turns into a huge knot and pulls my whole body into a little ball. And that's the way he finds me, a sad twisted little lump in an orange chair. I'm a mess. I expect a big stern lecture. Maybe he'll even call the police. He pulls up a milk crate and sits down on it. He looks a little silly, to tell you the truth, but I don't want to say anything. His knees are up to his chin almost. But then he just looks at me and smiles. I have never seen a smile like that. It's as if the sun just came out in the cellar. I giggle, and he giggles too. I have never heard a grown-up giggle before. I never knew they could.

"We're both wearing the same thing," he says. At first, I don't know what he is talking about. But then I see we are both wearing blue shorts and red-and-white-striped tops. Even in his shorts and polo shirt he looks important, as if he could command a whole army from his back porch. I like the big mustache on his upper lip, and he has eyes like I had never seen before. Steady eyes that look at you and really see you. I want to hug his neck forever, but I start crying instead like a silly baby. He pulls his milk crate a little closer. "Were you having fun today?" I nod yes, feeling guilty as sin. "It's okay to have fun," he says. "I like to have fun, too."

"When I have fun, others have to suffer," I say.

"Is that what you think?"

"That's what my Nana always says."

"And what do you think?"

"I don't know," I say. "I didn't mean it."

"Of course you didn't. Fun is only fun, after all. Am I right?"

"Yes," I say, "but Nana is mad and Mommy is sick. I'm going to catch hell."

"Do you want to know a secret?" he asks.

I nod, not sure what to expect.

He leans in a little closer. He smells good, I think, like bread baking on a cold winter's day. And then he tells me, "You can't make your mommy ill. You can hide and disobey and maybe spill your milk sometimes, but that's all you can do."

I like what he's saying, but I'm not sure I'm allowed to like it. I feel a little naughty, like when I steal a cookie and stick it in my underpants for later.

"If your mommy is feeling bad, it's really not your fault," he tells me, asking, "Do you understand?"

"Yes," I nod, but I'm not really sure. I think maybe he thinks I'm a much older kid. Maybe he thinks I'm nine. But I don't want to be impolite, so I nod yes with my head but my gaze slides down my legs to the floor.

"Annie," he says, and I look up at him, at his nice eyes and his big smile. He doesn't say anything, but I know it's time to go home. Even though the cellar is a little cool, it feels all warm and cozy like my bubble bath. I don't want to leave, but he holds out his hand and we go up the steps together. I look back at him, and he smiles and says, "See you again, sometime?"

Nana is waiting for me with the hairbrush in her hand. She doesn't whack me, though. She just lays it on the table and I have to look at it the whole time I eat my tuna sandwich. I don't care, though. I know I'm not a bad girl even though later, when she's not looking, I hide the hairbrush in the hamper with the dirty clothes.

Nothing Can Make You Unhappy
— Waiting for Dad

Nothing can make you unhappy.
Nothing and no one has the power to make you
feel bad, judge bad, want bad, be bad.

My grandmother told her life story with all the paranoia and superstition of her generation. I could have grown up hearing stories of how
my great-grandfather had managed to make his way to America from
the Jewish ghetto in Manchester, England, or how my great-uncles had
capitalized on the growing Hispanic population in New York City and
built a family fortune by importing and packaging rice and beans. Nana
could have told me how my grandmother's mother had perfect pitch;
that, in fact, all the women in the family had great singing voices and
that I came from a family of intellectuals. I could have heard about
how Nana, as a practical nurse, had delivered hundreds of babies on the
lower east side of Manhattan and that my grandfather had once saved
a child from drowning in a small inlet off the Long Island shore.

Instead I heard, over and over again, the saga of the family feud
that started with Uncle Al and Uncle SW (whose name could never be
spoken). How Uncle Al was the good boy who went to school, cleaned
his room, never forgot his mother's birthday. How Uncle SW was the
family scamp, who always gave his mother heartburn. How Uncle Al

put every penny he had saved into a business and when Uncle SW turned up penniless, Uncle Al gave him a job — not just any old job but a decent job at a good wage. But Uncle SW cheated Uncle Al and tried to turn people against him, eventually stealing a large sum of money and moving far away to California. As a result, I was told, my great-grandmother had died of a broken heart. I used to look at her sepia image peering out at me from the oval photograph that hung in Nana's bedroom, eyes dark and sharp under her piled-up hair, and imagine her heart shattered into little pieces under her stiff dress, falling out of her chest, leaving a heart-shaped hole.

"Look what you've done to your mother," my Nana says, motioning to the closed bedroom door. "This chaos is killing her." I had refused to eat my lunch. How could I eat and still go swimming? You can get cramps and drown if you swim on a full stomach. I stuck to my lookout position by the back door, in my new green bathing suit and flip-flops, with my towel tucked under my arm. I have been waiting there for three hours for my father to come home and fill the little plastic pool with water from the hose. My mother is having "one of her days" when she won't or can't get up out of bed. She lies in the darkened room with a cool washcloth over her eyes hour after hour. It is supposed to be my fault.

"How you can think about swimming when your mother is lying in there is beyond me," Nana tells me. She has washed all the laundry that had been piling up for weeks, and now she is ironing everything. Back and forth goes her arm, turning out my blouses and skirts, Mom's dresses, even a gigantic tablecloth that still has tomato sauce stains on it. "She gave up her life for you," she says, as the steam hisses and sputters. "Could have been an actress."

I look up the driveway again. No sign of my father. Across the driveway, the house next door is stirring. Someone is lifting the shades and opening the back door. Pots and pans bang, a symphony floats out the windows. Then Bruce comes out and sits on the back porch with his yellow pad and pens. I move for the first time in hours to get a better look. "Can I go out and play, Nana?"

"Leave that man alone."

The truth is,

The fact is,

No one can make you believe that you can cause unhappiness.

The fact is,

The truth is,

It only looks that way to people if they believe they have the power to make unhappiness.

Consider the Possibilities

ᗰ

If we want a better world to live in, let's at least
contribute one happy person to it — ourselves!

At the local high school, it was possible to learn about doing your own taxes, or belly dancing, or ceramics, or English as a second language, or "How to Be Happy Without Changing the World." At first "How to Be Happy" didn't have as large a crowd as belly dancing, but after the fourth week, it doubled in size. Word had gotten out — the teacher was outrageous. Some said he was off his rocker. Others wondered why they hadn't heard of him before. The high school administration considered asking him to tone it down, but no one wanted to be the one to confront him. The teacher, a slightly plump, slightly balding, very solid-looking man, was sitting in a chair in the front of the classroom. *Bruce M. Di Marsico*, the program read. It was time to start, but people were still chatting, getting comfortable, standing in the doorway.

"The big mystery to all of us is why are we all so unhappy," Bruce began. And then he stopped. Everyone looked at him. The conversations stopped, the standees sat, the shifting ceased. He had their attention. "But unhappiness is not so mysterious," he continued. "Whenever we are unhappy, somewhere behind us is a voice that is saying: 'That is indeed something to be unhappy about.' This is what we call a belief, and people behave as they believe." He looked around, sensed a vague ripple going through the group at the opening statements. A few people shifted in their chairs. Some leaned back ever so slightly. Others leaned forward. It was going to be an interesting night.

"How does a belief affect feelings?" Bruce asked. "Here's an example I like that explains it very well, I think: Imagine a family on their doorstep. A mother, father, two daughters. They are saying goodbye in front of their home as the older daughter leaves to go to college. A stranger is passing. Imagine the different feelings they might have. The mother is distraught. Her baby is going away to school. Why can't she go to the college in town? Is she really ready to be away from home? The father has mixed feelings. He's going to miss his little girl. They were really starting to get close. He feels he is just getting to know her. But she has so much to look forward to — new friends and experiences, intellectual growth. He's excited for her more than anything else. The younger sister is overjoyed. Now she will be the center of attention, and she will have her own room. The phone will be all hers at last. The stranger passing by is indifferent. The scene means nothing to him. One event. Four different emotional responses. If the event itself could cause the feelings, wouldn't everyone feel the same? As we can see, the feelings each has are based on their judgments. If we believe a thing to be good, we feel good. But when we feel bad, it is because we believe we must. We also feel like we have no choice."

He paused then and asked for questions. No takers just yet. Bruce paused to let his words sink in. He spoke without notes in an unbroken stream, with very little hesitation. He seemed relaxed and happy, not trying to prove anything or please everyone, but speaking with complete certainty. The group hung on every word, albeit exhibiting a range of expressions from completely deadpan to skeptical acceptance to wide-eyed wonder. "So, let's try a little exercise," he continued. "Let's say the person you love is fooling around with someone else. How many think they would be unhappy about that?" Nearly everyone raised a hand.

"So, let's go around and say why. Who wants to start?" he asked them.

A woman raised her hand. "How can I feel secure with this person?"

Bruce nodded. "Just yell it out," he said, when several hands shot up. "No need to ask permission."

"What does that say about me as a man?"

"What if I catch a disease?"

"I'm feeling relief. What's wrong with me?"

"See how we already have four distinctly different reasons just within this room," Bruce pointed out. "What does that tell you?"

"That we've all had experience in this matter," said a young man, laughing. His girlfriend shot him a surprised glance.

"Well, that wasn't exactly what I was going for," said Bruce, smiling. "What about this? The obvious reasons are not so obvious, so we dig deeper, ask the next question and the next. We can start by asking why: Why would you be unhappy about that? Questioning the unhappy feeling is the most ridiculous question to many. Because I have to be, don't you? But I don't ask the question to say we shouldn't be unhappy — it's a real question. After all, don't we all want to be happy and happier? And when we uncover the essential belief, it often comes down to this: 'If I don't get unhappy, I will never do anything to change it.'"

He stopped then, taking a long drink from the Pepsi he'd brought with him, and asked them to think about other things that people get unhappy about.

"Death is number one with a lot of people," said one woman.

"So, let's take the death of a loved one," Bruce said. "Why would you be unhappy about that? One person might think, where will my next meal come from? Another might say, who will keep me company, listen to me, watch out for me? If I wasn't unhappy about it, does it mean I didn't love them? Again, I am not saying we shouldn't be unhappy and I am not saying we should want 'bad' things to happen, but imagine, just imagine, a world where we are not unhappy about things."

A woman sitting in the back of the room had become so agitated, she could barely sit still. "Obviously *he's* never lost a loved one," she told the person sitting next to her. But when Bruce asked if there were any questions, she folded her arms tightly across her chest and didn't say anything. She didn't have to. A buzz started around the room as people argued for and against the idea that we don't have to be unhappy about death.

"Are you saying that death is not a bad thing?" a man protested.

"How do you know death is a bad thing?" Bruce replied. "Has anyone ever come back to talk about it? What if we believed otherwise? Imagine the changes that belief could cause in our lives if we could ever just start by suspending the so-called *knowledge* that death is a bad thing, that death is the end of everything we care about. Just consider the possibilities. Consider the possibilities of a world with happier people. There's a good chance if people were happier, there would be no lying, cheating, exploiting. There would be no wars, no killing. Unhappiness takes a very heavy toll."

"But don't you think unhappiness serves a purpose?" asked the same man. "You said a while ago that we believe if we weren't unhappy, we wouldn't change. Maybe that's part of being human."

"Meaning that the only way humans can change behavior is to get unhappy?" Bruce asked.

"That's what I'm saying," said the man, shifting in his chair. "I'm wondering about that."

"Do you like that view of human beings? That they have no choice when they want to change but to become unhappy? Does anyone?" asked Bruce, looking around the room. "It's kind of like spitting in our blueberry pie when we want to change to cherry pie. You are happily eating your blueberry pie, or insert any behavior that you are doing — and suddenly another choice appears. There are those of us who happily simply stop eating blueberry and switch to cherry. And there are others who must spit in their blueberry pie to give themselves permission to move on. Do you know people like that?"

The man laughed. "I see what you mean. I'm definitely the spitter," he said. "And my wife is the switcher. It drives me nuts!"

"Or maybe that's one of the things you love about her," Bruce suggested. "So, what makes that difference between people? Clearly, it isn't the event. Could it be what they believe about themselves? And, even if it does seem that unhappiness helps us to achieve some things, it may not mean what we think it means, or it may not be the way we really want to live. Many a person has become a millionaire because he or she was afraid of poverty, but did the fear leave them once they were rich? Or did they worry day and night that they might become poor again?"

"They probably worry day and night," the man said.

"Would it have been possible to achieve such wealth without un-happiness?" Bruce asked. "Could they have become a millionaire just because they wanted it?"

"I don't know," the man said. "That sounds too easy."

"What if it is easy? What if our desires were really the only thing that ever motivated us?" asked Bruce. "And the unhappiness is a result of not trusting that? What if we use unhappiness like a gun held to our own head? It's another way of saying we wouldn't just change because we want to. We need to be threatened or prodded or pushed in some way. And if no one else is doing it, I will do it to myself."

Bruce noticed a young girl sitting in the front row with an expres-sion of pure wonder on her face. Her right hand seemed to be slowly rising and when he looked her way, she actually pulled it down with her left hand and giggled. "I see your question," he said, laughing. "But I don't hear it." The young girl leaned over to her father sitting next to her and whispered something in his ear. The man smiled and asked her question: "My daughter would like to know if this applies to kids, too. Do kids have a choice about their feelings?"

"Of course," Bruce replied, "and I am so glad you asked the question. Anyone who is capable of making choices — even as fundamental as 'Do I want to suck my thumb at this moment or don't I?' — is a thinking being. Children of all ages make choices on some level about how they are going to react to things. Older children, who can talk, will answer questions about their unhappiness just like adults do. And so often, for kids and adults of all ages, it gets down to *the* basic belief: I am afraid if I am not unhappy about such and such that I am not a good person! So many of us try to prove we are good people by becoming unhappy. Even kids. Especially kids!

"When we are children, we learn to use unhappiness to get what we want. We all remember tasting certain foods when we were children that tasted horrible to us. We would gag and make faces and refuse to eat it. When we were children that worked. Our parents relented because they didn't want us to be unhappy. As an adult, is it still true? Do we still gag on spinach, turn up our noses at okra — to make it okay to not eat it? After doing this over and over again, we forget after a while how it all began. Many of us are stuck on beliefs that we have had since we were one — beliefs that we just picked up from our parents, or our interactions with them. We look around us and see so much agreement. And once we have agreed that we have to be unhappy, there is not much else to do but blame.

"If I can't see that it's some belief of mine that is causing me to be unhappy, what is the first thing that happens? My finger points to someone else. It's your fault I'm miserable. We can spend a hell of a lot of energy trying to get someone else to change his ways so we can be happy. So the question is, does our happiness or unhappiness come from us or from the world? One of the most fantastic things we can do for ourselves is to take something we are unhappy about and really question it. What I am hoping most to leave you with is a question. I am definitely not saying that we should not be unhappy. What I am saying is: Don't we all want to be happier? Is our unhappiness really necessary? Even when disaster strikes — we may not be happy with it, but do we have to be unhappy? That's the question I want to leave you with today. Do we have to be unhappy? Consider the possibilities if we don't."

On his way home he thought about the class. He loved thinking about a world without unhappiness and the possibilities it presented, especially when it came to loving our own desires, loving what is, and allowing ourselves to be loved in return. In happiness, we move freely and fearlessly, like many children do before they learn to be afraid. He remembered the morning that he went out to get the newspaper and saw his next-door neighbor, Annie, toddling out the back door of her house. It was around six o'clock in the morning, and she must have been about two at that time. He looked to see if anyone was behind her, but no one was there. She made her way down the back steps through a combination of sliding and crawling. When she had made it, she dashed into the backyard and danced a wild dance of innocent freedom, her tender little bare feet kicking up the morning dew.

When she was through, she found that the first step was too high for her to climb up. He watched her as she stood there looking at the steps. He thought about all the choices available to her. She could try to climb the stairs or not. She could become frustrated or upset or not. She could give up and go do something else. She could simply wait. And that's exactly what she did. She sat down on the bottom step and waited for someone to help her. And he did. Wouldn't it be nice if things always worked that way — if someone was always standing in the wings to help out? Perhaps. But wasn't it nice to know that our happiness doesn't depend on it!

Bruce's Method

All feelings are the beginning of gladness.

Some things he wrote to work out some concept. Some things he wrote to help his students understand how to use his method. Some things flowed in poetic profusion from his pen. Some tumbled out in crisp miracles of clarity. Others appeared to be an impenetrable tangle of convoluted thought but if patiently followed unraveled mysteries into simple truths. He said only one thing, but there was always something else to say about it. That one thing was the answer to a question he had been asking from the time he was a young child. Why are people really unhappy? Do they have to be? Can people really be happy, no matter who they are, no matter what has happened to them?

He loved mysteries, conundrums, and surprises — things that challenged his intellect. Finding out the truth about unhappiness, a feeling he knew well as a child, was the greatest mystery of them all. Somehow the answer came to him. Did it come in a dream, in an epiphany, or was it born in him, like it is in all of us? Of course, he would say, we all know the truth. Some of us say yes to the truth; others argue. What is the truth about unhappiness? Everyone knows the truth about their own unhappiness. If you want to know why someone is unhappy, ask them: "Why are you unhappy?" They will tell you, "I am unhappy because . . ." If you and they believe they have to be unhappy because . . . , that will be your answer. "I am unhappy because I lost my job." But, if you know that losing a job can't make anyone unhappy, the question becomes a different question. The question is no longer "Since we know we have to be unhappy, why are you unhappy?" Now the question is "Since we know we *don't* have to be unhappy, why are you unhappy?" Then we can truly know why we are unhappy. And we can begin to see how and why we choose unhappiness.

Again and again when he questioned people about their unhappiness, he heard that people were unhappy because they "wanted" to be, meaning they believed they should be. They believed unhappiness served a purpose and that purpose was — without exception — the attainment of happiness, even perfect happiness (happiness with a capital H). "Unhappy" could mean the simplest annoyance to murderous rage. It was simply a term for the feelings people have about things that they believe they need to stop in order to *ultimately* feel good. He heard that they were afraid to abandon unhappiness, believing that unhappiness was preferable to happiness — fearing that happiness was some kind of craziness and unhappiness makes us sane, makes us human, even. If I weren't unhappy, they would say about some loss, it would mean I didn't care. It would mean I wanted it to happen. I'd be against myself, lost, alone.

Over the years he discovered that any unhappiness could be traced back to a belief through a series of simple questions — questions that could be asked only by someone who did not accept the inevitability of unhappiness, someone who was willing to hear all the answers without judgment. That someone could be anyone. He wanted everyone to know that.

He wanted to help people see that their unhappiness didn't just happen to them, that they had a choice about how the events of their lives affected them, even events that had already happened. When he helped people work through a problem, it reminded him of peeling an onion. The outer layers were the who-what-why-when-and-how — all the reasons and justifications behind the unhappy feelings. The questions helped to peel away each layer of justification until there was no justification left, only the beliefs behind the unhappiness. Eventually, the whole onion could be peeled down to the core belief, which could then be questioned and exposed as just that — a simple belief, not a fact, just the person's belief that they had probably subscribed to long ago.

That simple truth — that unhappiness and other bad feelings didn't have a life of their own but were caused by beliefs — could enable anyone to deal with any problem if they knew this. Bruce wanted to help people to always have a way out of every unhappiness. He believed that anyone could change if they had a reason that really mattered to them. He truly believed that seeing the truth about unhappiness changed people if they let it. But they had to want to change. They had to want to see. It was all up to them. There was no method on earth, no remedy, no pill, no intervention that could cause a person to change if they did not agree.

People were sometimes afraid of his questions and what they revealed. Some were so afraid they ran away. Some raged against him. Many others loved him as if he were their father, though they were the same age or older. Some were intimidated in his presence, uncomfortable with the power of his teachings. People thought he could read their minds, that he was judging them. He wasn't. He was devoted to the truth about unhappiness — that we can be free of it — that it is not something that happens to us like the color of our eyes.

He lived joyfully within this knowledge and refused to compromise on its meaning or neglect its reality. He could not. It sat on his shoulder while he ate breakfast. It rode in the car with him as he drove to his sessions, out to dinner, to the movies. It went to sleep with him each night and arose with him in the morning. He cooked it in the food he loved to make for friends and family. He laughed it, sang it, spoke it, wrote it every chance he got. He knew and loved it so purely that it became a part of him. It radiated throughout his being and colored everything he did and said. And those who knew him felt their hearts flower into light in his presence.

People treated him like a guru sometimes and were dismayed when he didn't act like one. They expected him to be different, this man who seemed to know them better than they knew themselves. He chain-smoked, drank soda by the gallon, loved rich food. He could sit up all night watching Charlie Chan movies or helping someone sort out a problem. When he bought himself a sleek white Corvette, one of his most beloved students went into a rage. Materialism didn't jibe with his image of Bruce, the man who had for all intents and purposes taught him to discover himself, taught him to be happy — not just glad, but gloriously, joyfully happy. The student argued and complained for hours at Bruce's dining room table while others watched in fear and disbelief, more than a few having the same thoughts. Bruce simply did what he always did. Through his questions, he helped the student deal with his anger, and they agreed to disagree later that morning in a 4 a.m. test drive at 140 mph.

In the presence of unhappiness, even when directed against himself, Bruce wanted only to help his friends and students, and even strangers sometimes, to be happy. He often told them that a person's belief in the necessity of unhappiness was the great self-deception of all. To help someone see this, and move beyond it, was to him the greatest love possible.

"What are you unhappy about?"
Can Really Be a Question

The first question: What are you unhappy about?

They're fighting again. I can hear their ragged voices chasing each other through the house. My father's words are sharp chipped icy things. My mother's beg him to stop, just stop, just leave her alone. Can't you just let me be? I cover my ears, pressing them flat to my head. When I count to three, I tell myself, they will be laughing. One, two, and three — my hands release and there is silence. He is speaking low now, measuring his tone, each word mean and heavy: "What are you so unhappy about all the time?"

The sound of my father's steps bounces off the stairwell walls. The back door slams so hard my books fall off the shelf above my bed. He is gone again, and Mom and I are alone with each other — I feel guilty for the relief of it. Mom's door is closed for two days this time. Nana comes again on the bus from New York City. She draws the shades and speaks in hushed tones as if someone is sick or dying.

When Mom comes out to dinner on the third day, there are four of us at the table — me, Nana, Mom, and a huge black shapeless mass that steps on my spirit and squeezes my stomach with an iron grip. I want to ask, I am dying to ask: Mommy, can't we just stop this? What would it hurt to laugh and sing, to go out for ice cream after dinner? To play a little softball in the yard? You love softball and ice cream.

You could throw me the ball and I could try to hit it like Daddy taught me. You could chase me around the yard with the ball trying to tag me, and we could both fall down laughing in the cool grass. Remember how we used to do that? Even Nana will smile in that disapproving way she has, and then we can all have ice cream with chocolate syrup and whipped cream. I'm dying to ask, but the black thing won't let me.

"Mom, are you mad at me?" I ask instead, desperate to break the spell, picking the safest question I can think of. They all look at me. The black thing quivers and gets a little smaller.

Nana opens her mouth to speak, but Mommy holds up her hand for silence. "Of course not, darling, why would you think that?"

Why would I think that? I feel it rather than think it, and it's a feeling that is as familiar to me as my own breath. "But you are mad, aren't you?"

She has to think about this. "I guess you could say I'm sad, but not about you, never about you. You're my joy and my consolation," she says, reaching across the black thing to stroke my hair, caress my cheek with her cool hand.

"Why, Mom, why are you sad?"

My mother looks at me. Her eyes fill with tears, her mouth turns down. The look says, "You'll understand when you're older." The look says, "We have no choice." The black thing nods in agreement. We finish our dinner in silence.

Happiness Is

⌒*ᴍ*⌒

What if, Bruce thought, what if I were to write everything I ever wanted to say at this moment on this pad of paper, here in my living room. Today.

What if, he thought, what if today was the last chance to say it, to say it completely, to drain it from my heart and mind, to give it away. Right here, today. What would I tell them if they asked me, what is it? What is it you want to tell us? Tell us, tell us in two pages. Tell us in two paragraphs. In two words. Tell us once and for all. I would tell them:

Happiness Is.

Nothing in the world gives happiness.

Nothing or a lack of anything causes unhappiness.

Happiness is.

I don't have to be unhappy.

I simply do not have to believe that I will ever be unhappy again.

I do not have to believe that there is anything that is happening in me or around me or to me that can cause me to be unhappy.

I do not have to believe that there ever could be.

I do not have to interpret or understand or discover or consider or be open intellectually or allow the possibility for my own sake or for the sake of the truth or any value: that I have to be unhappy or that I may be unhappy.

The words flowed effortlessly from his pen like a meditation, but he was aware of a slight tugging at the edge of his consciousness — a distraction to his general feeling of well-being. He looked at the words he had just written. *I do not have to believe that there is anything that is happening in me or around me or to me that can cause me to be unhappy.* So what is it? he asked himself. What is bothering me? His students would be coming soon, a new group from his practice in another town. He had thought long and hard before opening his home, but now that he had decided, he would take the consequences, come what may. He knew that his method, simple as it was, was profound and life-changing. That could be very threatening even to the most confident person. Was that what was bothering him? That there would be arguments? He was used to that. That people would become afraid and consequently out of control? That was something he could deal with. Nothing real came to mind.

Then what would I be afraid of, he asked himself, if I were not bothered? His favorite question. Still nothing came to mind, nothing exceptional, that is, but something so obvious he had almost missed it. Wasn't that always the way with our beliefs, which are so natural and comfortable? He was afraid that if he were unconcerned, he would not be vigilant, that something bad would happen that he would not see coming.

Why do I believe I would have to be unhappy about that? Because I should have known better. It would have to mean that I am bad for myself, for my own happiness. There it is again — the belief that I could be bad for myself. Why do I believe that? There were so many reasons. From childhood. Ancient history. Superstition. Everyone he ever knew believed that. Self-protection. Honesty. Any sane person would be afraid of that.

The question is, he thought, do I believe it today? Just say the truth, no strings attached. Just between me and me, here and now. No. I don't believe I am bad for myself. So, we'll see what this brings. I am doing this today, and if it doesn't work out, I will do whatever I do about it. He relaxed then and let his pen drop again to the paper.

You can be happy.

Happiness is being glad for who you are.

Happiness is admitting that you like that you want what you want.

Happiness is admitting liking that you don't like what you don't like.

Happiness is admitting liking that you change your mind whenever you think that's best.

Happiness is admitting liking that you don't change your mind until you really change your mind.

Happiness is admitting liking that you don't like not knowing how to have what you want.

Happiness is admitting liking that you don't like being mistaken.

Happiness is admitting liking that you feel just the way you like to feel about everything you do.

Happiness is admitting liking that you feel just the way you like to feel about everything that happens.

He put his pen down.

That's it, then, he thought. That's the end. Or is it just the beginning?

My Parents

People choose their beliefs. Every belief.
People choose what they have hope in and what they have no hope in.
People decide what they want and don't want.
People choose to believe that they can or cannot do something.
People choose what they feel and think about anything.
People are free everywhere, and yet they choose to believe that they
are constrained in their opinions, beliefs, attitudes, decisions,
and options.

My parents, Eve and Martin, met at the local college sprawled at the north end of town, where Eve was studying art and Martin was pre-law. They had known each other in high school but ran with different crowds, a symptom of their inherent incompatibility. Eve's friends liked macrobiotic food and green tea, and spent the long afternoons and evenings of bottomless youth discussing the meaning of life. They could be seen most Fridays waiting for the bus to New York so they could hang out in Greenwich Village listening to poetry or jazz, if they could afford it. They really wanted to know if there was a God.

Martin and his friends didn't leave town much except to see a ball game or a rock concert. They could often be found smoking dope in the local parks or drinking beer in someone's basement. They loved sports but lacked either the natural ability or the determination to be jocks. They saw the idealism of the times as a sign of weakness and focused their attention on escaping the family plumbing or contracting business, hoping to be lawyers or accountants.

Unfortunately for my parents, they were attracted to each other. Eve used to say their life together was like a favorite picture puzzle where more and more pieces got lost each time the picture was assembled. Something always seemed to be missing. In their early years, when she was in a state of bliss imagining the long loving years stretching before them, fantasizing about their first child, their first home, her vision of them together, the beautiful adoring couple — Martin was secretly bored and scared. After the wedding, which was much bigger than he wanted, and after the honeymoon, which was too long and too expensive, he woke up to discover that he was a married man. He was expected to come home after work and be a husband. Everything was supposed to revolve around the two of them. The things he loved the most — after his wife, of course — had to be put aside. So no more basketball games in the park across from work, no more beers at the local pub, no more Tuesday night poker games, no more carousing weekends that ended just before work started Monday morning. No one had told him that.

They tried that first year to convince each other to become what the other needed. They resolved that they would always strive to work things out between them, no matter what was happening in their lives. So he agreed to come home each night after work for dinner. She agreed to let him play golf on Sunday afternoon as long as he was home for dinner. He agreed to accompany her to poetry readings in the city. She agreed to stop complaining about Tuesday evening basketball. He agreed to be cordial to her Wednesday night book club. She agreed he could go out drinking that night. He agreed they would have a child before they were thirty. She agreed they would have only one child.

He started law school at night. She began painting miniature canvases with vivid color and precision, building little scenes with layers of paint upon a single word. Home. Love. Time. Marriage. Their rules started to shift and fade with more late nights at the office and the demands of night school. They kept the trappings of their life together intact. He cleaned out the garage and painted it. She redecorated their bedroom. They were a popular couple. They socialized regularly with other couples, people they had known since college. Their lovemaking was comfortable and regular, their conversations revolved around the details of their life. She would have liked to go deeper, to pull him closer. She blamed herself when he fell asleep as she read him one of her new poems.

In the years that followed, their early resolutions slipped away as they dragged their lives along on a pallet of unspoken desires. When they were thirty, he had his first affair. She had her child. In the hospital, they brought in her daughter bound up in a pink blanket and laid the bundle on her chest. She could hardly breathe with the weight of it. When the baby started to fret, the grandmother lifted it upon her knees, rocking ever so slightly, chanting, "Now, now, let's not trouble Mother." Eve wanted to protest, but she was so tired, so tired, and where was her husband? She fell into a deep sleep while her mother watched and rocked with competent detachment.

She had delivered a full three weeks early and he was unprepared, still allowing himself to be unavailable as he spent afternoons with his lover. He had meant to end it close to the time, but it was too late. When he arrived that evening, Eve was in a deep sleep. His mother-in-law, clutching the pink bundle, cast a feral sniff in his direction and icily proclaimed the child would be called Annie, after a dead relative he had never known. He loved his little girl but rarely could get beyond the wall of protection his wife and mother-in-law had erected that first day in the hospital when he was not there.

Thus began the decade of "what ifs."

Unhappiness Is a Choice —
Me and Dick and Jane

Unhappiness is a choice.

I have to be honest. For the first four or five years of my life, I was blissfully happy. No, I won't even say blissful. Even that is too limiting. Let me say it this way: I simply was happy. It was my natural state. I know this very well because I remember the day I first got unhappy, and it was a completely unfamiliar feeling.

I'm not going to say that I remember being an infant or a two-year-old or even a four-year-old. My clearest earliest memories are of Dick and Jane, characters in my childhood reader. I carried the spirit of Dick and Jane inside me every moment of every day. I bought their protected pretty water-colored world hook, line, and sinker. I was a Dick and Jane groupie.

In our world, the milkman appeared every day in his starched white uniform, bringing sparkling bottles of wholesome milk. Our smiling, attractive mothers wore pretty dresses and baked cookies in their sunny kitchens. Our handsome, healthy fathers were happy in their work and spent countless hours of quality time with their children. We regularly visited our grandparents in the country where Grandmother always had a freshly baked cherry pie and Grandfather showed us how to appreciate farm animals. We had our favorite teddy bear, and our teachers were endlessly patient. Dick and Jane and I were loved and cherished by the people in our world.

I remember that feeling of safety and goodness in my life. Looking back at it, I can say my life was nothing like Dick and Jane's. There was a cold war between my parents almost from the day I was born. We did very little together as a family. My mother often brooded, and my father stayed away for long periods of time. My grandparents were stiff and strange. It didn't matter. I believed in Dick and Jane's world. I shared their belief that everything was taken care of. And then I stopped believing that.

When my father left the first time, my mother tried to pretend that nothing important had happened, as if his presence all the short years of my life had been a dream that I could wake up from with no more serious side effect than a vague feeling of something missing. In fact, there was nothing vague about it. When he wasn't in his bed in the morning, I stood at the door to their bedroom waiting for him to appear. On Saturday morning, I sat in my place at the table, waiting for him to come and flip pancakes for me. The truth was that abruptly the core of consistency, such as it was in our fractured family life, was stripped away. I wasn't supposed to notice.

They wanted me to take sides. Standing between them, I could feel the pull from one to another. For the first time in my life, they fought in front of me, mostly about money. From my mother's perspective, it was never enough, and the reason was always about me. I needed a new coat or I needed to go to the dentist or I needed clothes for school. They would scream and yell, and my mother would pull me to her, saying, "Why are you doing this to us? You are ruining our lives."

Even though Dad came back a few months later, I was constantly afraid that he would leave again. Over time, there was a new feeling, as if during the night someone had put an extra blanket on me that was a bit too heavy. My world had sprung a leak. I was no longer part of the Dick and Jane world where things were predictable and safe.

I began to be afraid. I was terrified of things I couldn't see. When they tried to cover my face at the doctor's office before removing a mole on my cheek, I screamed hysterically. (I still have the mole.) In swimming class, I wouldn't put my face under the water because I had to close my eyes to do it. In my bed at night, I curled into a tight little ball and burrowed deep within the covers.

Nobody knew about my transformation from a member of the protected species of Dick and Jane into a scared little kid. I believed that my place in the universe was at risk. After all, if Daddy could be ejected from our world, why not me? So I watched myself very carefully. I tried to be good with all my heart and bit back my fears as best I could. I hid any desire that seemed unpopular unless I just couldn't help myself. If I failed to suppress myself and some passion spilled out, no one really reacted negatively unless my grandmother was around. Nevertheless, I still felt a kind of low-grade guilt that became one of my familiar feelings. Little by little, I got used to the new me. It never occurred to me that I had a choice.

Although it may not seem obvious at first, people are actually unhappy because they want or choose to be.

All people choose what they believe is best for themselves and can do no other.

People choose what to feel emotionally.

People choose their postures, their mannerisms, their speech, language, inflections.

People choose what they learn, their tastes, opinions, attitudes.

People choose their superstitions and religions.

People choose to believe that what they believe is a proof of anything.

People choose that what they believe is relevant and pertinent.

People choose what they think about their lives, their dreams, their memories, their thoughts, affections.

People choose whatever they think about anything.

The Miracle of Miracles

*B*ruce took his writing table and his favorite pen and went to sit on the back porch. He had his cigarettes and his soda and there was Berlioz playing as loud as the afternoon would allow. *Harold in Italy.* Breathtaking. He considered the empty page as if it were a blank canvas. The writing was already inside his head in its entirety. Like a dream, it would present itself to him in terms that he could understand. In his head, it was a feeling, an urge, flavored with meaningful intent. It would roll down his arm, he knew, into his hand and make its mark upon the paper.

He didn't know what he would write today, but he knew that he would write and that it would be about what was in his heart to say. There was no purpose in his writing except to get the words out of his head, out of his heart, onto the paper. He wasn't writing a book. He wasn't sure who, if anyone, would ever see the writing. But he knew the writing would change him and move him forward. That this could happen seemed to him to be miraculous. He put his hand down to the paper and the words came.

What is a miracle? A miracle is a creating of something from nothing. In the act of this creation (the miracle) knowledge is created (where there was no knowing) of the fact of the miraculous event. The knowing and the event are the same miracle. The true knowing of happiness is the miracle.

He looked out at the day. He loved all the days that he was lucky enough to see and smell and know. He loved the sunshiny days as well as the wet and gray days. He loved the snowstorms and the nor'easters. He even loved the muggy summer doldrums. Every day was a good day to be alive. To be happy.

What is the greatest miracle? The revelation that happiness is all that is, and that unhappiness is caused by merely believing it is wrong to be happy. The knowledge that we can question why people believe they must, or should, or need to be unhappy is a miracle.

What is not a miracle? Any so-called miracle that purports to reveal an angry or sad god, or some other unhappy heavenly being, is merely the same old deception of unhappiness. The truth is that all people have the right to be happy, and it is not necessary to be unhappy. It is only believed to be.

He thought of his students, who would be coming later for the group. In letting go of their unhappiness, they experienced the grace of happiness flowing into their hearts. They had started to look for miracles in their lives, almost to expect that miracles were close at hand. What did they want from miracles? Some of them didn't even believe in God. They wanted permission to believe that it was okay to be happy, but they were afraid. Inevitably, when faced with the prospect of not *having* to be unhappy, they immediately saw the possibility of *never* being unhappy. Because they were still unhappy in so many ways, that realization frightened them. Someone would always say: "If people were happy, and wouldn't get unhappy no matter what, what would keep them from doing bad things?" A good miracle would set them free, they thought, let them know that God approved of their happiness. A good miracle would keep them safe from evil.

What is evil? There is no evil since nothing causes unhappiness. People merely believe in evil, something that ultimately causes the unhappiness of the innocent. All are innocent since no one can cause anything about which anyone must be unhappy. The most that can happen on this earth, or in this universe, is something that people do not want; not something that should not be, which is what is meant by evil.

The fundamental question, he realized, was "Is it good or bad to be happy?" This was a question that people had to decide for themselves. He could help them with their fears and he could help them decide, but the ultimate, glorious decision was theirs alone. Some of them would know that the miracle had already happened. They would know the miracle every day, endlessly rejoicing in the gift of happiness and the knowledge that no one has to be unhappy. Others would still be looking for the miracle and disappointed in God's silence, in the lack of proof, and they would experience profound sadness and anger without really knowing why. The miracle would float unseen just above their heads.

What is the value of a miracle? First, to realize that we are blessed, lucky, freely given the gift of the miracle, which we were not owed. We realize we are happy, and we have the right to be happy. Second, the wondrous opportunity to admit that truth. The opportunity to respond. We can have the happy response of being awed and glad for the chance to experience the miracle, and more, the chance to admit that we did indeed experience a miracle. It gives us the chance to show or become who we want to be, happy.

The Party

All people are allowed to be happy at all times, forever. This is happiness: to know you are always allowed to be happy no matter who you are, what you do, and no matter what happens to you.

And there were the parties that pulled me in with their great magnetic embrace. The first one I dared to crash sprouted in my sleep late one spring, populating the lawn next door with green-and-white-striped canopies, a profusion of lovely lemon-colored lanterns, and fringed hammocks that floated between the trees.

I am trying with all my might to stay at the breakfast table, barely able to endure the soggy mess of milk-soaked cereal and bananas in my bowl. I can hear the caterer's delivery truck, the hosing down of lawn chairs, people calling out to each other next door. The party is happening. I'm sure I belong there.

Mom doesn't think so. "You are not to go over there," she says as she sets up the tables for her Saturday poker game. "We weren't invited."

My jaw sets and I can feel trouble tickling the corners of my mouth, almost making me giggle out loud. I'm only seven, but I know how to play my cards too. I help Mom make little finger sandwiches that I'm not supposed to eat. I help dust and vacuum the living room, all the time plotting how I will make my escape, what I will wear to the party.

At noon, the ladies sweep past me into the living room and take their places. I get wet kisses and pinched cheeks. They ooh and ahh over my growth since last month, how I look just like my mother. And was I shy or what? I know it's rude, but I'm not interested. I am itching to be next door. The last time I peeked, Bruce's yard was filling up with people wearing jeans, tie-dyed shirts, long flowing dresses. They're bringing presents and flowers, fruit and bakery boxes. Everyone is talking and smiling. People are laughing and hugging each other. Under a huge tree four musicians are playing stringed instruments.

I finally escape to my room. I think I can even smell the food from Bruce's, where they have not one, but three, barbeques set up. If I listen carefully, I can hear the ice cubes clinking in the glasses. People are singing now. I can hardly stand it. Down in the living room, I know the poker players are washing down chopped chicken liver, bagels and lox, and finger sandwiches with coffee that Mom calls "cabinet coffee" — something she pours into coffee mugs from a bottle she keeps in the liquor cabinet. Soon they will forget me completely.

I put my new white eyelet pinafore and white patent leather Mary Janes in a grocery bag stolen from the pantry, and sneak it out to the garage. Then I go into the living room where the ladies are already talking about how their husbands are never home and their children are turning into juvenile delinquents. Mom is staring at her cards so hard, she jumps a little when I whisper in her ear the way I'm supposed to when she's busy. "Mom, I'm going out to play."

"Don't go too far," she whispers back, giving me a squeeze. I know I'm good till at least six.

In the garage I change into my party clothes. I had a bath this morning and I even put on a little bit of Mom's Chanel No. 5. I have on my new white socks with the ruffles and you can't see my skinned knee because I put some of Mom's pancake makeup on it. I go and stand at the edge of the crowd, pretending that I belong there. I wonder what the party is about. I can tell they are celebrating something, but I'm not sure what. People are speaking together and laughing in small groups like grown-ups usually do, talking about their jobs, their children, what movies they have seen. But I can tell they are excited about something. I never saw so many adults smiling so much at the same time. Then the musicians put down their instruments and Bruce starts to speak.

"You are a very unique people," he says. *"You are the beginning of a movement unknown in history. I would like you to be in touch with the significance of that fact. From this place where we are now will spread an idea, a question unheard of before. From here will grow the possibility for people to be happy, truly happy. People who never believed it was possible. There are people who are so fearful that they will even fear that possibility. There are many who have not even dared to hope to be truly happy out of the fear that those hopes will be crushed and they will be worse off for having dared to hope. Help one another to be happy. Unless you help one another here, how will you help others? You cannot always say 'Tomorrow.' Someday, if you are to be happier, you will say, 'I will — now!'"*

Everyone is listening to Bruce so closely that when he pauses, you can hear leaves rustling in the trees overhead. A lot of people are holding hands, and a nice man asks me if I want to stand on a chair so I can see better. I would, but imagine if Mom were to go into our kitchen and see my pointy head coming out of a crowd of Bruce's friends. My life would be over instantly. I look across the driveway to my own house to see if anyone is looking for me. But no one is. I wish I could stay here forever and grow up in this crowd and one day become one of them. Then I will really know the secret of their celebration.

Bruce continues, *"Do not deny your specialness. You have within you the seeds for a beautiful garden. Spread them fearlessly. Some seeds will not seem to grow. Others will seem to need extra care, and others will disappear to grow where you may never see the fruit. But, wherever they take root, and for however short a time they seem to grow, know that there was the chance for something that there never was a chance of before that."*

Finally Bruce notices me. We look at each other and he smiles. I feel self-conscious and squirmy, so I check out my shoes in case they have scuffmarks. When I look up he is still smiling at me. He looks like he expects me to do something wonderful, like take off flying over the housetops. I am wondering myself, when suddenly my heart feels like it's rising like soda pop bubbles right up to my mouth. My lips smile so big I think they might burst.

The musicians start to play again. They make sounds that seem to leap from bow to bow to plucked strings right into the open air that seems to be waiting. People have tears in their eyes. But not me. I have gotten what I came for. The party is in me.

The Inappropriate Girl

Unhappiness is believing you know you are bad for yourself.

Happiness is the freedom to be as we are, however we are: richer or poorer, in sickness or in health, gaining or losing, winning or failing, wanting or not wanting, approving or not approving, forever. Happy is what we are and what we'll be if we don't believe we are wrong to be as we are.

Once upon a time there was a little girl whose name was Linda, I write. I cross out Linda and put Alexandra. I always loved that name. Once there was a little girl named Alexandra. She lived in a big blue house on a big wide street.

Our teacher had asked us to write a story that was descriptive. It was supposed to be fifty words. You aren't supposed to count "a," "an," and "the."

Alexandra had the biggest brown eyes you ever saw and pretty little pink fingernails and the longest eyelashes you ever saw. (Thirty-eight words already. The story is almost finished.) Alexandra had a little brown dog named Bones that she loved more than anything. One day the dog ran away. Alexandra cried and cried until her mother bought her a shiny red bike. The End.

I read the story to my mother, and she laughs and claps her hands. "Very good," she says, "but why don't you try to make it even more descriptive?"

The story is due on Reading Day, which is Wednesday. Mrs. Sanderson, our teacher, is going to let us read our stories up in front of the whole class. On the bus, I read my story over and over, and I like it less and less. I think about how to make it more descriptive, like Mom said. Finally, I cross out the part about the dog running away and write: One day the dog ran into the street and got crushed by the ice cream truck. All its guts squished out like spaghetti. (That is more like it.) When Alexandra came home from school, her mother had bought her a new bicycle to take her mind off Bones. Alexandra fell off the bike and scraped her knees all red and bloody. The End. (That's better.)

Brian Mitchell is the first person to read his story, one about a striped cat that has seven kittens. One has blue eyes and is white with a brown circle around its eye. One is yellow with a pink nose. Every kitten is a different color. "Very descriptive," says Mrs. Sanderson, and everyone claps. Then Elsa Eubanks reads her story about a shiny black colt with long, long legs that makes friends with a long green snake. Everyone claps and claps when the snake rides bareback on the horse.

Then it's my turn. The first sentence goes over well, I think. The second sentence gets a nod from Mrs. Sanderson. When I read the part about the ice cream truck the whole class goes wild. Silly Audrey Sloan even screams and slams her silly hand over her silly mouth. "Well," says Mrs. Sanderson. "Well, isn't that descriptive." Then I read the part about the guts and everyone starts making gagging sounds. Then Mrs. Sanderson says, "I think that will be all for now, Annie. Who's next?"

"But I haven't finished my story," I say, and everyone in the class stops gagging and just looks at me.

"Well, Annie," says Mrs. Sanderson, folding her hands on her desk like she does whenever recess is over. "I think your story is upsetting the class. Why don't we talk about it later?"

"But you said we could read our stories," I whine. "It was supposed to be descriptive. Wasn't it descriptive?"

"Well, yes," says Mrs. Sanderson, getting up from her desk and steering me back to my seat. "But perhaps it was a bit too descriptive. Some of your classmates were getting upset."

I shrug her hand off my shoulder and look around the class. Peter is passing a note to Andrea. Michelle has her head down on the desk. Eileen is picking her nose behind her math workbook. They don't look any more upset than usual.

I stand up very straight. "I would like to read my story like everyone else," I announce in my loudest voice. Mrs. Sanderson's hand is back on my shoulder, instantly gripping me with fingers like talons. "Follow me," she squawks and motions with a quick dart of her eyes for the teacher's aide to take over the class. We go out into the hall. "Annie," she says. "You did a good job on the story, but you must not argue with me when I tell you to do something. Do you understand that?"

"Yes, Mrs. Sanderson," I say, lying through my teeth.

"If you can collect yourself, why don't we go back and listen to the other children's stories. We are wasting a lot of time, don't you think?"

"I don't think so," I say, digging myself a big old hole. "My story is as good as anyone else's. Brian's story about the cats was just boring." I look at my shoes.

"Well, thank you for your opinion, but I am the teacher here. Am I not? I would like to go back in now. You can leave your story on my desk. I will read it tonight and we can talk about it tomorrow. Do you think you can do this?"

"No," I say, folding my arms. I may have stamped my foot a little, too. And that's when I go to the principal's office. I sit there for the rest of the day rewriting my story. I try but by the end of the day, all I can change is the murder weapon. In the final version, the dog gets creamed by the garbage truck. They send me home with a note to my mother.

Mom has to read the note four or five times. She puts the note down and looks at me as if she is going to say something. Then she picks up the note and reads it again. "I don't understand this," she says. "It says here you disrupted the class and caused Mrs. Sanderson to have to stop what everyone was doing."

"I wanted to read my story," I say, starting to cry for the fifth time today. "Mrs. Sanderson wouldn't let me."

"Well, it says here," Mom says, "that the story was meant to upset the class. I don't understand. The story you showed me last night was very sweet."

"I changed it," I tell her. "On the bus. I was trying to make it more descriptive, like you said." I show her the version from the principal's office.

She laughs. "Blood and guts," she says, "are certainly descriptive. I guess Mrs. Sanderson didn't like your story. She said it wasn't appropriate. I'm supposed to explain this to you. Mrs. Sanderson says that you wouldn't admit that you were wrong to upset the class."

"I wasn't wrong," I say. "They just didn't like my story."

We look at each other, two of the most inappropriate people we know. "Did you like your story?" she asks me.

"Well, I didn't like the part where the dog gets killed," I say, "but it's just a story."

Mom laughs and laughs. "Out of the mouths of babes," I hear her telling Aunt Billy on the phone later.

Mom helps me rewrite the story, but I don't ever read it in class. Mom calls Mrs. Sanderson and tells her I understand everything and there is no need for further discussion. A few days later Mom gets a call from the school psychologist. Mom is supposed to bring me in for testing. We make the appointment, but Mom cancels, saying she is sick. They make another appointment and Mom cancels that one too, saying she is unexpectedly called out of town.

The next time we have to write a story, I show the final version to Mom first. Mom says I have to find my voice as a writer. It's the one thing we do together where I have Mom's undivided attention. At the end of the year, I win the prize for having the most stories. Mrs. Sanderson doesn't let me read in class anymore, though. Mom says that's okay — that all writers have to learn rejection. By the time I'm grown up, I should be totally immune.

Happiness Is Not a Reward for Good People

Happiness is not a reward for good people.
When we love someone, we want good things as a reward to them
*   for the good they do for us or others.*
To want them to be happy because we see happiness as a great
*   wonderful "thing" for them seems natural.*
But happiness is not a thing. It is their feelings.
To think that happiness should be a reward for their kindness or
*   love is to ignore that they create happiness by themselves.*
You can reward anyone as much and in any way you want, but
*   they have to do the happiness part of your gift.*

I remember when I knew for sure that my parents didn't love each other anymore. Right before my eighth birthday, Mom and I drive to the mall. Instead of getting out of the car, Mom just sits there, her eyes like stone fixed on some point just out of her reach. It's a week before the start of school, and we are going to buy clothes and my first wristwatch. A special day, that recedes into impossibility as Mom's grip grows tighter and tighter on the steering wheel. It's like her will to move has evaporated.

Finally, I get out of the car, walk around to where Mom is sitting, take her by the hand and lead her to a pay phone where she calls a cab to take us home. We pull up just in time to find my father bringing his suits on hangers out to the car, already piled high with everything he must think belongs to him alone. The three of us stand there in the driveway before the open trunk, me still holding my mother's hand, my mother's eyes never leaving the ground.

"I'm leaving, Eve," he says loudly, as if speaking to a deaf person. "I want to take Annie with me. You can come with me now, sweetheart," he says, reaching out to me. "I'll wait right here."

I just stand there, frozen. Could this really be happening? Could this be my father, his handsome face twitching, the soft brown eyes hidden, extending one terrible beautiful hand toward me, the other slamming the trunk closed? And my mother, in her lovely summer halter dress, her fists clenched, the rage visibly moving through her delicate frame?

"Are you insane, you bastard?" she spits out, throwing her arms around me, crushing me to her chest. I think it's the worst day of my life.

My father drops his arm and steps back. "You're not fit, Eve," he says. "You'll prove it in time. Annie, you can come to me any time. You're a big girl. Just call me and I'll come get you." He drives off without looking back.

All I can think is, I'm just a kid. Don't they know I shouldn't be hearing this? At the same time, I feel a little guilty thinking how I won't miss the long silences at the dinner table that I had tried to break with news from school or even the local headlines. No more muffled fights in the night, the sound seeping beneath my door. No more closed doors in the middle of the day or late-night phone calls saying he was not coming home. All would be replaced by — what? I can't imagine it.

"She's a child, you idiot, you fool. How dare you!" my mother whispers to the empty driveway. He is really gone.

There is only one thing to do.

Know that you are happy, lucky, and taken care of naturally.

There is never anything to be worried about.

Nothing to fear, feel sad about, or be angry over.

When we see those we love become unhappy, it is natural to feel un-happy also, but know this:

Unhappiness just can never happen to anyone.

The next afternoon, Nana moves in. She comes in a cab this time all the way from her old life alone in a two-room apartment in Manhattan. The furniture arrives later — solid dark woods that own the room in a way the previous white wicker never could. More than anything I want to be close to my mother, to talk about what we will do now, how we will live, what it all means. I become afraid of leaving the house. In the schoolyard, my stomach twists and churns and sometimes I just have to run home where I often find Mom still in bed. I climb in with her fully clothed and slither into her arms, nestling my face in the warmth of her hands. They smell faintly of Jergens lotion. I breathe it in, and it makes me feel safe and good. I wish Nana could do something like that for Mom, but Nana is too busy being angry. She only wants to blame Dad, and she and Mom fight about it all the time. If I only knew what to say or do to make it all better.

The Incredible Wrongness of Being

Unhappiness is the belief in the wrongness of being. To be unhappy is to feel that you are wrong to be who you are. When a person believes he has to be unhappy, what he is believing is that he has to experience being against himself. The belief in unhappiness is the belief in being wrong for oneself.

*I*t's been a year since Dad left and it's my birthday again. Mom and I are having a party in her bedroom. She leads me by the hand to her vanity table where the cake is set up with nine candles blazing in the darkened room. In the triple mirror, I can see my partitioned reflection blowing and laughing, with Mom behind me clapping her hands.

But I'm nervous because Daddy is picking me up at seven o'clock and it's already a quarter to. We're going to have Chinese food in New York City and I get to pick out all the dishes. I'm wondering how to ask Mom if I can save the cake for later when she turns me around to show me my present on her bed. There's my Brownie uniform that I've been so worried she wouldn't be able to get for me in time for the meeting next week. There's the brown dress and the beret and even a red plastic Brownie purse. And then she hands me a little box with my Brownie ring with the red stone. I get that happy sad feeling again. I love my Brownie dress but I'm not sure it's okay for me to have it. I can already hear Nana saying, "You take good care of that. Your mother went through a lot to get that for you."

I wish I could stay here with her. Even more, I wish she were coming to dinner with me, Daddy, and Michelle, Daddy's new girlfriend, but that would never work. Even I know that. "I thought your Daddy was taking you tomorrow," she says. I wish she didn't always get things mixed up. Nana says I'm a selfish child who takes advantage, that Mom would be fine if only Daddy and I would behave.

When Dad comes to pick me up, Mom stays in her room. At dinner all I can think about is Mom sitting in her room with my cake and birthday presents. I'm at the table eating lobster Cantonese, my favorite, but my heart and soul are in Mom's bedroom. I wonder if the candles are still burning. Did she blow them out herself? Did she make a wish for me? What if she didn't blow them out? What if she burns the house down with my birthday candles? Can that happen? I'm not sure I should really be here. What if Mom starts to have trouble breathing and she forgets what to do? Pretty soon the food won't go down anymore and I just feel like lying down under the table. Daddy gives me my very own camera for my birthday, with film and everything. We take my picture so I will always remember this day.

On the way home, I'm really worried about Mom. What if something terrible happened while I was gone? What if Mom is so mad at me she will never speak to me again? I can't get the thought out of my head. Daddy notices and pats me on the hand, but Michelle is mad. I can tell even though she's trying to hide it. I know she's thinking that I'm a sulky brat, that nothing ever pleases me. I wish I could tell her that I'm just worried about my mom, but I'm not supposed to talk about her.

When I get home I can't say goodbye to Dad and Michelle fast enough, and I'm in Mom's room before his car is out of the driveway. When she smiles at me, I feel all the sickness draining out of me. I can see she's been crying, but I am so relieved there's not going to be a big scene tonight. We eat birthday cake together, and I try on my Brownie dress and dance around her room telling her it's the Brownie birthday dance. I want to sleep in Mom's bed, but she tells me she's going to be up reading for a long time. It's hard to leave her room to go to bed. I'm still afraid something bad is going to happen.

Before I go to sleep I say my secret prayer. "Please, God, I promise I will be good if Mommy will be happy some day. Amen."

A Child's Spirituality

"The Kingdom of Heaven is within you." That means that all you ever need and want to be happy: that is, the power to be at peace and happy forever, is within you. All you ever wanted was to be able to be happy. Then, okay, be happy!

I'm supposed to be Jewish but I really don't know what that means. Jewish kids go to temple and Catholic kids go to church. I know that. Sometimes kids won't play with me because I killed Jesus, they say. I don't understand why they say that, but somehow I know those kids don't even understand what they are saying. Their parents tell them to say it, I think. The kids really like me. I can tell. No one in my family talks about religion, except when Daddy tells about the concentration camps. He gets all upset and Michelle says, "Calm down, Marty, you're scaring the child."

I like the Catholics. My friend, Maryanne Gugliamo, is Catholic. She has a picture of Jesus Christ on her bedroom wall. She showed me how his eyes follow you around the room. I love the picture of Jesus. He looks so kind and beautiful, and I get this warm feeling whenever I look into his eyes. Too bad Jesus is only for Catholics. When I eat dinner with Maryanne and her family, they all join hands and Maryanne's father says a prayer. Maryanne says the food is blessed then. I like the feeling of having blessed food inside me. It makes me feel as if maybe I could be a good girl after all.

On my way to school, I pass at least four churches, no temples. Sometimes I see people go into the churches in the morning and I wonder if it would be okay if I peeked in just for a minute. I'm scared I'll get into trouble because I'm a Jew. But then Maryanne tells me that Jesus was a Jew before he invented his own religion and that Jesus wouldn't mind if I went into one of his churches. She promises to take me into her church. She practically has to drag me up the long flight of stairs to the church doors. They're the biggest doors I ever saw, with life-sized people carved into the wood. I want to stand there and stare at the doors, but Maryanne is pulling me inside already.

It smells nice in the church, and the first thing I do is look up. There are people painted on the ceiling and it's so high I almost fall over looking at it. Maryanne shows me how to make the sign of the cross with water from a bowl, but I don't do it.

"I can't," I say. "I'm not allowed."

She shrugs her shoulders and gives a little curtsy at the back of the church, and then she walks right up to the front as if she owns the place. I'm afraid to go much further than the back row, and Maryanne keeps turning around and motioning for me to come with her. But I can't do it. What if they find out there's a Jew in their church? Can you get arrested for that?

I pass by this church every day on my way to school. It gets harder and harder just to walk past it. It feels as if something is pulling me inside. So one day I walk up the steps and just stand by the door to see what happens. Since I don't get struck by lightning, I decide to go in a little ways. It's a hot day, but the church is cool inside. I guess God doesn't need air-conditioning. I sit in the very last row and try not to look Jewish. Next time I go back to the church, I move up a few rows, and after a few weeks, I'm right in the middle of everyone. If God is watching, he could definitely see me there by this time. There's a great big cross at the front of the church with Jesus Christ hanging on it. I know for a fact that I should not look at the cross, but I want to look really badly. Every day I move closer and closer to the cross until finally I'm in the front row. People are kneeling in front of that cross. I can see their lips moving, and I wonder what they are saying. What would I say?

It takes me weeks before I actually look up at the cross. I'm sitting in my favorite row, the fourth from the front, and I'm looking at my hands. I can feel, I think, I can really feel that Jesus is looking at the top of my head. He wants me to look at him. He has a surprise for me. I'm not sure how I know this. It's as if he's whispering in my ear. So I finally look and then I can't stop looking. It's as if my heart opens up like a giant flower inside my chest. Jesus and I are looking at each other, and I know both of our chests are filled with the same giant heart. My eyes feel enormous too, and I want to sit here and look at Jesus all day. I feel as if I just found candy in the pocket of my coat. As if I got chosen to be the lead in the school play. As if Mom smiled at me and told me I'm her best girl.

When I leave the church, the feeling goes with me. And I know I can always come back to get the feeling again if it goes away. And Jesus told me a secret, too. Jesus said, "It's all right."

Feeling the presence of God is a natural, actual phenomenon for human beings. God is Happiness, pure and simple. God has made, and still makes, Himself available to each and every human being of His creation. Whether people believe He should or not, He does. To be happy is to be one with God.

The Monday Night Group

Unhappy Beliefs:
I am supposed to be —
You are supposed to be —
They are supposed to be —
Life is supposed to be —
The world is supposed to be —
God is supposed to be —

I'm supposed to be in bed, but it's Monday night — group night at Bruce's house. I know this because he told my mom that people would be coming each week and to please let him know if the noise disturbs us in any way. My mom said what a polite man Bruce is. I just wish they were as loud as they could be. I've been listening for hours from my bedroom window, and I can hardly hear anything.

I know they'll all go into the kitchen for coffee and cake. Then they'll sit around the big table. If I can stay awake, I can hear little bits of what they say. Last week, I heard Bruce say loud and clear, *"Anxiety is an unhappy belief, not unlike any other."* I really wish my mom could hear that because I know my mom has anxiety. That's why she has to stay in her room all day and night. She used to stay just in the house, but since Dad moved in with Michelle, she spends most of her time in her room. Mom is always talking about what she wants to do and how she can't do it. How she lost Daddy because she didn't do the right things. How she's afraid of losing me, too. I wish Mom could hear Bruce.

Mom says that anxiety is a disease, not like the kind you catch, but like the kind you can't help. She's always telling me to do well in school, comb my hair right, make sure my clothes are clean and pressed. Mom says you have to be the best you can be — it's your responsibility or your fault if you don't get what you want out of life.

On Mom's bad days, she cries a lot. "I feel so bad," she says over and over. When Nana asks her what about, she can't answer. It's as if she's in pain, but nothing seems to take the pain away, not even extra-strength aspirin. Nana says Mom should take pills to make her feel better and that makes Mom really mad. "I'm not crazy," she shouts. "I'm just a little blue." And then she goes into her room and doesn't even come out for dinner. Bruce says feeling bad means you don't think you deserve to be happy, that feeling bad is the same as feeling that you are bad. Sometimes I write the things Bruce says on a piece of paper and slip them under Mom's door or under her pillow. I don't know if she reads them. Sometimes I find one in her wastepaper basket and I take it out, smooth it with my hands, and put it under her mattress.

Mom tells me secrets sometimes. She tells me she has nothing to look forward to except nothingness. I don't know what nothingness is, but it doesn't sound good. I wish Mom wouldn't tell me secrets. It makes me sad, too.

What If the Answer to Your Problems Is Already Within You?

We are unhappy when we believe our very life, our heart, our self is against all that we live for: our personal happiness.

The "library group," as Bruce called it, met in a small town library on Long Island. He would make the drive every Wednesday afternoon, cruising over a network of highways, tunnels, and bridges in his large comfortable car, drinking Pepsi and smoking cigarettes while he prepared his lecture in his head based on notes he had made the night before.

He liked to keep it simple, building each week on the message of the week before, and he liked to answer the unspoken questions that settled like a cloud around the group. These were the questions that most would be thinking but no one would raise — questions they judged too stupid to ask, or too challenging. He loved these questions the most. These were the questions that usually got to the core of why people clung to the old unhappy routines year in and year out, questions like "If I'm not unhappy about things, why would I ever try to change anything?" or "If I am happy with everyone, won't people walk all over me?"

The group was small, only eight men and women, but a good cross section of ages and occupations: a young couple who were recently engaged, a grandmother, a thirtyish secretary who was always late, a local carpenter, a clergyman and his wife, and one of Bruce's students who lived and worked in the city. The group lasted for two hours. He would start with his half-hour lecture and then open the group up for people to work on problems with him one on one while the others listened. In this format and setting, people usually avoided working on problems that were deeply personal. No one ever discussed sexual problems or problems with abusive partners, for example.

It really didn't matter. His approach worked with any kind of problem, no matter how small or how large, how simple or complicated. The simple truth was that people were unhappy because they believed they had to be, and every bad feeling could be examined from that perspective. Mild annoyance about a traffic ticket or uncontrolled rage over being cut off in traffic — both had some belief underlying the bad feeling. The belief might even be the same in both situations. "This shouldn't have happened to me. This is a bad thing in and of itself. If I weren't unhappy about it, it would mean I didn't care. That would be like saying it's okay that people drive crazily or that cops give tickets when they shouldn't."

As he took his place in the corner of the library set aside for the weekly group, he thought about last week, the fourth session of the eight-week course entitled Introduction to the Option Method. He had spent the first three weeks explaining how his method worked and demonstrating by working with problems that people raised. The group had been going well, with the usual dynamics of one or two people being the most talkative, a few others interjecting here and there, and at least one person completely silent throughout.

Then something extraordinary had happened in the last half hour of the session. In twenty minutes, he had helped Jim Reynolds, the carpenter, work through his twenty-year problem with insomnia. Jim had been one of the people in the group who were especially receptive to the method. From the very first meeting, he was entranced with the idea that the only thing standing in the way of his happiness was to examine the beliefs behind whatever it was he was unhappy about.

Jim felt that he was already a pretty happy person, but he needed help with some long-term problems, which he considered to be deep-seated and hard to deal with. Insomnia was one of those problems.

Over the past twenty years, Jim had averaged only three to four hours of sleep each night. The problem had begun in his high school years and was one of the reasons he had chosen a profession where he could work for himself. He could never be sure if he would be able to get up on time. He scheduled his work life so that his first appointment was at 10 a.m. So far that had worked out for him well enough, and he had gotten used to falling asleep only to wake up in the middle of the night and not be able to go back to sleep most nights. But now, nearing the age of thirty-five, it had started to take a toll on his concentration on the job and his energy level. He was thinking of starting a family, as well, and was concerned about his ability to work more hours and increase his income.

That day, Bruce had been talking about phobias and the fear of being out of control. When he opened up the floor to the group, Jim raised his hand just enough to get Bruce's attention. Basically a shy person, he was clearly hesitant about becoming the center of attention.

"Okay," Jim said. He took a deep breath and folded his long arms into a tight knot in front of his chest. "I've been thinking about this problem since you started talking today. I don't think I would ever have brought it up. But I'm desperate. I've tried so many things to change this thing about myself but I've never succeeded. It just seems to be part of me."

"What does, Jim?"

"Insomnia. I haven't had a good night's sleep in years." He relaxed a little, then, at least enough to unfurl his arms and settle his hands into his lap.

"What happens when you go to bed?"

"It goes in phases," Jim continued. "Sometimes I actually do sleep well, but most often I go through weeks and weeks where I'll fall asleep right away but then I'll wake up at two o'clock or three o'clock in the morning, sometimes 4 a.m. if I'm lucky, and I just can't fall back to sleep. I used to lie there, but it bothered my wife so much, now I get up and watch television in the other room or read."

"How do you feel about not being able to sleep?"

Jim thought about the question for a minute. "I don't know," he said. "In some ways, I've learned to live with it, and sometimes I tell myself that this is my natural rhythm and that's just the way it is. Other times, which is most of the time, I feel oppressed by it."

"What do you mean by oppressed, Jim?"

"I feel like it's got me under its thumb and there's nothing I can do about it." He laughed at that. "Silly, huh, like it has a mind of its own."

"Well, sometimes, things we can't seem to control do seem that way. What do you mean when you say there is nothing you can do about it?"

"Well, short of taking drugs, I mean. I know there are relaxation techniques you can do, but once I'm lying there awake, I can't stand being in bed anymore."

"What can't you stand about it?" Bruce asked.

"Just the feeling of wanting to go to sleep and not letting myself do it."

"So you want to go to sleep and you are not letting yourself. What do you mean by not letting yourself?"

"Well, I think I must be doing something to cause it. I must be keeping myself awake in some way."

"In what way do you think you might be doing that?"

"Well, sometimes I start trying to figure something out as soon as my head hits the pillow. I like to do that for a while, but then I'd like to stop and go to sleep. But I don't stop. I just go from one thing to another all night almost."

"How do you feel about doing that?"

"I get frustrated."

"What do you mean?"

"I mean, I feel like I can't control myself. I want to shut my mind off, but I can't seem to do it. That drives me crazy."

"Jim, let's talk about why you are bothered first and then talk about why you believe you can't shut your mind off. Why does it drive you crazy that you can't shut your mind off?"

Jim laughed. "Because I should be able to."

"Why do you believe you should be able to?"

"Because somehow I know that I can."

"Then why don't you?"

"I guess I don't really want to."

"Yes, maybe at that time you really want to be thinking about the things you're thinking about. That's more important to you than sleep at that moment. Could that be true?"

"I guess it could be," Jim considered.

"What kinds of things are you thinking about when this is happening?"

"Oh, usually some job I'm working on where there's something I can't figure out."

"Do you figure it out then?" Bruce asked.

"Actually," Jim said, grinning a huge grin, "most of the time I do, or partially anyway. I'd just like to be able to do that during the day when I'm trying to figure it out."

"What's preventing you from doing that?"

"Well, nothing, really."

"Then why don't you do it then?"

"I guess I am kind of putting it off. These are usually the things that I'm not sure I can answer and I don't like that feeling."

"What feeling is that?"

"The feeling of not being able to do something."

"Or not do something, like falling asleep?" asked Bruce.

"Yes, I really hate the feeling of not being able to do things I want to do."

Bruce nodded and leaned forward, asking Jim, "What bothers you most about that feeling?"

"Well, I guess it's keeping me from moving on, going where I want to go. That's the main thing. It keeps me from moving on."

"What is there about not moving on that bothers you?"

"I don't really know how to answer that," Jim said. "I just don't like standing still when I know something has to be done. I don't like waiting for anything. I don't wait in line for anything. I'd be the guy pacing around looking at his watch every five minutes."

"Okay, then, what is there about standing still when you want to move forward that bothers you?"

"I don't know. I just can't stand being incapacitated."

"What do you mean by 'incapacitated'?"

"I guess just being prevented from doing something I want to do."

"What would you be afraid it would mean about you if you were incapacitated and you weren't bothered about it?"

Jim had to think about that. "If I weren't bothered, well, I don't know. I can't imagine it. I can't imagine not being bothered."

"Imagine if it were possible not to be bothered. If such a thing were possible, what would you be afraid of?"

Jim closed his eyes and was silent for a few seconds. Then he said, "Oh."

"Oh, what?"

"I see it now. If I weren't bothered, I guess that would be okay, then," said Jim. But then he thought about it a little longer and added, "If I weren't bothered, I guess I'd just be passive. Everything would be okay with me. But it's not okay."

"Why would it have to mean that?" Bruce asked. "Could you imagine wanting to move on, but not being able to, but still wanting to anyway and just being in that state? Without being bothered?"

Jim smiled. "That's an amazing thought. I'm so used to being bothered about everything that isn't the way I want it to be, I never considered that I didn't have to be that way to change something."

"So, getting back to insomnia? How do you feel about it now?"

"Well," said Jim. "I feel different about it. First of all, I can see that this fear I have about figuring things out contributes. If I could get over that, I wouldn't be saving all my unresolved problems until I'm in bed."

"And, what else?" asked Bruce.

"I can see, too, that the same fear applies to my insomnia. I get frustrated when I can't sleep because I am being prevented from doing something I want to do. But I don't have to feel that way about it. The frustration isn't getting me to sleep any faster. If I weren't frustrated I could try just wanting to sleep. It's really my only choice anyway."

Today Bruce's lecture was entitled "It's Too Good to Be True," but before he even got to it, Jim asked permission to tell the group about how last week's session affected his insomnia.

Jim was beaming. "I wasn't sure if we had really gotten anywhere last week," he said, "but when I went to sleep that night, I had a whole different attitude. First of all, it was really okay with me if I slept or not. I gave myself permission to stay up all night if I wanted to, to work out any problems I wanted to. Before I knew it, I was asleep. I'm not going to say I slept through the entire night, but I slept at least six hours, and every night it gets better and better."

Instead of being happy for Jim, the group generally was skeptical.

One man suggested that maybe it wasn't real insomnia. "Insomnia is a medical condition that takes years of therapy to sort out," he said authoritatively.

Others wondered how the seemingly innocuous interchange of the week before could have had such amazing results. "The questions seemed so obvious," the secretary said. "I would have thought Jim would have asked himself those questions a million times."

"You would think that, but I never did," Jim said. "All these years I've just been feeling frustrated with my stubbornness about going to sleep, feeling as if it were my fault that I wasn't sleeping. I treated it like a disease, like something that had me in its power. I don't feel that way anymore. If you really listen to yourself answering the questions and realize that those answers, as dumb as they sound, are really coming from you, are really what you believe, it has to change you."

"It's too easy," said the clergyman. "I don't trust it. I hope this doesn't happen, but I feel that you'll go back to sleepless nights sometime in the future."

"You know," said Bruce, "every year, thousands of people travel over continents to talk to gurus in faraway countries. Every year marks another year in a series of years and years of therapy for some. There's a belief in our society that the real answers are hard to find, that the more effort expended, the more valuable the information. I'm not saying that this isn't true sometimes and that those are not good and valuable experiences, but what if, what if, the answer is right under your nose? What if the answer is within your reach this very moment? What if the answer is as simple as telling yourself the truth? What if the answer is already within you? Wouldn't that be nice to know?"

They all nodded, but he saw they were in doubt. Except for Jim. Jim just smiled.

There's Something About the Night

Rest and wander freely or fly directly in your freedom.

"There's something about the night," Mom says. "It's like a blanket you can pull around you and take everywhere you go. But you have to get the right time of night. It's not good enough just to be in the darkness. You have to find that special time after the world shuts down and before it opens up again. When everyone is asleep, or supposed to be. That's when the dark is the darkest it can be, when we can all be invisible. That's the time when no one is supposed to be doing anything but sleeping. Nothing else is expected until the light rips through the darkness — until the light catches us again."

With Daddy gone, Mom doesn't seem to want to live like a regular person anymore. It's like she wants to turn everything inside out or upside down. When everyone else is up and around, living life, going to work, meeting with friends, Mom is asleep. When everyone else is asleep, Mom gets up. She goes out sometimes, too, in the middle of the night. I can hear her creeping down the stairs, hear her sneaking the back door open. I can feel the house releasing her and settling back into silence once she's gone. I wish I knew where she goes.

Nana says to leave Mom alone, but I can't do that. I miss her so much. When I come home from school, I go upstairs to change my clothes while Nana is watching her programs, but on the way out to play, I slip into Mom's room. First I usually just stand inside the door letting my eyes get used to the light. Then, when I can see the big bed with Mom in the middle of it, all curled up in a ball with her head under the pillows, I crawl toward the bed. At first, I was afraid Mom would wake up, but she never does. That's because of the little white pills Mom takes now. The pills scare me. I worry that they won't know when to wake Mom up, or maybe Mom will take too many pills and she won't wake up at all. Mom says that all grown-ups take pills to help them sleep, but I don't think that's true. Nana is always snoring on the couch by eight o'clock, and she won't even take an aspirin.

So I crawl over to the bed and just kind of sit on the floor next to the bed where Mom's hand usually hangs over the edge a little bit. I sit so my head is just under her hand, her fingers touching my hair ever so lightly, and I tell her all about my day. I leave nothing out. I start at the beginning with what I wore to school and what I had for breakfast. I tell her about all the quizzes and what questions I got wrong. I tell her about what my best friend, Maryanne, tells me at lunchtime, about the notes she passes to me in class. I tell her about how I didn't get picked for punchball at gym and how Nana ironed my gym uniform all wrong so I was the only one who had creases down the front. When she's all up-to-date, I crawl back to the door and press my ear against it, listening just in case Nana came upstairs, and then I go out into the sunlight and ride my bike, squinting my eyes like when we just get out of the movies.

When I was a baby, I missed everything that goes on in the night, but now that I'm almost twelve, I can wake up in the middle of the night if I want to. Just like Mom. I listen for her every night and some-times I stay up waiting for her to come home. Sometimes she just goes and sits in the hammock. If I go into Mom's room, which faces into the backyard, I can watch her lying there, rocking back and forth, smoking cigarettes. I can hear her humming sometimes, simple songs I never heard before. They sound sad and beautiful and just kind of trail off into silence. Sometimes she takes the car. She rolls it ever so slowly out of the driveway with just the little lights on. It's like the whole car is in on the secret. And then down the road I can see the big lights open up the night on the way to who knows where.

I decide I'm going to go with her. I wait until the Easter break so she can't try to tell me I have to get up for school. Every night I say goodnight to Nana in my pajamas but as soon as Nana leaves the room, I change back into my clothes so I can be ready. The first night she only goes and sits on the front porch. The second night, she doesn't go out at all. The third night I don't know what happens because I'm so tired from waking up and listening for her that I sleep through the whole night. Finally, on the fourth night, I hear her creep down the stairs and go to the garage and I'm up from bed and down the stairs like a bunny. When I get into the car, Mom almost jumps out the window, she's so startled.

"Annie, oh my God, you scared me to death. What in the world are you doing up at this hour? You're all dressed and everything!"

"You're up," I say.

"Yes, but you're just a child. You need your rest. Go back to bed now," she says. She gets out of car and comes around to my side and opens the door.

I stick myself to the seat like glue.

"Annie, you can't come with me. I'm just going for a little ride. I'll be back before you know it."

"I want to go with you, Mommy. We never go anywhere together. Never." And, of course, I start to cry. It doesn't work. She takes me by the arm and pulls me out of the car, marches me up the stairs and makes me get into bed. She sits with me, though, until I fall asleep. That's a good feeling.

The next night, in the middle of the night, Mom appears in my room. I'm sleeping, but I wake up as soon as the door opens. She motions for me to be quiet and get out of bed. I start to look for clothes to put on, but she shakes her head and hands me my robe and some sneakers, and we go down the stairs together this time, and get into the car and coast out of the driveway. This is the most exciting thing

I have ever done in my life. Here I am in my baby doll pajamas and pink quilted bathrobe roaring down the highway at a hundred miles an hour. And there's total silence all around us. We don't listen to the radio. We don't talk. Every once in a while, a big truck goes by, or a car or two. I ask Mom where we're going, finally, but she'll only say, "To the best place you'll ever know."

It's pitch black outside, and we drive and drive until after almost a whole hour, Mom turns off the highway onto a small road and we open up all the windows. The smell of ocean air fills the car. "Are we going to the beach?" I ask. "In the middle of the night?" I'm almost beside myself with hardly believing what is happening. Mom parks, and we walk to the boardwalk and just stand there looking at the blackness. I can hear the ocean. I can smell the ocean. It feels like an immense black forever thing. I have a sudden urge to run back to the car, but I'm afraid to turn my back on it. I'm a chicken when it comes to the ocean. It's okay when everything is calm and the waves make little lapping noises against the shore. But when the ocean arches up into a giant I-don't-know-what and crashes down all foamy and uncontrollable, I just want to run in the other direction. And that's in broad daylight. When Mom takes my hand and says, "Let's go closer," my legs just refuse to move.

I really, really don't want to go. "You don't have to if you don't want to," Mom says. "Let's go back to the car." She doesn't seem mad or anything, but I can't allow myself to ruin Mom's night. So I let her take my hand and walk with her closer and closer to the vast blackness until finally we stop at the very edge and just stand there. I am so scared I'm shaking. I feel as if I'm about to be gobbled up alive by this huge wet thing in front of me. This huge, enormous thing that is deeper than the deepest thing filled with millions of creatures of all shapes and sizes, some with eyes in the back of their heads, some with giant mouths filled with spikes for teeth, some with long tendrils that can wrap around you and pull you in. But Mom isn't scared at all. My mom, who spends her days hiding under the covers and never leaves the house when other people are in the world, is not scared. My mom hugs me against her, telling me nothing bad is going to happen, over and over. Nothing bad is going to happen. She says it over and over until she is almost singing it. Nothing bad can happen. Nothing bad. Nothing bad. Nothing nothing nothing bad.

"You're so scared," she tells me. "It's funny, but coming here is the only time I am not scared." And I can feel that she is calm. It calms me down somewhat as well, but I'm still not prepared to turn my back on the ocean and walk back to the car. So we walk backwards together, kicking the sand up into the air with our toes, running backwards and laughing when we trip over our feet and fall into the cool sand, trying to get back to where we can look forward again.

I will stop being afraid and I will continue to go. But now I need to know whatever I want is okay to want. I'll do what I want most.

Daddy Isn't Daddy Anymore

~*M*~

You and everyone else are absolutely innocent and completely
forgiven for everything.
True forgiveness is knowing that there is nothing to forgive.

Daddy isn't Daddy anymore. Not really. Especially since Michelle. They're living together, you know. Now, mostly, he's Michelle's boyfriend. Everything in his life seems to be about Michelle. Not that I'm jealous, but even his name is different. At Daddy and Michelle's house, he's called Marty. Mommy and Nana always called him Martin or Your Father. And at Daddy and Michelle's, the rules are completely different. I have an actual bedtime, not like at home where I just go to sleep when I'm tired. I'm not allowed to eat between meals, and my homework has to be done before I'm allowed to watch television. Daddy says structure is good for me, that it will help to keep things on an even keel.

Not that we don't have fun. Daddy and Michelle are lovey-dovey like on television. They do tons of things together. Daddy is always doing some project for the house. It's as if he was always here and was never really a part of our family. Michelle has a whole bunch of nieces and nephews, who are always coming over to play. Michelle likes having a lot of children around. She's full of love for everyone, even me. Of course, Daddy is the center of her universe. I'm glad to be there in this warm, loving, safe place, but I'm also kind of sad. I try to hide it, but Michelle notices. I hope she's not mad.

I overhear Michelle on the phone one day saying I'm a thorn in Daddy's side. She says it very kindly, as if she's trying to be understanding. "Marty would be so happy if things were different," she says into the phone. "He worries about Annie all the time. How would she take it if her mom ends up in a mental hospital? It's hard on him."

Sometimes Daddy and Michelle sit me down and try to talk me into coming to live with them. I could have such a great life, they tell me, without having to worry about Mom's problems. I know they mean well, but talking about Mom this way makes me feel very uncomfortable. I put my mom in a safe place in my heart where no one can reach her.

It scares me because they're grown-ups and are supposed to know about things. I'm dying to run home and make sure no one has taken my mother away, but I have to stay until Sunday night as always. I love Daddy, but he isn't the same one who used to give me my bath. I can still remember the feeling of his hand resting on my shoulders as we walked together. That's when I used to belong to him. Now I'm just a visitor in his life. Someone who makes him sad. Someone who doesn't fit in.

Last Sunday, I asked if I could talk to Daddy alone. I think they both thought I was insane although no one actually said anything. After dinner we went into the living room, which is only used when company comes over. Daddy stretched out on the floor, and I sat next to him. "Well, pumpkin," he said, "I'm all ears." But I didn't know what to say, except that I wanted to talk with him more. I could see that he wasn't really understanding why this was so important to me. I started to get the feeling that I was doing something wrong, so I gave up. I didn't want to be a thorn in his side. Then I got to stay up late and watch Johnny Carson in their bed with them, as if they were both my real parents. I had that happy sad feeling again, but I think I hid it pretty well.

Daddy and Michelle want to do nice things for me. They took me shopping for school clothes last year, and this summer they arranged for me to go to day camp. It's a special thing, I'm told, because Daddy isn't even paying for it. Michelle took money out of her own bank account to pay for me. A little school bus comes to pick me up. When we get there, everyone gets out and runs in different directions, except me. I just stand there because I don't know what to do. I was never at camp before, and it feels very, very strange to me. I really start to miss my mother, and even though I'm one of the bigger kids, soon I am the only one crying. The counselor asks me if I want to call my mom, but she dials Michelle's number and I have to try to explain what is wrong *now*. I can't speak because of the lump in my throat. I lie and say I have a stomachache and one of the counselors drives me "home" to Daddy and Michelle's house.

I'd really like to call my mom but it's not the sort of thing I should do at Daddy's house. Michelle is nice, but I can't talk to her about how I am really feeling. I don't want to hurt her feelings. I feel ashamed of myself for being such a baby and so ungrateful. The next time I'm supposed to go to camp, Michelle gives me a choice. I can go or stay and help her do the laundry and the food shopping. Everyone thinks I should have preferred to go to day camp with the other kids, but I have one of the best days at Daddy's house ever. Even so, sometimes I just feel as if I'd rather not go to Daddy and Michelle's house. I just get tired of being an outsider. Michelle says that Daddy is getting a second chance at life. I wonder how old I'll have to be before I can have a second chance.

Let's make it simple. Whatever you have been, considering what you believed and how you perceived things, you were being the way you were supposed to be. You couldn't have been different. If that helps you to understand your life, it is because it is true.

Just because you don't get what you want doesn't mean you were not the way you should have been. Nature doesn't punish you for not being what you should have been. Remember, to believe that you are bad is to believe that you are not allowed to be what you are, or have been or will be. You are allowed to believe that, but you are also allowed to know that it isn't true. You can't be bad, and you are the one who has to allow yourself to know that.

The Cause of Unhappiness

*If someone feels or behaves a way that you don't like, what about
it can bother you? Why can't you feel the way you like at least?
Can they prevent you from feeling the way you like about things?
Don't be afraid they can affect your feelings in a way that doesn't
already agree with your values. All they have done is become a
reminder to you of what you value, unless you become afraid.*

I love school, and even though I'm shy and suspect that everyone else
is smarter than me, I feel more at home in school than anywhere else.
School is my haven. Until this summer. I never should have listened
to Ginny. There's a summer youth center in the gym every day where
kids can go to play games and just hang out with each other. It isn't
really my thing, but my new friend, Ginny, is going, and it's raining.
Why not go? We end up dancing to golden oldies all day, and I really
have a pretty good time.

We start to think about leaving when a girl I have never seen before
comes over to me. "You," she says, standing before me, one finger
pointed at me, the other on her thrust-out hip. I have never heard
so much venom in one word. I don't say anything. I just stand there
looking at her. "Sandy's going to slap the shit out of you," she says,
and with that she turns on her heel and disappears into the crowd. I
feel my skin tingle and heat flare up to my scalp. Where was Ginny?
Another girl I barely know comes over then to tell me Sandy is wait-

ing for me outside. I can't believe what's happening. Who are these people? Who is Sandy? Are they all nuts? I realize I'm trapped in the gym because there is only one way out. I would have to pass by Sandy, this sudden enemy I never even heard of before today. I don't even know what she looks like, but apparently everyone seems to know about the threat.

"Sandy asked to borrow my ring," a lanky tenth grader tells me. "She wants to leave a mark when she smashes your face in. She's mad because you're trying to take her boyfriend away," he says.

"Who's her boyfriend?" I ask, befuddled. This is such a joke. I don't even like boys. They like me, especially now that I've started to fill out, but I really haven't figured out what to do with them yet. Sandy seems to know and she isn't going to let me interfere. I consider getting a teacher to help me, but somehow that option doesn't appeal to me. Something tells me there is only one way to deal with the situation.

I go out into the schoolyard. I see her immediately, blocking my path. The girl who had delivered the warning is standing next to her. A few others are scattered around at a safe distance. I walk up to her. "You wanted to see me?" I say. Then she hauls off and slaps me across the face. It's the first time in my life that anyone has ever hit me. It stings but I'm surprised that it doesn't hurt more. And then an amazing thing happens. I feel completely untouched by her, not unaffected, just untouched. I look her square in the face and say: "I'm not going to hit you back. You can't make me stoop that low." And I shoulder past her and walk home.

School is starting next week. Mom tries to get me to go clothes shopping, but I'm not interested. She gives me money for school supplies, but I just keep putting it off. I barely eat or sleep. I feel sick to my stomach most of the time, and that feeling I had in the gym will not go away. My skin feels too tight for my body. I feel electrified. I keep thinking that Sandy is going to come and find me and finish off the job. Someone out there wants to hurt me. It scares me.

When school begins, I wake up and drag myself off to the first day.

My usual excitement and anticipation about school has completely disintegrated. For the first few weeks, I don't see or hear from Sandy, until one day in the girl's bathroom, the door opens and there she is. Or I think it's her. She looks different. She's smaller than what I remember. She just looks at me and steps back. After that, she seems to be everywhere. I turn around in the cafeteria and I see her looking at me. I feel someone's presence behind me and I turn around to see her just standing there. After a few weeks of this, she finds me in the girl's bathroom again and this time she speaks. "Do you want to be friends?" she asks.

I can't believe my ears. No, I don't want to be friends. "I don't like bullies," I tell her.

She just stands there and looks at me and I actually start to feel sorry for her. If her idea of making friends is to attack people, what's in store for her? And what's in store for me, if I'm afraid of her? She's just a scared little girl, I realize. She can't hurt me and somehow in some way I had something to do with that. I had thought I was her victim, that she had some kind of power over me. Now I feel that I'm the one with the power, but I don't like that feeling any better. I recognize something about myself. I don't belong here, in this relationship with this girl. She sought me out, but she is mistaken. I don't want to play her game. It isn't me, and I never want it to be me. The fear drops away like an outgrown dress. I step out of it and walk out the door without looking back.

The Lesson

*B*ruce went to the front of the room and wrote on the blackboard.

The Seven Understandings of All Unhappiness.

Number One. Unhappiness is the feeling of a belief about a perceived or imagined phenomenon. Unhappiness is not an experience caused by the phenomenon or anything else.

Number Two. Unhappiness is experiencing your own belief that an event is bad and/or should not be happening because you believe IT causes unhappiness.

Number Three. Believing something causes unhappiness is the very reason it seems to "cause" unhappiness.

Number Four. Believing that something can cause unhappiness is the only cause of the fear of it. By "fear" is meant loathing, need to avoid, need to cure, need to kill or eliminate, disgust, hatred, terror, horror, repulsion, disdain and all such similar feelings.

Number Five. Believing someone or something is morally wrong or evil, psychologically "sick" or behaviorally inappropriate is to fear that person or thing as if it could cause unhappiness.

Number Six. Unhappiness is fearing that unhappiness can "happen" or be caused by anything.

Number Seven. Unhappiness is believing that something is necessary, something has to be, should be, ought to be, or must be other than what it is.

He put the chalk down and looked at the group. They were scribbling furiously. He picked up his notebook and left the room. They continued to scribble down the causes of unhappiness. One by one they laid their pens on their desks and waited. By that time he was in the parking lot walking toward his car. After five minutes, small conversations broke out. "Where did he go?" "Is he coming back?" "Sure, he's coming back."

Then, "What's this supposed to be? Is this some kind of a test?"

Bruce backed his car out of the parking space and headed to a local diner.

"Who is this guy, anyway? This is what we paid $20 for? Is he kidding? What is this rubbish?"

"Who does he think he is?"

Bruce ordered a cup of coffee and a jelly donut.

"Don't you get it?" said one man. "Look at what he's written up there. What more is there to say?"

"Come on, it's not that easy. If everyone believed that, we'd all be insane. Everyone would just do whatever they wanted to do to everyone else because — look at what he says up there — it's just our beliefs. There is no bad behavior."

"Talk about bad behavior. Who scribbles on a blackboard and then walks out of a class? This is absurd."

Bruce looked at his watch. Twenty minutes. It was time to be getting back.

Several class members had gone out into the hallway to discuss the Seven Understandings of All Unhappiness. A few who were especially annoyed had phoned the program director to complain bitterly and demand their money back. Some left angrily, sure that they had been taken advantage of. Most figured it out and just waited.

When he entered the class again, there were six fewer people, four very angry people, six slightly irritated and embarrassed people, and nine curious and intrigued people — a good combination for an interesting discussion.

He sat down in front of them and asked, "Any questions?"

The Meaning of Life

What is the purpose or meaning of life?
Each person will answer this for himself or herself.
How you answer determines how you live.

I grew up watching and listening to Bruce and his friends coming and going. Their voices would drift up to my window where I'd be playing or studying or sleeping. At meals I would often see them coming and going through the back door, and sometimes, if I were lucky, I would run into them in the driveway, back from one of their trips. Then I could actually ask where they'd been and I might even help unload the car and be rewarded with a seashell or a piece of rich dark fudge from some faraway candy shop.

For grown-ups, they seemed to have a lot of fun, and they certainly had more fun than I did. I would surreptitiously watch them loading the car for a beach outing or a picnic. They would put so much into the car, I would expect them to be gone for days, but they'd be back late that night or even in the early morning hours. I'd listen to the sounds of their return from a half sleep and be glad they were home safe again.

This summer things are different. They load up the car early in the day but they never leave. This goes on weekend after weekend. There are no lawn parties, and fewer people come and go. There's no music coming from their open windows. They plant nothing in their garden. Summer days bloom gloriously, perfect for a hike or day at the beach, but the car stays in the driveway. On the 4th of July when everyone congregates in parks all over town to watch fireworks, Bruce's house seems uninhabited. As the hazy summer settles over the town and winter is forgotten, I realize I haven't actually seen him for a long time. I used to see him walking out to get the paper every day or setting off on one of his long walks, deep in conversation with some friend or family member.

Then one evening just as the crickets are setting up their evening song, I hear the car start and peek out my window just in time to see Bruce in his bathrobe being helped into the backseat. His wife gets in with him, and a friend drives their car away. He must be lying down because I can't see his head through the back window. I don't see the car again for two days.

After that, things are changed. I still see him sitting on the back porch writing, but he doesn't go out in the backyard or the front porch the way he used to. I see him walking to the car with a cane, and it hurts to watch him walk. I still see them coming and going, but there are no more daylong excursions, no more attempts even to pack the car. No more groups. Nana says what a shame it is, and Mom says she thinks he had a heart attack. I ask her how she knows, and she surprises me by saying she spoke to his wife, who came by one day to deliver a piece of misdirected mail. "Don't fret so, Annie, people do get over heart attacks. Some live to be ripe old people." But I can see that Bruce is not going back to be the way he used to be, and I wonder so much what he is writing now on his yellow pad.

What is the purpose of the meaning of your life? Is your life for you to be happy, or would you prefer your life to be for something else, or nothing? Would that make you happy? Whatsoever you seek, you still seek the cessation of unhappiness and the satisfaction of happiness.

After you have what you want, what would you feel? After justice? After truth? After health? After riches? After peace on earth? Then will your happiness be allowed? Any goal or ideal is the means by which you are ultimately seeking happiness. You believe these things are necessary first. If you don't believe true happiness is possible or desirable without them, why?

You do all that you do for happiness. You may not have realized that.

Dear God

Desire happiness for you and everyone.

Dear God,

Wouldn't it be nice if everyone could just be happy? Wouldn't it be great if just for one day, Nana could smile at me, give me a hug, ask me what I want for dinner instead of shoving whatever she planned to make a week ago under my nose and then getting mad at me if I don't want it. Wouldn't it be nice if Mom could just stop moping around the house and realize that Daddy is never coming back and good riddance? Wouldn't it be nice if she could just have fun? Go on a date. Go get her nails painted red. Wouldn't it be nice if we could just laugh once in a while?

And wouldn't it be nice if Daddy and Mom could still talk nicely to each other? If they could even hug once in a while? If Daddy didn't say nasty things about Mom behind her back? If Nana wouldn't glare at Daddy every time she saw him? Wouldn't it be nice if Daddy could bring his girlfriend over and we could all go out for ice cream together? And wouldn't it be nice if the teachers weren't mad at us all the time? If they actually listened to what we had to say? If half the kids at school didn't make fun of the other half? Wouldn't it be nice if the so-called scaggy girls had really cute boyfriends and if the beautiful girls at least dated some of the shop guys? Am I the only one who thinks this would be nice?

And what if everyone wanted to help people who had less than they did? If everyone who saw someone mistreating someone else stepped in and said, "Stop that. Stop that right now." And what if everyone who heard a lie said, "That's a lie." And everyone who didn't hear the truth said, "Tell me the truth. I want to hear the truth." And what if people could just change places with their neighbors once in a while. Go and live in their house and see what it's like. What if people wouldn't tolerate living next door to someone for ten years without even once talking to them? Without offering them a bunch of flowers or some homemade cookies?

And what if white people could live one day in a black person's skin and vice versa. What if the smart ones could change places with the dumb ones, and the strongest ones could feel what it is like to be weak for just a little while? What if people could really see miracles? Not big miracles, like the parting of the Red Sea, but people-sized miracles, like walking away from a car crash, or even kid-sized miracles, like finally learning to tie your shoes after trying and trying so many times.

So, God, if you could make me happy, I will be good for the rest of my life. I won't lie (not that I ever have). I will be good to my family. I'll be the best friend anyone ever had. If I could just be happy, I'll do whatever it takes. I'll be really kind to everyone even when I don't feel like it. I'll treat everyone just the way I'd like to be treated. I'll be a good girl, forever, I promise. If I could just be happy. Please let me be happy.

Love, Annie

If They Could Hear

God loves what he is doing: Your life.
God loves what he is doing:
*   the beats of your heart, your feelings, your desires.*
Do you love what he is doing?
Do you love what you are doing?
If you love everything that comes from you,
*   then you are both doing the same thing.*
If you do not love everything or anything that comes from your
*   heart, then of course you and God are doing different things.*
You won't even like what you will become then.

Bruce's clients rarely discussed God, but it was always about God
— about love and acceptance — about being allowed to want what they
wanted and not want what they didn't want — about being good, doing
the right thing — about loving themselves and trusting in their good
nature — about believing they deserved to get what they wanted, no
matter what. If that's not God, what is?

He wished he could wave a magic wand so they could know it
was all right. But there was no magic wand. There was only the truth.
And that was okay.

What would it take, he wondered. What would it take for the
average person who has been unhappy most of his life, what would
it take for that person to be blissfully happy? What would it take for

a person who has believed he is a bad person for his entire life, what would it take for that person to know that he is not a bad person? What would it take for that person to stop believing he is bad? Why did they believe it in the first place?

It happened when they were so young, so impressionable, he thought. A young child trying to learn how to be, how to please Mommy and Daddy. When Mommy and Daddy get angry, when they say, "You are making me unhappy with your behavior," when they are believing, really believing, that the child is making them unhappy, the child may think he is learning something. And then this child comes to his office twenty years later, thirty, forty, fifty years later, with the problems of a grown-up. "My love life isn't what I want it to be." "I am afraid of losing my job." "What if I can never have children?" "I just learned I have cancer." "I'm sad about the loss of a loved one." The child is still there, behind the sophisticated complaints, behind the complications of adult life, behind the grief, sadness, anxiety.

Then he would ask them, "What can I help you with? What are you unhappy about? What is there about that, that you are unhappy about? What about that? And that?" When the central cause of the unhappiness was exposed — "I am unhappy that I can't get what I want." "I am unhappy that bad things happen to me." "That good things don't happen to me." "That I may lose what is dear to me." When the belief behind the cause was revealed, he would ask them: "What is there about not getting what you want that you would be unhappy about? Why do you believe you would have to be unhappy if this happened, or didn't happen, or that happened? What then?"

"Well, there would be something wrong with me," they would say. "I am a bad person." The child speaks again. The child who still believes that he is bad, because he believes he should believe that, because why? Can we know and does it matter? Why would an innocent child believe he is bad for himself, and how can that child be healed of that belief?

What God (or nature) doesn't love:

Nothing.

The belief that you could be a disappointment to him.

The belief that you could have feelings that are not natural for you.

The belief that a lack of his love exists.

The belief that he does not love you.

The belief that he will not always love you.

The belief that he would want to be nothing to you.

If only, he thought, if only, that child within that adult could look up and see the adult acting out his greatest fears. If only that child could say to the adult that he has become: "It's okay, Big Me, the One I Have Now Become. I was just a child when I believed that." It seemed so convincing to a little child, a child who depends on parents and teachers and older people to take care of him. When you are a child, you believe people. You trust with an acceptance and openness that you will never again experience as an adult. If only, he thought, that adult could look at the child within himself and say, "It's okay, Little Me, the One I Used to Be. You don't need those old beliefs anymore. You're a different person now."

If only the Child and the Adult could hear the voice of God. What would they hear? If they could hear God, they would know they could never be bad, could never be undeserving of happiness, could never be unloved. If they could hear.

Hell Is What You Make of It

All people seek happiness. When happiness seems impossible, then people seek to avoid the greater unhappiness. All other things are sought as a means to the greater happiness, or to avoid the greater unhappiness.

We feel happiness or unhappiness according to what we believe we will feel. We would always be happy if we did not believe we had to be unhappy. We can never get unhappy about something we don't believe is something to get unhappy about.

Apparently, it's hell night on Madison Street. Nana won't let me go in Mom's room. If I press my ear against the door, I can hear Nana whispering urgently to Mom, begging her to do something. I haven't seen Mom since school started almost a month ago. She won't leave her room and I'm not allowed in. Now I can hear them yelling at each other, too.

"I'm not going to stay here and watch you throw your life away," screams Nana.

"Then leave, you old bitch," Mom sends back.

My hand flies to my mouth as if I had said it myself. I can hear Nana stomping to the door, so I quickly pop into the hall bathroom. The door to Mom's room slams behind Nana, followed by the sound of objects bouncing off the door.

"I'm calling him," Nana shrieks, and she goes downstairs to call my father. Michelle is going to be really pissed. This is the third time this week. I start to shake. Daddy is really going to be mad. The next thing I know an ambulance is coming up the street. Its lights are flashing and everything, as if someone is dying. Is Mom dying? I run to her room and bang on the locked door. "Mommy, let me in," I scream, which brings Nana up the stairs.

"Stop that this minute," she orders me. "Your mother has enough on her mind."

"But, the ambulance. Why is the ambulance here?"

She grabs me by the shoulders and tries shaking me, which is hard because I'm now a good four inches taller than she is. "Wait until your father gets here," she sneers, as if I were six. "Go downstairs and wait for him. He'll deal with you, young lady."

I'm at the back door waiting for Daddy, and I can see that the ambulance is at Bruce's house. The attendants are coming out the door with Bruce on the gurney. He is covered with a blanket, and there's an oxygen mask over his face. They are moving fast, but they set the gurney down in the driveway for a minute before putting him inside the ambulance. Bruce's wife and his best friend come down the stairs and stand by the gurney. I expect them to be crying and wringing their hands, but the three of them are talking calmly, like they do this every day. I start to think that maybe Bruce is not that sick, based on their behavior, but the attendants look very grim. I can hear them talking on their radio about a heart attack. On the other hand, at my house, where no one is dying, people are going insane.

Then Daddy comes and gently starts to pull me inside. "This is not for you to see," he says, and covers my eyes, which nearly drives me nuts. "No," I say, a bit too loud, and to my embarrassment, everyone looks over at us, even Bruce. I can see he is too tired even to lift his head, but I can see his eyes. They smile at me. They really do. I can feel his pain then and the effort he is making to try to send some little part of his immense peace to me where I stand across the driveway. I can feel my own heart expanding and before I know it, I smile so big I have to cover my mouth. He winks at me. I feel so happy. There is absolutely no explanation for it.

Nothing in the world gives happiness.

Nothing or lack of anything causes unhappiness.

Happiness is.

Later on the ambulance comes back for Mom. It doesn't come with lights flashing. It rolls up the driveway quietly, secretly, as if it knows that this is just some neurotic housewife who thinks she can't breathe. "Let's pretend she's really sick so she doesn't have to face the truth," it says. "Let's pretend there is really something wrong with her so she doesn't have to be embarrassed." But she *is* embarrassed. First, she won't let them put her on the gurney. Then she tries to pull the sheet over her head. "It's four o'clock in the morning. The world is asleep," says my father, who has been trying to calm her down for hours. She won't look at me, and Nana keeps trying to push me out of the way.

"Why can't they just leave the oxygen tank?" Mom cries. "That's all I need."

My father leans down to whisper something in her ear, and I can see her grab his hand. He takes her hand and gently places it under the sheet. "Let them take care of you," he tells her. "You just need rest."

"I'm dying, Martin, I know I'm dying. Please don't let me die." I hear her say it tonight, just as I have heard it so many times before. It seems like such a simple statement, but when it's not the truth, it would take years to explain.

The belief that our beliefs are irrelevant makes us fearful, and it feels as if we need help. We feel like victims of our emotions because we don't realize that our emotions are determined by our beliefs about the causes of unhappiness. We can question those beliefs and then either affirm or change them. We no longer need to feel like victims. We can understand the choices.

And then she's gone. Daddy says to pack a few things; we're going to his house. I feel as if my heart has been torn apart by wild horses. Daddy just seems relieved to have it over with. Nana is mad about everything — that Mom let this happen to her, that Daddy didn't calm her down, that I'm up at four in the morning. Daddy wants to console me, but he doesn't know how anymore. I just want to go to the hospital and find them both.

Maybe Unhappiness Does Work

In a way, people are unhappy because they "want" to be. They believe they should be. They believe it is good and necessary to be unhappy about whatever they believe that applies to; in degrees, to some experience of not getting what they want — what they believe they need or should be.

This is the way people choose unhappiness as a feeling. You could say unhappiness is a term for the feelings that people have about things that they believe they need to stop in order to feel good.

"It's your fault," Nana is telling me. "All your moping and complaining did this." I hear her and I know I'm supposed to feel bad. The words circle around my head looking for a place to work their way into my brain. I don't let them. I'm twelve years old — too old for her tricks. I'm home from Daddy's to pick up more clothes. Apparently, someone decided I'm supposed to stay with Daddy and Michelle until Mom gets better. "You don't have to if you don't want to," Dad says, but what can I say?

"Can we go to the hospital first?" I ask for the third time today.

"In a while," he says, trying to make it sound soon, but not too soon. That scares me more than anything.

At Dad's house, I know I've made a big mistake right away. I can tell Michelle doesn't want me there, even though she tries to hide it. There's a big discussion about where I will sleep as if no one had previously realized that I did that. The next day they register me for school, which is a lot bigger than the one I go to. At my school, I could always walk or take the bus. This school is too far to walk to. I have to take a bus to get there. The first day I miss the bus because I'm waiting in the wrong place and Michelle has to drive me. She tells me I have to be more responsible, pay attention. I don't know what to say. All I can think about is Mom in the hospital. I wish I could just go to the hospital and stay with her.

It's very hard to be in school. Every day I have to throw up as soon as I get there. I don't know any of the teachers and all the kids seem older than I am. All the adults seem angry. The Spanish teacher threw a book at us because we don't listen. "Eschuchen," she says. "Yo tengo dolor de mi garganta. I have a sore throat."

"You tango dollar de me gigantic," we all say.

"Listen, listen," she says, pointing to her ear, "dolor, dolor." She rolls the "r" like a growl.

"Dolor," we all say.

"Sí. Sí. Garganta. Garganta," she says, pointing at her throat.

"Garganta," we all say.

"Yo tengo dolor de mi garganta," she says, as if it were the most natural thing in the world.

"You tango dollar de me gigantic," we all say. I know how to say it right, but the class has already decided, long before I got here, that this is the way we speak Spanish. A boy in the front starts to giggle and then the whole class is in stitches, even me. That's when she picks up the workbook and sends it slicing through the air above our heads. It hits the back wall and slides to the floor. She makes one of the boys bring it back to her and then mercifully the bell rings and it's third period.

The teacher stands by the door with her arms folded and gives each of us the evil eye as we file past her. I stay up half the night worrying about it, convinced that the next day the principal will call me to his office and I will be expelled. But the next day, there's a new teacher there, a man who looks like he pulls tractors in his spare time. No one seems to want to mess with Señor Blaustein and I am very relieved. I have enough problems as it is.

Things are getting a little easier. I have a friend, Barbara, who lives nearby. We take the bus together, and I hang out at her house after school sometimes. I never invite her to my house, which really isn't my house at all. I don't even have a room of my own. Dad set up a bed and dresser for me in a corner of the basement. Everyone oohs and aahs like it's so nice and cozy down there, like I'm so lucky because I have so much space to myself, so much privacy. It's spooky is what it is. No one knows it, but I keep the light on all night. There's way too many hiding places to keep track of.

After three weeks, I still haven't been to the hospital. Finally I'm allowed to call, but when I hear her voice, my throat closes up so tight I can't say anything. If I speak, I'll have to cry like a baby and everyone is watching me. Mom sounds sleepy like she just woke up and forgot how to talk. "How is school?" she asks, and I still can't say anything. I wish they wouldn't all watch me. "Okay," I whisper. I want to ask when she's coming home, when can I see her, but I don't ask because I know she doesn't want me to. Dad says everything will happen in good time. No one seems to think that this should be a problem for me.

At school they teach us about menstruation and having babies. They show us a film where the mother comes into the girl's bedroom, which is all pink and fussy with ruffles and café curtains. The mom gives the girl a box all wrapped up like a birthday present and inside is a box of Stayfree pads. Their timing sure is good because soon all the girls are saying that they have their periods. Barbara keeps asking me, "Did you get it? Did you get it?" It's the only annoying thing about her. Secretly I'm waiting for my mom to come to my room and give me the pretty box wrapped up like a birthday present. But my body has other ideas and one day I see bright red blood on my panties. Even though I know what it is, it scares me. I know the truth but somehow

I think this might be something else. Somehow I think there are different rules for me.

Now I've been at Dad's two months. I never did get to see Mom in the hospital and now they tell me Mom is home but I still can't see her. I don't understand this, and when I ask Dad about it, he tells me Mom still needs to rest. "Don't you like it here?" he asks me. How can I tell him liking it or not liking it doesn't matter to me? I just want to go home. I get strep throat and Michelle has to pick me up at school. I'm sick for a week. Mom sends over a stuffed bear with a card that would be perfect for a six-year-old, but she doesn't come to visit. There seems to be an unspoken rule about that. I wonder how sick I would have to get before Mom would come. Not that I mean to do it, but I get sick over and over again. Mumps. The flu. I even get a toothache. Michelle is not pleased with me at all. She seems to think that I'm doing this on purpose.

They take me to the doctor. The doctor asks me if anything is bothering me. Michelle is sitting right there, so how can I say that I miss my mom? I'm afraid my mom is going to die without me. No one would listen to me anyway. I'm just a kid who thinks too much. The doctor gives Michelle little pills, which I have to take every day. They are supposed to make me happy. And I do feel better for a while, but the pain is still inside me somewhere deep and fuzzy where pills can't go, waiting for its chance to have a say.

The belief that unhappiness is preferable to happiness — happiness being seen as some form of being crazy — is the dynamic of all unhappiness.

The belief goes like this:

"If I weren't unhappy about it (the loss, or possible loss), it would mean that I wanted it to happen. If I weren't sad, it would mean I didn't care."

I haven't smiled in months, but last night Daddy and I had a tickle fest. He started it while we were supposed to be watching *Cagney & Lacey.* He walked his fingers across the couch and before I knew it he had gotten me in my most goosey place. Michelle kept telling him to stop, that I'm too old for that, but I guess I have a pretty silly-sounding giggle because it got her going and pretty soon we were all laughing like hyenas. And then the funniest thing happened. I thought of Mom and I stopped laughing. No matter how much Daddy tickled me, I couldn't laugh any more. I had become tickleproof. Everyone just looked at me like "There she goes again."

Breaking Away

If you believed that at this time tomorrow you were going to become very happy, how would you feel now?

I pass my thirteenth birthday at Dad and Michelle's. I have a little party with a cake. I get to invite one friend and stay up till 11 p.m. reading my new book, *The Source* by James Michener, a very important writer. And I get the bike. Dad and I go shopping for it together. It's the coolest bike I have ever seen. It has three speeds and long red, white, and blue streamers that hang from the handlebars. I ask how far the bike can go, and Dad and the salesman both look at me funny. "As far as your little legs can pedal," says the salesman. Dad laughs and pats me on the back. I ask if I can ride my bike to school, but Dad and Michelle both think that's not safe, even though a lot of other kids in the neighborhood do it. I'm only supposed to ride the bike in the neighborhood, like the little kids do. I'm beginning to think that Dad and Michelle don't make too much sense and I make a conscious decision to stop listening to them. Barbara says that parents can be toxic.

I love my Dad and Michelle, but I can't talk to them. At dinner, Dad rants and raves about this and that, and I'm afraid to say anything. He's upset about the town government, how property taxes are so high. He's upset about how kids dress today and about how nuclear weapons are going to wipe us all off the face of the earth. He's especially upset about the Jews in the concentration camps. No one in our family was ever in one, but Dad can't get over it. He keeps telling me about it as if it should matter to me. I guess I'm supposed to be a Jew, but no one ever taught me what that means. Dad says that six million Jews were in the camps. I secretly think he's exaggerating, but Barbara shows me where it's written in her encyclopedia under Hitler. I'm supposed to feel as if any day I could be taken to a camp.

In *The Source*, James Michener writes about the Jews in a way that makes you proud to be one. I start to get excited about belonging to this great group of people, having a spectacular heritage, even if it means being picked on and maybe even killed. But then I remember who I am — the Jewish girl who hangs out in the back of the Catholic church, who doesn't even really know what the major Jewish holidays are, and I feel frustrated and disappointed. As if there's a perfect place for me to be but somehow I can't find the way.

"How come your mom didn't come to your birthday?" Barbara asks me. She doesn't know that Mom is sick. Every time Barbara asks about Mom, I make up some story about how she's redecorating my room or working on a big project or having the house painted, all reasons why I have to stay with Dad. "She wanted to," I say. "She just couldn't make it this time." At least I didn't lie.

We're at Barbara's house after school trying on her mom's evening clothes. I'm not ever supposed to be there when Barbara's mother isn't home, but that's the best time. We can snoop to our heart's content and even steal a smoke in the basement once in a while. Barbara is an only child like me. Her father died when she was seven, and her mother never remarried. She has a boyfriend, though, who takes Barbara and her mother out to dinner and the movies, even bowling, as if they were a real family. But Barbara's mother won't remarry until Barbara is grown up, she says. Barbara acts as if that's the way it's supposed to be, but I know that's special. My mom won't remarry either, but Dad says that's because Mom is unrealistic. She keeps thinking they'll get back together again.

Barbara's mother is really tiny, so her clothes almost fit us, except in the bosom area of course. Not that we're flat. Barbara is already wearing a bra, and I should be. Now you can see nipples through my undershirt sometimes. It's extremely embarrassing. "You should have a training bra," Barbara says, and we both laugh.

"I'm waiting for my mom to take me shopping," I say. I'm wearing a red sequined dress that on me goes almost down to the floor and black patent leather high heels.

"Let's call your mom," she says suddenly. "You can tell her about your new boobs." But I'm afraid to call. I'm supposed to let her be for now. "I vant to be alone," Barbara says dramatically, flinging the end of a fake stole over her shoulder. "But seriously, Annie, sometimes people only think they should be alone. What if your mom misses you and would really want to hear from you?"

"I think my mom would come and get me if she felt that way," I say, but I am wondering now. What if Mom is really wondering why I don't call or come to see her? I know Mom can be a real hermit when she's sick, but she was always glad to see me. I can't understand why things are different now. "I'm gonna call her," I say. "Where's the phone?" And I start to clomp across the room in my high heels. But Barbara has other ideas.

"Does your mom like surprises?" she asks, giving me one of her devilish grins.

"Yeah, kinda," I say, "as long as it doesn't involve people popping out of closets."

"So what if we just kinda show up one afternoon? Would that freak her out?"

"I don't know," I say. "It depends on her mood. But how would we even get there?"

So we start to plan the surprise. We look up my address on a street map and find out it's less than two inches away, ten miles or so we guess. I'm amazed to see the straight line I can draw from Dad's house to Mom. All this time I've been feeling that Mom is beyond my reach, but there she is, just two inches above us to the right. I can go home if I want to. There are probably even buses that go there. We decide to try it on the bikes.

Just thinking about going home again and seeing Mom makes me feel so happy, I can hardly stand still. We dance around Barbara's house in our sequined gowns, twirling, laughing, and singing, "Here she comes, Miss America." I crown Barbara Miss 7th Grade and she crowns me Miss Nipples in the Tee Shirt. For the first time in months, a heavy weight is lifted from my heart and I am looking forward to something — to being with my mom again, just us in our house on Madison Street.

People feel now what they believe they are going to feel in the future. They feel whatever feelings they believe will "happen" to them. They feel now whatever they believe it will be "natural" to feel in the future.

Disappointment at the End of the Road

This is happiness: to know that everything that is, up till now, is not wrong. You are still free to want anything to be different or not from now on. It is not wrong that it is what it is, and it is not wrong to want it to be different.

Barbara and I train for the event like two Olympic hopefuls. Neither one of us has ever gone more than twenty minutes at a time on a bike. We estimate that it will take at least two hours to get to Mom's house. My plan was to talk to Mom and get her to call Dad and tell him to let me come home. Barbara urged me to call and just talk to her, but I was afraid that Mom wouldn't let me come and see her. Dad and Michelle have told me so many times that Mom was too sick to see me or even talk with me. I'm desperate to see for myself.

The hours between 3:30 and 5:30 p.m., when I'm allowed to go to Barbara's and study after school, is our prime training time, as well as the weekends, whenever we can concoct alibis. We hit our first milestone of a half-hour round trip pretty easily, but staying on the bike longer than that kills our rear ends. We force ourselves to alternate between standing and sitting for long stretches at a time, and we each pledge to do forward lunges that we learned in gym every morning to build up our leg muscles. After about two weeks we build up to an hour-long ride with no stops. We decide we would add in a fifteen-minute break to drink water and stretch before getting back on the bike.

The first time we try that we end up falling asleep in the park until almost nightfall and make it back just in time to slide in under our curfew. Eventually, by adding incremental time on the bike with two rest stops of only ten minutes, we achieve a two-hour journey. This is bringing us pretty close to my neighborhood — just a few more blocks and I'll be home. We set the first Saturday in October — exactly one year after I had left home — as the date we would make the journey for real.

I'm so nervous at breakfast that morning that Daddy and Michelle almost send me back to bed. I make up a ridiculous story about tryouts for the school play.

"Oh, how wonderful," chirps Michelle. "What play is it? How come we didn't get a note from the school? Is Barbara trying out too? How are you getting there?"

Me: "*Sound of Music*. Forgot to give it to you. Yes. I thought we would take our bikes, just this once. Can I be excused?"

They agree, as long as I'm home by four.

Then I bolt for the door but not before overhearing them telling each other that I have finally settled in. This is the first time in my life I have ever told a bald-faced lie, although I have to admit I've been lying to them for months by not telling them what I've been up to. I think about all this as I roll my bike out to the curb and ride the short distance to Barbara's house, almost turning around and confessing the whole scheme.

When Barbara sees my face, the first thing she says is, "You spilled your guts, didn't you?"

"No, but I wanted to," I admit.

"Why, in God's name? They would just ground you, keep you from going. It's not right that they've kept you away from your mom. You want to see her, don't you?"

To my surprise, I start defending them and we get into a big fight. Barbara calls me a pudding-faced coward and I call her a dumb ox. Then she tells me she's ashamed to be seen with me and I tell her I never want to speak to her again. I start to storm out of the room, when Barbara's mother pokes her head in to see what all the fuss is about. She looks from one of us to the other, and neither one of us can think of a thing to say. "Well, then, let me see you make up," she says. "Clearly, if neither one of you can say what the fight is about, it's not worth fretting over. Am I right?" And she is right, we admit for her sake, and later we even admit it to each other.

"Do you really think I have a pudding face?" I ask sheepishly.

"No, I think you're really pretty, much prettier than me. Do you really think I'm dumb?"

"Of course not. You're way smarter than me. I'm just really nervous. What if my mom is really mad at me? What if my dad and Michelle catch us on our bikes a mile from here? What if my grandmother opens the door and calls the cops?"

"Calls the cops!" Barbara says. "Why would she do that? Why do you always imagine the worst, most way-out thing that could happen?"

I don't know how to answer that, except that somehow in my life way-out things did happen and I can never predict or explain how any of it came to be. When we finally take off on the bikes, nothing feels right from the very start. Instead of feeling that I'm getting closer and closer to home, I feel like I'm getting farther away. All of a sudden, there seem to be more hills than I remember. My butt hurts after only fifteen minutes, and my legs strain when I try to stand up and pedal.

When we take our first break after a half hour, my legs already feel like tree trunks. I feel like I'm carrying the weight of the world in my backpack. We stop at the park after an hour to rest for fifteen minutes. I'm feeling so mopey by then, I can barely drag myself back to the bike and start pedaling again. All I can think about is how mad Daddy and Michelle are going to be. But neither of us are quitters, so we keep pushing through. Finally, after having to take twice as many rest stops as we planned, we roll up my driveway on Madison Street.

I can see right away that no one is home. It's the last thing I expected. Mom is supposed to be home from the hospital, but the car is gone, the back door is locked, and the shades are drawn. It looks like no one has been there for a long time. There's a hill of newspapers on the front lawn and even a few packages on the front porch. We don't know what else to do so we just sit on the back step and wait. Barbara is worried that she's going to get into big trouble with her mom if she doesn't leave soon. I just can't face it that my mom isn't here. I have no strength left to do anything but sit here on this stoop until she does come home, even if it's months from now. I'll eat here and sleep here. When winter comes, the snow will fall over and around me, and I will turn into a frozen lump.

"Would you think I'm a really bad person if I started back?" Barbara asks. "I'm really scared my mom is going to have a cow if I don't come home soon."

"No, go ahead," I say, actually relieved to be alone, to give that huge lump in my throat a chance to wring itself out in a good cry.

I fall asleep for a while and when I wake up, someone is standing in front of me, calling my name. It's Bruce. I am shocked to see him after all this time. He looks okay, but older somehow and paler. I can tell by the way he is looking at me that he knows everything. He sees the painful look on my face and my bike dropped on the lawn where I left it. We go across the driveway together into his kitchen, and he fixes me a bowl of Campbell's chicken noodle soup. He even puts crackers on a little plate just like Mom does. Saltines. I love them.

He tells me my mom is in a rest home in upstate New York. Nana had told him this several months ago before she left to stay with friends. I am so shocked, for a second the whole world goes white. And then I am so angry I must have turned bright red, because Bruce gets a cold cloth and holds it to my forehead. He asks me what I would like to do and how can he help me? So we cook up a scheme where he will drive me home and drop me a few blocks away so I can ride my bike home just as if I had really been at the rehearsal. It's nearly 4:30 p.m. and they had expected me home a half hour ago, so we decide I will call and say I'm going to be late, but that I will be home soon. Michelle asks to speak to the adult in charge, but I pretend I don't hear her and hang up. I don't care anymore what they think. They lied to me. I plan never to speak to them again.

The Opposite of Wrong

⌒⧫⌒

When things are not the way you would prefer, that does not mean that they shouldn't be happening. It means that they are not what you want. It doesn't mean your life is not what it should be. There is no way it should be, and you do not need to make it be any way.

Your life is exactly what it is, and if you're wanting it different, then that doesn't mean it should not have been or should not be whatever it is. Your wanting it different means that you want it different. Whatever is you up till now is allowed. Whatever you want or choose now is also allowed. You are allowed to be what you are. Your life is allowed to be what it is. Your future is allowed to be whatever it shall be.

*I*t takes only fifteen minutes or so to drive across town. We don't say anything at first. I'm still in shock from the news that my mother is in a rest home hours away from here. I don't even know what that is, but Bruce explains that it is a place where people go to spend time with people trained to help them feel better. He knows the place where she is and he tells me it's like a country club with comfortable private rooms on grounds filled with serene walking paths, a lake, and lots of beautiful trees.

"My mom loves trees," I tell him. "She thinks they have spirits in them."

"So maybe your mom feels at home there," he says. "They're doing the best they can to help your mom feel better. I'm sure your mom would like to see you, but sometimes the doctors feel that patients are better off not seeing family to give them a chance to rest."

"But they all lied to me," I say, starting to cry. "How could they do that?"

"I don't know why they lied," he says. "Could you accept that they were doing the best they could in the situation? Sometimes people lie because they don't know what else to do. You don't like to lie either, but you lied today because you had reasons, am I right?"

He is right, I have to admit. But I still feel bad.

"What bothers you most about their lying to you?" he asks.

It doesn't seem like a real question. All I can say is, "People shouldn't lie."

"You may not want people to lie, but saying they shouldn't is something else, isn't it?" he asks.

"Well, they shouldn't, should they?"

"What do you mean when you say 'they shouldn't'?"

I really have to think about that. "Aren't parents supposed to tell the truth?"

"Well, we may want them to, but why are they supposed to?"

"Because it's the right thing to do?"

"And what makes it the right thing?"

I start to get a little annoyed. I can't imagine why an adult, especially such a smart one, doesn't know that it's wrong to lie. But I can't help remembering my lies of just a few hours ago. Even now I'm lying by sneaking back to Dad's house in Bruce's car. But I don't feel good about it! I don't know what else to say, so I say, "It's just not right to lie."

"What does right mean?" he asks.

"Well, right means the opposite of wrong," I say, feeling really proud of myself. But I'm not going to get off that easy.

"And what does wrong mean? And don't say the opposite of right."

"It means something you do that you get punished for."

"I see. So punishment is a part of this?"

"Don't you think that people should be punished if they do wrong things?"

"Do you?"

I realize that by agreeing, I would also have to think that I should be punished. I don't like that. Then I have a bright idea. "How do you get people to act the right way if you don't punish them when they do wrong?"

"And why do people have to act right?"

"Can't I just want them to?"

"Sure, we all want what we want, right? But why call it 'acting right,' 'acting wrong'? Isn't it really just about what we want? Why should people be punished or rewarded one way or the other?"

"Because."

"Because why?"

"Why are you always asking why?"

Bruce surprises me by laughing. I thought he was going to be angry. "I ask why," he says, "because I want to know what's true for you, not what's supposed to be. Let's get back to your feeling bad about their lying, which is why we are having this conversation, right? What if you weren't bothered about their lying?" He asks me, "Would that be okay with you?"

I have to do something funny with my mind to figure that out. It reminds me of one of those tests where you have to figure out which shape doesn't fit. Is he testing me? "If I didn't care whether they lied, they'd do it over and over, and then I would never know anything. They'd think it was perfectly okay to treat me like that."

"Why would it have to mean that?" he asks. "Why can't you care and not feel bad?"

That stops me in my tracks. All of a sudden it's as if a lightbulb goes on over my head. I had thought that feeling bad and caring were the same thing. "You mean," I say, "if I don't feel bad, I can still get what I want?"

"Well," he says, smiling, "we don't really know, but what you are saying is that you believe your feelings have something to do with that. So, if you weren't unhappy, what would you be afraid would happen?"

"I guess I'm afraid that nothing would happen. Nothing would change."

"What do you mean?"

"Wouldn't they have changed already if they wanted to? If I'm unhappy, at least they can see they are hurting me."

"Well, maybe it would matter to them if they saw that. But is it worth it? Do you want your happiness to be attached to what people do and don't do?"

"I guess I thought it had to be. So what do I do instead?"

"Whatever you want to do. For example, what does it feel like if you imagine yourself going home this evening and saying, 'Daddy and Michelle, I forgive you for lying, and from now on, I would always like you to tell the truth.' What does that feel like?"

I'm not so sure I could ever do that, but when I think about doing it, I feel good. And amazed. It's like there's a whole room in my brain full of things to do but the door has been locked. I wonder what my life would be like if I could go in that room whenever I wanted.

"You'd be doing the best you can to get what you want, wouldn't you?" he asks me.

If thoughts could glow, this one would be building a little fire in my heart. I often feel as if I should be doing things differently, especially when it comes to the adults in my life, who are so often unhappy. As he helps me take my bike from the trunk, I ask him, "Is this what you do? Is this therapy?"

He considers that. "This is the way I talk to people to help them with their unhappiness," he says.

I like that. It seems like the most important thing a person could ever do in life.

Lies Love Company

When I get home, there's a crowd waiting for me. My dad and Michelle, Barbara and her mother are sitting in the rarely used living room. They all look at me with the same eyes — eyes that see the wrong in me — even Barbara, who is blaming me now to save herself. I stand in front of the little semicircle of four on the beige circular couch, waiting to hear my sins over the glass coffee table.

"I'm deeply disappointed in you," says Dad.

"We're going to have to take your bike away," adds Michelle.

"We thought we could trust you . . ."

"To tell us the truth."

"Not only did you lie . . ."

"But you apparently tricked Barbara into going with you."

"Why did you tell Barbara you had permission from us to go?"

"And that we discussed it with Barbara's mother? You had Barbara believing she had her mother's permission."

"How could you have disrespected us so much?"

"Why do you hate us so much?"

"What do you have to say for yourself?"

"I didn't," I say, starting to cry in spite of myself. I wish I were back in the car with Bruce, where things made sense.

"Didn't what?"

I look at Barbara. What's the use? Barbara had saved herself. At my expense. Barbara had abandoned me.

"Didn't what?" they repeat.

"I just wanted to see Mom. You said she was there. She wasn't."

"That's not what this is about, young lady. Did you or did you not say you were just going to rehearsal?"

"I don't know," I say, knowing it always drives them crazy when I say that.

"Barbara's mother has asked us not to let you two spend time together," says Michelle. "She believes you are a bad influence on Barbara. What do you have to say to that?"

Before I know what I am doing, my eyes fasten themselves on Barbara's downcast eyes and won't let go. It's like my eyes have a life of their own, like they want to drill a hole in Barbara's head and let the truth out. This infuriates Barbara's mother. "That child is seriously disturbed," she screams. "That child needs to be severely punished."

Then they are all up off the beige couch. Dad is yelling at Barbara's mother. "Watch yourself," he says. "What kind of talk is that? Get out of my house!" Barbara is crying. Her mother practically picks her up and runs out of the house. Michelle keeps stroking my father's arm, saying, "It's all right, Marty," as if he were the one who was being attacked. I don't like her very much at this moment.

I get sent to my room without supper. Later, they both come in separately. Dad brings a bologna sandwich, which just gets stuck in my throat like a giant glob of peanut butter. Michelle gives me a hug and tells me she and Dad are only trying to do what's best for me. Neither one apologizes for lying to me. When Michelle leaves, she asks me if there is anything I would like to say to her. I think about it, but the only words that come to mind are ones I am sure I should not say out loud: I forgive you for lying. I forgive you for lying about where Mom is. I forgive you for not standing up for me today.

Even saying the words to myself has an immediate effect on me. I look Michelle in the eyes and smile. Two weeks later, they take me home.

Don't Believe Everything You Hear

Fear and unhappiness are caused by the belief that something other than fear is the cause of the unhappiness you see in the world.

*E*ven though Mom is still upstate in the hospital, I am allowed to go home because Nana "gave up her freedom to take care of an ungrateful child." She isn't happy about it. Mom is coming home soon, though, and we have a lot of work to do to get the house ready.

"Your mother is in a very delicate state," says Nana, handing me a mop. "Anything could upset her," she says (looking at me as if I were "anything"), "and send her right back to the hospital."

I am expected to come home from school every day and help with the cleaning. Mom shouldn't see a speck of dirt. Clutter, especially, is absolutely forbidden. Clutter, by its very nature, can drive a person insane. Nana doesn't want Mom to worry about whether the house is clean or the bills are paid or what we will eat for dinner. Everything has to be taken care of by Nana, who knows how to do things right.

Often at meals, we talk about how things will be when Mom comes home. "Your mother has been through a lot," says Nana. "She mustn't get upset about anything. You must do exactly as you are told and not hang on your mother day and night."

On the night before Mom comes home, I go into her room with a little bouquet of flowers from our yard. Nana has completely changed her room. The piles of books Mom always keeps by her bedside are gone. All her cosmetics and perfumes are hidden away in drawers. The familiar clutter of her night table, her favorite hand cream, her reading glasses, the crystal carafe and glass Daddy and I had given her one Christmas are all gone somewhere. The room looks like a hotel room and smells like Lysol.

In bed that night, I think about how excited I am that Mom is coming home, but I'm frightened that I might do something that will send her back to the hospital. Nana seems to be of the opinion that this is inevitable — that I am the reason Mom is there in the first place. That makes me mad. That's a damn lie, I tell myself and work myself into a silent rage imagining how I will tell Nana off when I grow up. Nana will be in a nursing home and I will be tall and married with my own car, and I will say to Nana, "Nana, you miserable old bitch, how could you say such hurtful things to a defenseless child?" That makes me cry, which makes me even madder. I toss and turn for hours, giving myself a headache and worrying that I won't be able to get up for school. Finally, I get up and sit by the window facing Bruce's house. What would he say? I'm not quite sure, but I know all the things he wouldn't say. He wouldn't say Nana is a bad person. He wouldn't say I am a beaten, defenseless child. He would say, "They are doing the best they can," and I would know it was the truth.

The house is so quiet, I can hear Nana's snoring as soon as I open my door. I sneak into Mom's room, find all her things in a box in the back of her closet, and put them out again. I spray her favorite perfume on the bedsheets, mess up the towels in the bathroom, which had been lined up in order of size, rip out the hospital corners on the bed. Then I get right into her bed, pull the too-starchy sheets up around my neck and sleep like a baby until it is time to get up for school.

Happiness Is for Other People

Only the person who diligently questions his own unhappiness is at all suited to help another. You can help others best when you have no tolerance for any unhappiness as if it were necessary — no fear of anything. To fear unhappiness is the biggest mistake and self-deception. It is denying that all our previous unhappiness was anything but self-chosen.

Sometimes it seemed to Bruce that his most disturbed clients were closer to real happiness than many others. At some level, there was a passionate rock-solid commitment to their beliefs. They were willing to rant and rave over it. They threw themselves into walls over it. They were willing to see their lives ripped to shreds over it. Yet, somehow, for them even the darkest hole that they had dug for themselves could be lit instantly with the light of happiness, a light they embraced or rejected, sometimes with quiet acceptance, sometimes with great passion. Many of his so-called "normal" clients tended to work through the same set of problems over and over, and when they invariably reached the core belief that revealed to them why they were unhappy, they seemed to cover it over like a dog with a bone, waiting to dig it up when they needed it, delaying happiness for some future time. As if it would always be there.

The client came in without his family. They usually came with him to his sessions but had called to say they were afraid to be in the car with him. On their last outing to the supermarket, he had grown outraged when another driver cut them off. From the backseat he had reached across his mother, who was driving, and punched the car horn with all his might. His mother was so frightened, she hit the accelerator and rear-ended the offender. The client's hand was broken in six places, and his family was facing a lawsuit. It was possible he would have to be institutionalized again.

"How can I help you today?" Bruce asked. They sat and looked at each other for a full fifteen minutes. Bruce looked at the patient's heavily bandaged hand. "What happened to your hand?"

The client laughed nervously. "I broke it when my mother drove into the rear end of the car in front of us."

"Is that so?"

"Yeah, do you mind if I smoke? Can I light it from yours?"

"Go ahead." Bruce handed him the cigarette. "Why don't you see if you can deal with some things?" he asked.

"What things?" the client asked, holding his hand between his legs.

"Wouldn't you like to be happier?"

"I don't know."

"What are you unhappy about?"

"You. Seeing therapists all the time."

"If you weren't so unhappy you wouldn't have to see therapists all the time."

"What if I was born this way?"

"You weren't, and even if you were, is that any reason why you have to stay that way?"

The client examined the tray that held Bruce's business cards. "Can I take one of these?"

"Be my guest." Then: "What if you don't want to be unhappy?"

Silence. Smoking.

"How are we going to let this real self that wants to be happy, be happy?" Bruce asked.

"What time is it now?" asked the client, turning the wooden desk clock around so he could see it. He picked the clock up, weighing it in his good hand. "This is heavy."

Bruce said, "You are going through life every day telling yourself that there are loads of things for you to be unhappy about. Maybe you don't have to be unhappy. Wouldn't that be great?"

No response. The client was busy trying to tie his shoelace.

Bruce tried again: "Let's talk about unhappiness."

"I don't think there's anything to talk about. My family should be here, not me."

"Let's talk about adjustment."

"We can talk about unhappiness if you want. But that's not me. *You* told me I'm unhappy."

"Why do you believe that things can interfere with your happiness?"

"People have control over me. You. You might put me in the hospital. What's wrong with me anyway?"

"I don't think there's anything wrong with you."

The client sat back in his chair, crossed his legs, took a quick drag off his cigarette. "So what's new?" he asked, lowering his eyes.

"Do you want to talk about unhappiness?" Bruce asked patiently. "Let's talk about what makes you unhappy."

"I'm not unhappy."

"You're happy?"

The client nodded, looking down at the desk.

"Will you always be happy is really the important question. Will anything stop you from being happy?"

"Happiness is something you are born with," the client stated.

"How come you told me you haven't been happy?" asked Bruce.

"I was kidding. I was bored."

Bruce knew better: "If you weren't unhappy, why would they want you to come?"

"My family thinks I'm crazy."

"It's because you seem so unhappy to them."

"What's crazy mean?" the client asked. "Insane?"

"Does it hurt you?" asked Bruce.

"No, I think they are all crazy."

"Does it bother you?"

"They influence my life, my job. But I'm not crazy. I'm happy. When my family was here, you made it look as if I'm always unhappy. I'm always happy."

"Except when you're not," said Bruce.

"You can't be happy all the time. What do you want me to do — go around with a smile on my face all the time? Like you do?"

"What's wrong with that?" asked Bruce.

"People think you're nuts."

"Are you nuts?"

"Who cares? I guess I'm a little nutty sometimes. They say I'm schizophrenic."

"But what does that mean? Isn't that some kind of unhappiness?"

"It's a chemical imbalance. I refuse to go around with a smile on my face."

They both laugh.

"Why?"

"Because people will think I'm nuts."

"They think you're nuts anyway," said Bruce.

"You're going to have me going out of here with a smile on my face," said the client, laughing.

"Would that be so bad? Why do you refuse to go around with a smile on your face? I am really getting the impression that a person in your state — who has gone through so much unhappiness — could be happy just like that." And he snapped his fingers.

A smile played at the edge of the client's mouth. "Isn't my time up yet?" he asked, putting out his cigarette. They looked at each other for a few minutes. The client got up and stood behind his chair, studying the edge of the desk. "Happiness is for other people," he said, "isn't it?"

"Only if you say so," said Bruce.

Laughing Even When It Hurts

To be impatient with unhappy people because they continue in their unhappiness may be believing that people should rid themselves of unhappiness. That would be to deny or forget that they are unhappy because they believe it is a necessary and inescapable truth about themselves. That they don't have that belief is an impossibility. Who would or could ever be unhappy otherwise? All unhappy people believe it is necessary to be unhappy. That's why we have to ask why.

Mom has been home two weeks, and I am starting to see that nothing has changed. I thought they were going to fix Mom in that fancy place up in the mountains. I thought Mom was going to be the old Mom who used to play with me and go out shopping and paint little pictures. Even the Mom who used to spend most of the time in her room would be okay. That Mom still used to be my mom. We still had our adventures. That Mom used to rub my back and play with my hair. We used to giggle sometimes when she wasn't crying.

This Mom is a stranger. She doesn't even smell like Mom. This Mom has an invisible fence around her that no one can go past. This Mom is like a windup Mom. She does all the Mom things. She does the grocery shopping. She gets her hair done. She even started playing poker again. She smiles and talks. But she doesn't laugh the same way. It's as if her laugh is coming from a different place. Not the place deep down inside that has no rules. This laugh comes from a jar on a dusty shelf, with the other preserves. I don't like this Mom. And we fight a lot.

"Are you going out looking like that?" Mom says.

"Like what?" I look down at my favorite faded jeans and Daddy's flannel shirt hanging out. I look really cool.

"You're not going to school looking like that."

"All the kids do," I say.

"Go up and change," she says, and then does the thing that really infuriates me. She smiles at me. We are at the breakfast table. Nana is making pancakes, and she stops what she is doing and turns around and looks at me. The look says, Do what your mom says or she will go instantly insane and it will all be your fault.

"I can't," I say, taking a giant step onto the ledge.

Mom keeps smiling. Nana puts her hands on her hips.

"My other clothes are all dirty." Before they can say anything more, I jump off the ledge. I grab my books and charge out of the house. I haven't had breakfast. My insides are all knotted up. I am so mad I can hardly breathe. I hate them. And you know what? The hell with school. I'm not going to stupid school. I'm going to do whatever the damn son-of-a-bitch hell I want. And I'll curse if I want to.

So I stomp down to the park and plop myself down on a bench and glare at the falling leaves. Then I jump up and stomp around the park, kicking the leaves into brilliant leaf storms and hurling sticks and rocks into the pond. I'll show them. I'll never go home. I'll never go to school. I'll live in this park and no one can make me leave. Screw them. Who do they think they are anyway? I'm sick of their bullshit. I'm so mad, I can hardly stand myself. Then I start to cry, of course, which makes me hate them even more, but mostly it makes me feel weak and sorry-assed. What a mess I am. What a gigantic baby.

I hear leaves crunching. I look across the large pond draped with weeping willows, and I see Bruce walking in my direction along the path that circles it. He doesn't see me yet. I sit on the bench and watch him, knowing that we'll be face to face in a matter of minutes. He is actually walking and smoking a cigarette at the same time. I never saw anyone do that before. And the way he walks, you would swear he owns this park and everything in it. I'm starting to feel calmer watching him because he is so calm, so sure of himself. He is getting closer, and I put my head down because I don't want him to see me crying. I know he sees me though. I can feel him looking at me. Then the sound of leaves crunching under his feet stops and I look up to see him standing on the path about ten feet away. He is looking up at the sun, which is just coming up high over the trees. I look, too, and a funny thing happens. I get the strange feeling that we are all connected. Me and Bruce and the sun — even the trees and the squirrels and the dead leaves on the ground. I look at Bruce's face. He is looking at the sun the same way he looks at me.

He starts walking again, but something is different. He is limping and dragging his right leg slightly. He keeps on walking, but I can see he is having a lot of trouble making it around the bend. I'm shocked at how much has changed in the last few seconds. As I watch him struggle through his walk, I know without a doubt that something is really wrong, and as he reaches the bench I'm sitting on, he stops and puts out his arm. I am just tall enough to slip under it and help prop him up.

"Want to be my walking stick?" he asks, laughing. There is nothing else I would like in the whole world, I suddenly think, as if I've been waiting for this my whole life. I think we are going to be heading home, but we don't. We walk around the path again, ever so slowly — me and Bruce and the sun, with the autumn leaves all around us.

"What's wrong with your leg?" I ask. He says a word I can't pronounce and explains it means that the veins are getting too small for the blood to force its way through. I ask if it hurts and he says not as much as it's going to. But he looks calm, and I realize I'm calm too.

How can you be calm when your legs don't work, I wonder, but I don't want to ask. It's not really a question. It's a surprise.

We walk home together, Bruce and me. Nana is standing in the driveway and she gives me the evil eye, but I just smile at her. She and Mom are in a place I don't want to be in. The place where no one has any fun, where you have to watch your every step in case you slip on a banana peel and crack your head open. I want to be in the place where Bruce lives — the place where people keep laughing even when it hurts.

How Can I Not Be Unhappy About the Loss of a Loved One?

Today Maryanne didn't come to school because last night her father died. No one expected Maryanne's father to die, says Mrs. Hatcher, our homeroom teacher, and that's why it's so hard for the whole family. We are all supposed to say a prayer for Maryanne in whatever way we usually say our prayers. The only prayer I know is "Now I Lay Me Down to Sleep," but that doesn't seem right. Maybe I could ask Mrs. Hatcher what a good prayer would be. The thing is, Maryanne is my best friend almost. I've known her since second grade. I ate dinner at her house maybe a million times. I know all her brothers and her sister. Her mom has driven me home from school tons of time.

In art class we draw with pastels, and I decide to draw a special picture for Maryanne. I draw a picture of Maryanne's family around the dinner table with me as a guest. There's a big bowl of spaghetti and meatballs in the middle of the table and a big salad bowl with croutons, the way they always eat it. There's Mrs. Gugliamo at one end of table and Mr. Gugliamo at the other. I draw a halo over his head for some reason, but then I think that's too stupid and I turn it into a hat. A big yellow hat. I try to start the picture over, but the art teacher, Mrs. Shaw, comes by and says, "Why, Annie, that's quite a family portrait you have going there. Good work!" So I figure, stay with a good thing. That's what Mr. Gugliamo always used to say. He had these sayings that he would bring out when questions came up. Should Maryanne quit the flute and take up the tuba? "Stay with a good thing," he'd say. "You're good at the flute." Should Mrs. Gugliamo bake brownies for the school bake sale or try that new recipe her mother gave her? "Stick with what you know," he'd say. "Your brownies are wonderful." I liked Mr. Gugliamo. He always laughed at my jokes, even the ones where I forgot the punch line. The whole family would try to guess what the punch line might be. But no one would get it, and Mr. Gugliamo would lean over to me and say, "Don't worry, Annie, it's in there somewhere," and he'd point to my head and wink. I liked him a lot.

And now he's dead. I figure I will take the drawing to Maryanne's house on the way home from school. When I do, this really tall lady whom I never saw before answers the door. I can see cars parked up and down the street and the house seems to be full of people, but the lady doesn't invite me in. She takes the picture, though, and says, "This is very sweet." She looks at the drawing, and I swear to God, her right eye squeezes shut just like a camera. She looks at me, then, a little differently, I think, and says, "I'll see that Maryanne gets this." I decide I don't like this lady. I can't understand why she doesn't let me in the house. I know Maryanne would like to see me. I always make her laugh. After a few days, I call the house, but someone I don't know answers and says, "The family is at the funeral." I think, I would have liked to go to the funeral, but no one invited me. I guess kids don't count when it comes to stuff like this.

But then one day Mom surprises me by saying that she and I are going to go see the Gugliamos. We get all dressed up and buy a cheesecake from the Italian bakery. My mouth is watering for the cheesecake, but when we get to Maryanne's house, that same really tall lady takes the cake and puts it on the dining room table along with a bunch of other cakes and cookies. It looks like the whole bakeshop got transferred to the Gugliamos' house.

I am allowed to go upstairs to see Maryanne then. She's sitting on the floor playing with her dollhouse. Maryanne hasn't played with that dollhouse since we were kids. I sit down beside her, and she tells me her Dad actually made her this dollhouse. I am amazed by that. Mr. Gugliamo was this gigantic man with these enormous hands. It's hard to imagine him putting together the tiny kitchen cabinets, painting the little walls, hanging up the little pictures. There's even wallpaper in the bedrooms. Did he shrink himself down to a tiny workman and put up the wallpaper with a tiny roller in the little house?

That reminds me, I wonder where my picture is. While we play "redecorate," my gaze slides around the room trying to find the picture. It's nowhere to be seen. Finally, Mrs. Gugliamo comes in and says my mom is getting ready to leave. "See you at school," I say, not knowing really what to say. Maryanne looks at me and shrugs. She looks like one of those kids from those really poor countries in the magazines. For only fifty cents a month, you can feed this child. I want to take her home with me, but I know that won't help. Her dad won't be there either. So I say, "I think this is the most beautiful dollhouse I have ever seen." Maryanne smiles, but she looks so sad. I wish I could just stay and play with her and the dollhouse until she really smiles again.

In the hall, Mom gives Mrs. Gugliamo a hug. Mrs. Gugliamo says, "Thank you so much for coming. It's so good to talk to someone who understands." You could have knocked me over with a feather. I look at my mother with my eyes almost popping out of my head. And then my mother says, "The hardest part is not being able to talk about it, so don't hesitate to call me." Someone has taken my mom's brain out of her body when we weren't looking and replaced it with another woman's brain, the brain of a woman who actually has a dead husband. My back is to Mrs. Gugliamo so I open my eyes real wide and look at Mom, giving her the signal. She ignores me and gives Mrs. Gugliamo a hug. I can never show my face here again. That's all.

Then I see the big tall woman again and I excuse myself from the hugging and go up to her. "Um, excuse me," I say, feeling like a little nobody. "Do you remember me? I dropped off a picture for Maryanne a few weeks ago? I was wondering, I didn't see it in her room." The tall lady folds herself down to my level, which is really funny until she takes my hands and looks me right in the eyes. She does that camera thing again with her right eye, and I can't help thinking of the FBI. "We decided not to give it to her just yet," she whispers. "It wasn't quite appropriate at this time. You understand, don't you?" I don't, but I nod that I do. Then I look over and see my mom actually crying on Mrs. Gugliamo's shoulder, and I think: Here we are, the Inappropriate Family. Like mother, like daughter. That's all. Just let me disappear. Let me just disappear into thin air.

Finally, Mom disengages herself and we leave. Our house is just a few houses away so we're walking home and she isn't saying anything and I'm about to explode, I'm so beside myself. And finally I just plant myself in front of her on the sidewalk. "What was that?" I almost scream it. "What was that back there?"

She just looks at me. "Annie, you really need to learn to have a little compassion."

That's what she says. Compassion. "Compassion for what?" I ask her. "Do you have a dead husband? Daddy is alive, Mom. Daddy is alive and living in the next town. How can you act with that woman as if you have experienced the same thing she has? Her husband is dead. I don't get it."

She keeps walking. She's not crying but her lip is quivering really hard and when we get to the door, she turns and looks at me. "I don't expect you to understand," she says. "Sometimes you can lose someone while he is still alive, and feel just the same as if he were dead. It's still grief. It's still a burden we have to bear, Annie."

"But Daddy is happy, Mom. If you love him, wouldn't that make you happy? And what if Mr. Gugliamo is in heaven? Isn't that supposed to be a good thing?"

She whirls on me so fast, I jump back and almost fall down the front steps. "You," she says, jabbing at my chest with her finger, "you don't know the first thing. You are a child. A thoughtless, careless child. You know nothing! When people lose the ones they love, it's natural to suffer. What kind of a person are you?"

We stand there in the cool night on our front porch staring at each other. I have never seen her eyes so cold. I am certain that at this moment she truly hates me.

"What did I do?" I ask her. "Why are you looking at me like that?"

"I don't know you," is all she says, and she slams the door in my face.

When I say my prayers that night, I ask God to forgive me for being a thoughtless, cold, unfeeling child. And I ask God to take care of Mr. Gugliamo and make sure he finds his way to heaven. I ask God to forgive me for not being sad when I am supposed to be sad. "I can't help it, God," I tell my ceiling, "but when I think of Mr. Gugliamo, I get this funny feeling in my chest like everything is all right. I guess you're not supposed to talk about it."

The Policeman on the Porch

*What kinds of things do we consider things to be happy about?
Something that "proves" to us that we are good for ourselves, or
something that takes away what "proves" to us that we are bad for
ourselves? Even good luck. What kinds of things do we consider
things to be unhappy about? Things that "prove" we are bad for
ourselves, or things that take away what "proves" we are good for
ourselves? Even bad luck.*

*The things that can matter to happiness or unhappiness can be
anything: thoughts or lack of thoughts, remembering or forgetting
desires or lack of certain desires, behavior or lack of behavior,
events that happen to or are caused by self, by another person,
by nature or God, or by the lack of another person, or loss of a
thing — in fact, anything that "means" whether we are good or
bad for ourselves.*

Other kids don't have to worry about coming home and finding police
cars in front of their house. They don't have to worry about what's
going to be happening on the other side of the door when they come
home from school. That's why I didn't join the Young Writer's Club
before now. Every week they meet in someone else's house. I couldn't
figure out what to do when it was my turn. But I've been thinking,
now I'm in high school. Mom has been okay for a while, weird but

okay. Maybe this is my year to be in the Young Writer's Club. So, I join the club and we make up the schedule and based on the number of kids in the club, we're going to have to meet at my house at least twice. That makes me nervous.

But the first time, it all goes really great. We get there right after school. Nana greets us with milk and brownies and then disappears into the ironing. Mom doesn't seem to be anywhere around. I think Nana drugged her. A little early nappie for Mommy. I can't prove that, but Nana gives me a sinful little wink and darts her eyes upstairs. This is a new thing — Nana being on my side. It makes me nervous, too.

I guess I got too cocky, too sure of myself. It's May and everything is in bloom. I'm walking around the bend with Brenda, Janice, Felice, Debbie, and Joanna. I'm thinking that the house will look nice with the daffodils up the walk and the trees all leafy and pretty. We young writers have been meeting all year and we're getting to be friends. Well, some of us are. Me and Brenda and Debbie kind of hang out together now. Felice is kind of snobby, being the prettiest one and thinking she is the "gifted" writer. I don't see how anyone who can make a sentence go six lines is gifted. I read it over five times and I still can't figure it out. Naturally everyone is falling all over herself all the time trying to get in good with Felice. And Joanna is too busy taking riding lessons every five minutes. She invited me once but Nana said horses don't like our family and went into this long story about how my great-grandmother had seen a horse trample a young child when she was pregnant with my grandfather. How my grandfather had gotten stepped on by the iceman's horse when he was just a little kid and his foot got all mangled. As if that wasn't enough, another horse had once run wild through the neighborhood, spooked when a fire truck went by and crashed through her greenhouse. And on and on. I tried to get Mom to overrule her, but Mom doesn't care about those things. She lets Nana make all the decisions about what I get to do and what I don't get to do. If I really want something badly, I have to go to a higher court, my dad, who is even more protective but loves to overrule Nana. But I'm saving him for when I want to go camping.

I should have known this meeting would be the one when everything blew up in my face. I really should have known last night when Mom burst into the kitchen where Nana and I are making these cute little finger sandwiches with the crusts cut off. She looks at all the sandwiches and starts that chattering she does when she's getting ready to have a major meltdown. All the time Nana and I are smearing cream cheese and cutting up those little green olives with pimentos and spreading goose liver and stuff all over these cute little breads, Mom is circling round and round the kitchen table, flitting from one subject to another as if someone had asked her to empty her brain of all contents or die.

She was fine last week. We went shopping together for shoes. In fact, she's been pretty good for months. She's even been talking about taking courses at the college. But tonight she's sounding scary. Not making eye contact. Hasn't asked what all these silly little sandwiches are for. She's making us nervous, and we completely lose count of how many sandwiches we're supposed to be making. The pile keeps getting higher and higher as Nana and I work away. You would think the whole school was coming.

Then she disappears, and the kitchen is suddenly so quiet, so calm, as if someone just turned off a cyclone. That should have tipped me off. Now, when we round the corner and I see the police car in front of my house, I almost expect it. The siren isn't going, thank God, but there's Nana out on the front porch talking to the cute one, Glenn. I've known Glenn since I was young. They always send Glenn when Mom disappears. I guess he's an expert or something.

I would really like to die on the spot, but what can I do? All the girls are asking me questions and I'm really starting to feel like I want to smack someone, especially Felice. "Wouldn't this make a great story?" she keeps chirping, without even knowing why the police car is there. For all she knows, they could be coming to tell me my father just got run over by a tractor-trailer.

I hear myself say, "They are just collecting for the Policeman's Ball." I don't even know if the policemen have a ball. We all troop up the steps and I say to Nana, "They can have my whole month's allowance." She looks at me as if I were speaking Japanese or something.

I keep talking to drown out their questions, and so they don't hear Glenn ask, "How long has she been gone?" And Nana says, "Her bed wasn't slept in." I wish I hadn't heard that. I wish I had checked her bed this morning. I wish I had kept track of her pills. I bet she's been flushing them down the toilet. I wonder how come the police car just got here, and I have to figure that Nana was probably hoping Mom would just show up as she sometimes does. But not this time. No ma'am. That would be too lucky. That would be too good to be true. So here I am with a roomful of some really nosy and gossipy girls, and I'll be damned if I'm gonna get all flustered and bent out of shape.

So we have our meeting inside while the policeman is out there on the porch writing things on his little pad. I get the sandwiches and everyone oohs and aahs over the sandwiches with their little colored toothpicks. I can't help but notice the stack is a lot smaller today. Mom must have brown-bagged it. Then Joanna gets this really bad idea that we should all do a fifteen-minute writing exercise about coming home and finding the cops at your door. I would really like to take her head off, but mostly by now I am really worried about Mom. Sometimes when she goes off, she doesn't come back for days and days, and when she does she never says where she has been. That's really annoying because Nana spends just about all her time standing at the front door watching for her. We can't talk about anything but where is Mom and when is Mom coming home. We can't do anything but wait for Mom. When I was a kid, Nana wouldn't even let me go to school when Mom disappeared. But now that I'm older, I go anyway, even if I have to climb down the side of the house. I'm not kidding, you know.

Then there are the times that Mom can't get home. She goes out and gets all panicked and thinks she's lost and hides out somewhere. Once we found her in the back of a church right around the corner. Another time she was in the frozen foods section of Foodtown with a bag over her head, rocking and singing. I don't like to think about those times. They freak me out.

So we all write stories about the policeman on my porch. Mine is about how he lived in the house when he was really tiny and he hadn't been in the house since because his mother died there and he lived in fear that he would have to answer a call there someday. But then that day came and he was so terrified that he would cry and how embarrassing that would be for a man, especially a cop. They're very macho, you know. But it was really okay because this little kid lets him in, and the little kid doesn't have a mother either, so then the cop has to be brave for the little kid. I think it's a good little story, but I can't help but notice the missing moms that come out in my writing. Write what you know. Isn't that what they always say?

Joanna's story is about how the cops have been called because of a peeping Tom and she goes into really graphic detail about what this peeping Tom is doing while he is watching this beautiful woman through the window. As if that would really happen. And Felice writes about how the cop is really in love with the sweet young girl who lives in the house and is so beautiful and gifted but doomed to death. Oh, spare me. Gag, yech. And so on until everyone has read her story and the sandwiches are all wolfed down and we're talking about what's going to be on the finals. And I finally get them out of there.

Mom is still not home, and it's getting dark. I can't stand the thought of her being out another night, so I get Nana to come with me to search the neighborhood. I just tell myself we are going to find her. It's hard though. Now that I don't have the girls to distract me, I'm seriously upset. You can't see it but I'm secretly kicking myself all the way down the block for thinking I could have friends over at the "crazy house." What is wrong with me? On the other hand, I'm wondering what I could have done to make Mom run off again. I go over my behavior for the entire month and I can think of at least three occasions when I was a really selfish brat.

We don't find Mom in any of the usual places so we go home, all beaten and depressed. And ashamed, I am ashamed to say. That's the worst part. I stay up most of the night worrying that she's beaten or dead somewhere and finally fall asleep, I guess, because I wake up and it's the morning. Saturday, thank God. I know immediately that she's home. She's in her bed with her head under the pillow, dead to the world. Her feet are filthy as if she's been walking around barefoot. Could that be true? She's got her clothes on under the comforter. Comforter. That's a good one. I should get one of those. I'm so pissed at her, I'd like to drag her out of the bed and make her tell me where she's been. I'd really like to tell her off. How she's the biggest disappointment of my life. How she's the most selfish person I ever met. How I am so tired of her crap.

I just wish I could fix things. Fix the thing that is wrong with me, with her, with all of us, that keeps us from being like other people, who are so happy and have so much fun and are so good to each other. I just want to fix it. I go to my room and I look in the box where I keep Bruce's notes to me. I close my eyes and fish one out.

Blessed are those who know they are happy. Happy are those who know they are blessed. To be blessed is to have the right to be happy. To be born is to be allowed to be happy. To know you are allowed to be happy is to be blessed.

To be born is to be allowed to be happy? That certainly includes me and Mom. I start to imagine that I am blessed and happy and the next thing I know, I am in Mom's room. I fill her wastepaper basket with warm soapy water and bring it over to her bed. Then I put a towel under her feet and ever so gently, so quietly, so slowly, I wash her feet until they look like baby's feet. And then I cry, for gladness at being allowed to be happy, and for all the tenderness that will never be lost from the world.

Mom's If Only Land

Inside my mom's head is a recording. It goes like this:

If only I had gone to college.

If only I had had that second child.

If only I had insisted that your father come home every night.

If only I had stood up to my parents.

If only I had learned a second language.

If only I had studied art in Paris as I wanted.

If only I had not married so young.

If only I had refused to go to that treatment center.

If only I had not taken all those pills.

If only I had been a better mother.

If only I had been able to work.

If only I had found a way to be calmer.

If only your father had been happy here.

If only I had found a way to be a better person.

If only.

In my house, the language of IfOnly is the only language that means anything. I've heard those words from the time I was a toddler from both my mother and my grandmother. If only my mother had not married my father, she could have gone on to be a great artist, and so famous and so successful she would not be in the position she is in today. If only my mother had gone to art school the way she planned.

If only she had not married, not gotten pregnant, she could have done all these great things, these really important things. And if only she had had more children, yes, more children, that would have helped bring her out of herself. That would have helped keep her on an even keel. If only that had happened, things would be so good, wouldn't they? And if only my father had not run off, had not abandoned his family, wouldn't things have been so great — wouldn't Mom have been okay then? There would be no pills, no weeks and months away at the rest home, no need to lock herself up in her room, no need to act so crazy, so strange. If only things had been different.

When I was six years old, I was chosen for the lead in the school play. I had learned all my lines, had my costume, was all ready for the performance. Then I got the mumps and Darlene got to play Rapunzel instead of me. The next year when my teacher asked if I would like to participate in the school play, I thought about it for a few minutes, and then I said: "I don't believe I should this year. If only the play were in the spring, that would be so much better. But I always get sick in the winter."

"Well, we can take that chance, can't we?" asked Mrs. Finkel, my teacher. "What's the worst that could happen? You'll have fun getting ready for the play, won't you?"

I liked that answer a lot, but when I told my mother, she was against it. "If only you weren't so prone to winter illnesses," she said, "I'd be all for it, but it's hard to say you won't get sick." I remember being so disappointed that my mother said that. I wanted her to be more like Mrs. Finkel and encourage me anyway.

I swore I would never live in IfOnly Land. I would never say, "I should have done." I would never say, "I wished I had." I would never say it, think it, feel it. I did, however, become a resident of WhatIf Land, which is really just the testing ground for IfOnly Land. If you don't watch out, you can spend your whole life bouncing back and forth between "What if?" and "If only." I don't want that to happen to me.

"Mom, why don't you take some classes at the college? They have a pretty good art department."

"I can't see myself there with all those kids," she says.

"Well, then, what about at the high school?" I wave a catalogue that had come in the mail. "They have a few really interesting classes. They even do trips to New York."

"Night school? Really, Annie. Isn't that for immigrants? For people who never finished high school?"

"Where are you getting that?" I ask, trying to control my temper. "I would take some of these courses. They look great. Maryanne's mother takes origami and she's a college graduate. Where else would you learn origami?"

"In Japan. Where else?"

"And what's wrong with immigrants?" I say. "Your nana and grandpa were immigrants and so were Daddy's. They were good people, weren't they?"

"I didn't mean that, Annie. It's just that I wouldn't feel comfortable going to school after all these years."

I don't expect to get anywhere, so why am I getting so annoyed?

"It's too late for me, Annie. Don't try to resurrect my life."

"Mom, you're only forty-five. There's plenty of time left. You could live a complete other lifetime. Don't you want to do something different, have some fun?"

"If only I were younger," she says. "If only I had been smarter."

And that's the end of the conversation.

Unhappy people believe: God is supposed to give us what we want so we will never be unhappy. God is supposed to give us what we need and make us believe we are not unhappy. God is supposed to make us stop believing we are unhappy or bad. God is supposed to give happiness by giving people whatever they believe they need to not be unhappy — money to the poor, health to the sick, success, lovers, new personalities. God is where my future happiness will come from.

Happy people say: God is the one to whom we are grateful for letting us know we don't have to be unhappy when we don't have what we want. We are glad that he has freed us from needing and fearing by letting us know we can free ourselves with his help (his knowing).

God is where my present happiness comes from.

Which do you believe? God is making me happy now? Or God may make me happy someday?

The Right to Be Happy

All people have the right to be happy. It is never wrong to be happy. Those who know it are happy forever.

You have the right to be happy no matter how rotten others think you are, no matter how sinful or stupid or selfish or sick or horrible or thieving or lying, or arrogant or shy or failing or murderous or monstrous. You absolutely have the absolute right to be happy always; no matter how others may hate you, or hurt you, or try to punish you. Those who disagree will be unhappy.

*I*t's Thanksgiving Day, and everyone is mad at me. I'm going to Maryanne's for Thanksgiving dinner. It took me weeks to get up the courage to say I was going. When I finally spit it out at dinner last week, Nana and Mom both drop their forks and stare at me. It is as if I said I'm pregnant or something.

"You would do that?" asks my mother. That's the end of that. The rest of the meal is spent with Mom staring at her food and Nana slamming plates around. They haven't spoken to me since, except of course last night when Nana came into my room to tell me I was killing my mother.

It snows Thanksgiving eve, just enough to make everything look pretty. I wake up happy and excited. I go to the window to see what's doing at Bruce's house, my morning ritual. It always makes me feel good. I can see them in the kitchen getting the turkey ready. Bruce is chopping something at the kitchen table. All of a sudden I get this crazy idea in my head that I can just go over and say, "Happy Thanksgiving." I'm fifteen now. Isn't it time for me to stop following my mother's rules? Don't bother Bruce, they've been telling me since I was born. What are they so afraid of?

I get myself dressed and ready to go. Everyone is still sleeping. It's my plan to get out of the house before anyone wakes up. That way I don't have to hear about it. I already feel as if my stomach is in shreds. My insides are in pieces. I wish I could just forget about them. I don't have to be at Maryanne's until one o'clock. I figure I'll just hang out somewhere.

So I do it. I go to Bruce's back door and ring the bell. They don't answer at first. Who could hear? Opera is blasting through the stereo. The kitchen is full of people doing Thanksgiving things. I'm about to run away when someone notices me. I think it's Bruce's brother. He opens the door and smiles at me. "Can I help you?" He doesn't recognize me. But then Bruce is waving at me from where he's sitting at the table. He smiles at me and I immediately start to cry. I want to tell him all about what a horrible girl I am not to want to spend Thanksgiving with my own family. How I ruined it for everyone. How my mother will probably sedate herself and stay in bed all day because of me. My grandmother will probably take the turkey, stuffing, cranberries, even the shrimp cocktail, and throw it all in the garbage. Then she'll go change her will for the third time this year.

"It's Annie," Bruce says. "Annie came to help us make Thanksgiving."

And just like that, I'm in. After not even having had a conversation with him for at least a year. Someone gives me an apron with a huge smiling turkey on it, and I help Bruce make the stuffing. He's doing everything sitting down, and I wonder why until he gets up to show me how to fry the sausage. His legs don't really seem to work that well. He shows me how to crumble the sausage into a huge frying pan. I'm still crying but no one notices. Bruce's wife puts a big glass of orange juice next to me and someone else hands me a toasted bagel. I feel as if I'm the guest of honor, as if they've all been waiting for me.

When we get finished frying sausage, we mix it all up with bread cubes that Bruce had been cutting up at the table, and add onions and spices and egg. I get to mix it all up with my hands. Everyone keeps saying how good I am at it, how I must have been doing it all my life. They show me how to stuff the turkey, and I do it all myself without dropping any on the floor. Someone pats me on the back, and Bruce winks at me. I'm starting to feel really good, really happy like it's Christmas. When Bruce looks at me, I get this special feeling deep in my heart. It makes me smile and blush. "Remember that time in the wine cellar?" he asks. I almost drop my teeth. I thought I had dreamed that.

Once the turkey is in the oven, Bruce says, "Come with me." We go into a beautiful little room at the front of the house where the piano is. He uses a cane to help him get there and hands it to me when he sits down on the piano bench. It makes me feel special to hold his cane, which is so important to him now. I sit next to him on the bench. He has such strong-looking arms and hands, more like a bricklayer than a piano player, and his playing is strong and sure. I think, I bet that's the way he does everything. Then he stops and offers me a chance to play.

"Oh, I don't play," I say. "I can't even read music."

"Sure you can," he says. "Just do what you do."

I like that. "Do what you do." I feel very embarrassed for some reason, but he's sitting right there waiting, so I do it. I put my two hands up and I just start to move my fingers. It sounds all jumbled, but in some way it sounds kind of nice.

"I'd like to learn to do this for real," I say. That makes us both laugh, and I feel so good again I have to remind myself that my mother and grandmother are right across the hedge feeling sick and sad because I'm such a bad person.

I notice a picture of a man sitting on a bench under a tree, and looking closer, I see a much younger Bruce. He looks almost the same except his face is a little softer, a little fuller, and he has a lot more hair. He is writing something in a notebook. I ask him, "Do you remember what you were writing that day?"

I expect him to have to think about it long and hard, but he says right out, "Sure I do. I once wrote this down for you. See if you remember. I was writing: Blessed are those who know they are happy. Happy are those who know they are blessed."

"I do remember, I tell him. "I especially like the part where you say, 'To be born is to be allowed to be happy.' Do you think that God wants us to be happy?"

"What do you think?" he asks me, as if I know.

And I do know. I know it like I know my own name, suddenly, like I know I'm Annie and I'm fifteen years old. And I also know it's just an expression somehow, for something that can't really be said in words. "Is that why you write all the time?" I ask him. "Is that what you're always saying?" He smiles a smile so huge, so brilliant, that I have to catch my breath. And then we both put our hands on the piano and start playing so loud and crazy that everyone in the house comes in, laughing and dancing around the living room.

A little later, Bruce walks me over to Maryanne's house, which is a just a few doors down. I can see it cost him a lot to walk there, but he doesn't seem to want to let me go alone. We talk a little about my mom and grandmother. He tells me about when he was a teenager and how he had to teach his mother to treat him like an adult. How she got mad and unhappy until she got used to it. It feels good to know that I'm not the only one who made her parents miserable. It's funny but after my morning at Bruce's I almost feel like I don't care if I do go to Maryanne's. I could go home and make the best of our little family Thanksgiving, even if Mom and Nana are still mad. I tell that to Bruce and he says, "Neither one is right or wrong. Just be happy, Annie, and do what you want. Your mother and grandmother will take care of their own happiness, too. That's their choice, as much as your happiness is your own choice."

I stay at Maryanne's an hour and then I excuse myself and go home. Mom and Nana are sitting in the kitchen eating food that Bruce's wife has brought over, because Nana really did throw the food away. I sit with them, so glad that they can receive kindness they understand from my other family across the way.

Happiness is being allowed to be happy.

Happiness is not believing it is wrong to be happy. Happiness is not believing it will become wrong to be happy.

Happiness is not fearing you will have no right to be happy.

Happiness is not believing you should be unhappy. Happiness is not believing you have to be unhappy. Happiness is not believing it is right to be unhappy.

It is evident. God permits you to be happy no matter what or when. Nature permits you to be happy no matter what or when. The only permission you need is your own — to be happy all of the time.

You don't have to deny your happiness ever. It is not wrong to be happy always.

The Woman in the Chair

You cannot be a way that isn't you. Period. No matter what anybody says.

You are allowed to do anything, be anything, feel anything, think anything, but no matter what it is, it will always be you and what you wanted to be. You also don't want to feel bad about it. In fact, you don't ever want to feel bad. You just have not believed this about yourself.

I never used to like any of the boys at school. I don't think they liked me either. They hardly ever spoke to me. They almost never looked at me. Maryanne said they looked at me all the time but I was too self-involved to notice. I'm not sure what self-involved means. I wonder, am I pretty? Maryanne says I'm pretty, but she's my friend. That's what friends say. I like my face, but I'm not pretty the way Maryanne is. Maryanne has this gorgeous long wavy hair and this little turned-up nose. My nose is all over my face, and my hair is kinky and wild-looking. If they look at me, it's because of my chest. Everyone says I have this killer figure. Secretly I like it when they say that, but at the same time it's embarrassing.

Maryanne has been on a date already, with a boy in geometry. They went to the movies and then they had a hamburger. His father drove them. I don't know what's wrong with me, but that doesn't even seem remotely interesting. The first time I got asked out was by this boy, Mark, one of the few Jewish boys in school. He comes up to me in study hall and sits down in the seat next to me. He just sits there until I finally have to ask him, "What do you want?"

"Want to go out?" he asks, all snot-nosey. He asks me as if it's a dare or something. I just look at him. "They said you're fast," he tells me. And then he tries to look down my blouse. Nice.

The truth is, the boys at school scare me. I never hear them say a kind word about any girl. They roam around the school like a pack of wild animals. They don't even look you in the eyes. They stare at your breasts or over your head and make rude mocking gestures when your back is turned. Lots of girls think they are in love with these boys. They mope around if the boy they love doesn't notice them, and when they do get noticed, they ignore everyone else. Last summer, Maryanne fell in love with a boy and I didn't see her for the entire summer. Until they broke up. Then she was back like nothing happened. Why do girls do that? I will never be that way.

I ask them what it feels like to be in love. They say things like, "Every time I see him, I feel sick," or "If he doesn't call me, I feel terrible." I start to wonder if feeling bad is required to be in love. I hope not.

Every once in a while a boy gets stuck on me. Even when I was twelve, eons ago, this weird-looking boy whom I had never seen before started following me around everywhere. One day I came home and there was a card for me on the kitchen table. Mom and Nana were all, "So what's this? Annie has a secret admirer!" The card was so sweet you could almost gag and there was this pretend-gold locket inside it. But the boy never tried to talk to me. What was I supposed to do? Fall in love right there and then and throw myself at him at the first opportunity? Like that will happen.

Daddy is always asking me if I have a boyfriend yet. And Mom and Nana keep buying me party dresses for my first date. So everyone is really happy when I meet Matthew. Matthew is a grade ahead of me and he's not like the rest of the boys. He has friends but he keeps to himself, if you know what I mean. He doesn't hang out in a big pack. I really never noticed him until one day he shows up using the locker next to mine. That's funny because this other kid has had that locker forever and he's still around. I saw him in the cafeteria. Anyway, Matthew seems to spend a lot of time at his locker because every time I go to mine, there he is. Rivers of boys pass by trying to talk to him, but Matthew just gives them a quick nod so they keep moving. Matthew doesn't talk to me or look at me, which I think is kind of odd, being that I probably see him more than any other kid in school now.

Then one day, there's a note stuck to my locker when I get there. The note says, "Dear Annie, check this box if you want to go the movies with me." There are two boxes. One says "Never in this lifetime." The other says "Why not? It's free." That's pretty funny. The note is not signed, which I think is kind of strange. How am I supposed to know who I'm turning down? So I'm standing there looking at this piece of paper, trying to figure out what to do, and here comes Matthew.

"What you got there?" he asks.

I like the sound of his voice right away.

"A note from some nut," I say, trying to shove the note in my pocket.

"Let me see it," he says, and actually fishes my hand out of my pocket like he has some kind of rights or something. I get this goosey feeling like someone just tickled me. He holds the note up and scrutinizes it. "Nice handwriting. Good sense of humor. But sloppy. How are you supposed to know who it's from?"

"That's what I thought," I say.

He turns the note over and over, and then he rips it up and throws it on the floor. "Loser," he says, and walks away.

I'm stunned and thrilled at the same time. "You're not supposed to throw paper on the floor," I yell after him. "You can get demerits for that." I scoop up the pieces and run to my class.

After last period, Matthew and I both get to the lockers at the same time. As I'm walking out of the building, I can feel Matthew behind me and then he's next to me. And we're walking home together, I guess.

"Get any more notes?" he asks me.

"No," I say, looking at him sideways.

"I hope you're not disappointed that you're not going to the movies," he says.

At first I don't know what to say. It amazes me that he would say that. It may be the nicest thing that any kid has ever said to me.

"No," I say. "I can go to the movies whenever I want. My father owns a movie theater." (Not true.)

"Yeah, but it's different when you go on a date," says Matthew.

"How is it different?"

"Well, for one thing, you don't have to pay."

"Why not?" I ask.

"Because the boy pays."

"Not when I date," I say as if I've been doing it for years. "I can pay my own way."

"Ooh, independent, aren't we?" he says.

And I have to laugh, the way he says it, with his whole body. I like Matthew. I'm not in love, though. That would be absurd.

"My father doesn't really own a movie theater," I say.

So Matthew walks me home every day and then one day he offers to help me with my algebra. He wants to come to my actual house and sit down at my actual desk as if everyone does that every five minutes. I'm not really sure if I'm allowed to have a boy in the house. And I'm a little nervous that Mom is going to do something really strange. Or that Nana is going to embarrass me the way she can sometimes.

So we just go in the kitchen and spread out our books, and I drag out some cookies and milk. Around five o'clock Nana comes in with a bag of groceries and almost jumps out of her skin when she sees me sitting there with a boy. She actually invites Matthew to have dinner with us, and I secretly pray that he will just go home. I'm sure he can live without having liver and onions with my crazy family. "Sure," says Matthew, "let me call Betsy." Betsy, it turns out, is Matthew's mother.

How weird is that? I love that. We get through dinner without anyone fainting. Mom is having one of her good days, except she keeps looking at the clock as if her "normal" time is about to expire.

Eventually, Matthew becomes kind of like a fixture in my life, even though after awhile he sees the gamut of my crazy home life. He seems immune to it, like he has some kind of deep-down understanding. The truth is, after Bruce, Matthew is the kindest person I know. We're not in love, though. That would be nuts. We don't walk down the hall holding hands. We don't date, exactly. We just do a lot of stuff together. And we talk on the phone half the night. Mom and Nana keep asking me where this is going and I finally have to ask them, "Where do you want it to go? I'm still a kid, after all. Gadzooks!" (My new expression.) They have so many opinions about what we should be doing. Has he tried to kiss me yet, because if he has, well then, that's all right, if it's just a kiss. But if he tries to put his tongue down my throat or touch me anywhere above the waist or below the waist (what's left?), I am supposed to run right to them and let them know immediately.

"Yeah, right. And gross, you know?"

Actually, the truth is, I'm the one who finally did the kissing. I've been thinking about what it would be like to kiss a boy since I was five years old. I remember when I used to secretly suck my thumb under the blanket at night. I would get such a completely cozy and satisfying feeling. But I knew it was wrong to suck my thumb forever, and one day I told myself to put the thumb aside. That some day I would have someone to kiss me on the mouth, and the feeling would be just like sucking my thumb. I really wanted to try this out on Matthew. So I ask him one day when we are walking home.

"Matthew," I say, "let's go behind that building and kiss each other on the mouth." He stops in the middle of the sidewalk and looks at me as if I said, "Let's strip off our clothes and run naked through the neighborhood."

"That's so retarded," he says.

"Why is it retarded?" I ask him, and then he pulls me over to him and kisses me right on the lips in front of the whole neighborhood. I'm stunned. And disappointed. It's nothing like sucking your thumb. It's just kind of, well, like mushing your lips into someone else's lips for no good reason. I laugh, completely hysterical, and Matthew just looks at me. "Gadzooks," he says, and walks away. I have to run after him, begging forgiveness all the way home.

Matthew seems as if he's willing to practice kissing with me all I want. We practice while we do our homework. We practice in the backseat of Mom's car when it's parked in the garage. We keep mushing our mouths together until we get it right. We try it with our mouths open a little, and we do that tongue thing that Mom and Nana said never to do. Pretty soon we get the idea that we would like to try other things. Our hands go lower and lower until finally we go below the belt line (the "equator," as we have come to call it). And that's when I wonder if I am in love with Matthew. My body is just one big mass of needing to be with him. We keep experimenting with our bodies. Matthew seems to know endless things to do short of actually going all the way. Eventually, I let him see my breasts but I have to practically put a bag over my head to do it. Okay, I actually pulled my shirt up over my head. We get so hysterical, we almost wake up the dead.

"I know all about it, you know," he tells me as we're doing our homework at the kitchen table.

"About what?" I ask, like the silly baby that I am.

"The wild thing," he says.

I know what he means, but I don't want to know. How could that be possible? "You're too young," I say, moving away from him as if he had leprosy.

"Don't be silly," he says. A lot of kids in school are doing it, you know, and a lot of them are a lot younger than we are. I haven't been a virgin for two years."

"What?" I can hardly believe it. "You did the wild thing when you were fourteen?" I pull away from him even more so I can get a better look. He starts to look different to me. Like a stranger in a way. "I thought we were both virgins," I say.

He laughs. "It's not a tribe, you know. Or a religion. It's a state of being that can easily be changed." And he chases me around the kitchen, making sounds like a lecherous old man.

"So who was she?" I ask him.

He winks at me. "Mathilda."

"Mathilda! You mean, the housekeeper? The very housekeeper who mops the floors at your house and cleans out the toilets? That Mathilda? The one we call Waxing Mathilda?"

He gives me that silly, crooked grin that tells me he's making it up. I figure he's just trying to cover up so I don't guess who it really is. I start to get a little jealous until Matthew admits it was really just one time at summer camp with a girl from another town. That's a relief! I do love exploring with Matthew, but I'm not stupid. I know where babies come from. Matthew says it's not a problem, that we could get birth control. But I could never bring myself to do that. Besides, I have my own form of birth control. I have *the picture*.

I fished it out of an old hatbox in the attic where Mom keeps the family photos. There's Mom sitting in a chair looking out the window at something far away. It's a side view but you can see the look in her eyes and the way she slumps ever so slightly, that she'd like to be there instead of where she is, but she knows she's stuck. In her right hand is a lit cigarette. In her left hand is a cup of coffee. And on her lap is what looks like a bit of laundry. But if you look closely, you can see it is a pink baby blanket. And if you look closer still, you can see the tiny head of a sleeping baby. On the back of the picture is a date, nothing else: October 1, 1970. My one-month birthday.

Mom says she was just having a bad day when the picture was taken. And I know Mom loves me. I know that Mom really wanted to have a baby, too. Bruce says we choose what we think about things, so I wonder, did Mom choose me? Or did I just kind of happen to her, like the flu?

So if there's one thing I already know about myself, it's this. I don't want my life to just happen to me. Especially when I have children. When I have children, and I will have them, I want to choose each one. I don't want to be some teenager with a baby she doesn't know what to do with. And I never want to grow up to be the woman in the chair who just happens to have a baby on her lap.

So I hope that Matthew understands that this is the me I want to be. I hope he chooses me anyway.

The Guru Next Door

Once I got up the nerve to knock on Bruce's door, I stopped hiding out in his wine cellar. It had been my big silly secret practically from the time I could walk. He knew I was there. I knew he knew. Since the first time he caught me there when I was seven, I had gone back again and again. There would be new things there that I knew were for me. My very own flashlight. It was sitting on the orange beanbag chair one day. It was a little one made of pink plastic with a strap. I still have it. A pretty little book with blank pages and a pencil to write or draw pictures with. And, of course, as I got older, more and more of his writings, on little slips of paper of all shapes and sizes, folded up in a little square addressed to "Annie." One day there was a plate of cookies and a glass of milk. It was still cold. He knew my schedule, but after that first time, he never came in while I was there.

The wine cellar is attached to the house, and you can actually get into the basement if the door is unlocked. Occasionally I try it, but most days it is locked. This one day, the last time I go to the wine cellar, right before my sixteenth birthday, it is standing wide open when I drop by after school. I would often do that to collect my thoughts and have some quiet time before I go home. The wine cellar had become a refuge, a place to go to feel safe and a little bit naughty at the same time. I always feel comfortable with myself in the wine cellar, never angry or confused or sad. As soon as I hit the dim interior, I slip into a reverie, kind of like a meditation. The feeling is exquisitely peaceful, and more and more I take that feeling with me when I go back out into the world. It's the feeling I remember from my first encounter with Bruce as a very young child. It's a feeling, I've come to realize, that belongs to me now — that I can take with me wherever I go.

So on this day, before I say goodbye to my secret place, I go through the open door into the basement. I see the basement pantry and the stairs leading up into the house. They have more food in their pantry than we have in our whole kitchen. It looks like a supermarket shelf — cans and cans of soups and tuna fish, bottles of oils and olives, and jars of fruit, homemade jellies and jams, twenty different kinds of pasta with names I had never heard of, stacks of soda, all the toppings for ice cream sundaes, nuts and syrups and marshmallow spread. Next to the pantry is a storage room with games and sporting equipment and shelves piled high with paint cans. There is a separate workshop with every imaginable craft, jewelry making and model airplane stuff and even a small kiln. I can see they have been working there. Someone has been painting scenes on wooden blocks. A little village is in the process of being built. There's a sign on the wall that says Be Happy and Do What You Want. I wonder if Bruce made that.

There's no one around. It's as if the basement is here today to be revealed to me alone. It speaks to me in my solitude, saying the world is full of fun down here below the stairs, where you least expect it. I had expected empty damp-smelling rooms like the space below our house, which is swept clean and repainted every few years. There's no family life in our basement. Bruce's basement is bursting with inspiration. Now I understand why I often see the basement lights burning late into the night and early morning. They are playing and building and fixing and probably eating ice cream sundaes piled high with nuts and cherries and sticky marshmallow crème.

I wish I could grow up to be the adults they are instead of like the adults in my life. I wonder whether I can be reborn into this family somehow as their little girl. Bruce would find me on one of his travels in foreign lands, maybe in an orphanage in Rome or abandoned near the Wailing Wall in Jerusalem. I would be waiting, and he would come along and see me waiting, and he would put out his hand to me just like that. And just like that I would take his hand and become part of his life. I would live in the big house and play in the basement and grow up to be just like him. I feel a little guilty thinking that. I love my mom and dad and even Nana. I just don't want to be like them.

I hear something upstairs, and I realize I better get going. I am almost out the door when I see a blackboard hanging on the wall. I have seen that blackboard before. It's the blackboard he uses to teach his students. I have seen it through the windows of the living room and kitchen, even in the backyard on summer days when they held class outside. It was always there. I read the message on the blackboard, and even though it is for adults, I understand some of what it's saying. And I know it's important. The message says:

Something happens (the event).

We believe it is good, bad or neither.

We are happy if we believe it is good.

We are unhappy if we believe it is bad.

We are neither happy nor unhappy if we believe it is neither good nor bad.

There are two kinds of motivation:

Wanting: Happy if you get it or avoid it.

Needing: Unhappy if you don't get it or don't avoid it.

Finally, the Method.

What are you unhappy about? Identify.

What do you mean? Clarify.

Why are you unhappy about that? Identify.

What do you mean? Clarify.

Why do you believe that you would be bad for you if you were not unhappy?

What are you afraid would happen if you were not unhappy?

It's the secret of life, I tell myself, right here in the basement of my next-door neighbor — the guru next door. I giggle a little to myself, thinking of Bruce that way. I had heard Bruce ask these questions, but I never understood that the questions were part of a method he had created. I thought it was just the way he talked. I loved the questions, especially "What would you be afraid would happen if you were not unhappy about that?" It was as if he were saying we didn't have to be unhappy. What if that were true? Then I notice there is a piece of chalk on the ledge of the blackboard. In the upper left-hand corner on the blackboard is a blank space. I pick up the chalk and look at the blank space, and then I stand on my tiptoes and reach up to that blank space and draw a single flower. I can't believe I have the nerve to do that, but somehow I feel as if the blackboard is part mine, as if it is the most natural thing in the world to add my voice, even if it is just in the shape of a flower.

I step back and look it over. It looks perfect, as if it has always been there. As I look at the flower and Bruce's words, I realize for the first time in my life that words must have enormous power. The things we say to ourselves can put us on one track or another track, and we probably don't even know it. I make a promise to myself that I will live the words on the blackboard and that the questions will be my treasure for all my life.

I run home to do my homework.

Holidays Are Dangerous Times

༄

Love is not something you beam at someone like a searchlight. It is being happy and knowing that you are naturally loving by doing whatever you want — knowing that you will give them whatever you want (no more, no less) without fear of not being loving enough.

It's Christmas Eve, and it's just Mom and me. Nana went to Atlantic City to blow her Social Security check on the slots. If she wins, we're all supposed to get new winter coats. I'm not going to get all excited though. Last year she said if she won, we would all get hand-knitted Irish sweaters for Christmas. Where does she come up with this stuff? Anyway, she comes back and there's never a word said about did she win or did she lose. And we got umbrellas for Christmas. Again.

This year I decided it was time I chose where and how I would spend Christmas. For the past eight years since Dad left, I've spent Christmas Eve at home and Christmas Day with Dad. This year no way I'm leaving Mom alone. I know she'll just sit around and mope. She's already turned down all the invitations from friends. Mom has a lot of friends, all girlfriends she's had since she was my age, even. But it's pitiful how insignificant our family is. All we really have is Nana and a few scattered cousins. Everyone else died or moved away.

Mom is an only child, just like me. Mom's aunts and uncles are all dead, except for one old lady in a nursing home on Long Island. She's been there like forever. New Year's Day Mom and Nana will make the trek, dragging tons of cookies and a load of old-lady Christmas presents, flannel nightgowns and those little frilly pillows stuffed with lavender. They always used to take me with them when I was a poor defenseless little kid. I'd get all dressed up in my special Christmas dress and I'd have to sit in a chair while they talked about how awful it was that Aunt Lulu lost her home and wasn't it sad her husband had to go before her. Then we'd all go into the dining room together and we'd eat the holiday meal. Everyone would make a big deal out of me in my cute dress and my jet-black hair and the longest eyelashes they'd ever seen. The best part was that Mom would always stroke my hair when they said that, like it was a prize afghan that had taken her years to knit.

The really sad part is that Daddy has this enormous family with scads of brothers and sisters. He has so many he can afford to be mad at one or two for years on end and not even talk to them. Daddy's family loved Mom, and we were always going to Daddy's family gatherings when I was a little kid, with Daddy's mother and father and all the aunts and uncles and cousins. I think Mom was probably the happiest I've ever seen her there. Then Mom and Dad got divorced, and it was like Mom got fired from her job at this big corporation where she had loads of people under her.

One minute it's all calls back and forth all the time and this birthday party and that family picnic, and then it's like bang, you're dead. And not just Mom. I got fired too. The funny thing is that all these people still exist and now they have all the same parties with Daddy and Michelle and Michelle's family. Sometimes I go, too, but it's not the same. It's as if there's a parallel universe or something, like on *The Twilight Zone*, and they all exist there and we exist here, and every once in a while I break through but don't really belong there and if I breathe the air too long I'll die.

So who can blame Mom if she freaks out every now and then? She probably thinks she's going to end up like old Aunt Lulu in the nursing home with plaques on the wall that say In Memory Of. What's that about? As if old people need to be reminded that they will die someday. Soon.

So I'm keeping an eye on her because I know holidays are dangerous. I talked to my homeroom teacher, Mrs. Carson, about this. I like Mrs. Carson so much, although she does embarrass me a little the way she makes a big deal over what a good daughter I am and all that. Mrs. Carson took an interest in me because I'm the only kid in her class pretty much that doesn't have any parents coming to school to talk to the teachers. That's just not something we do in my family. Daddy doesn't even know what school I go to, and Mom says she's going and then I come home to find her gone or holed up in her room again.

Mrs. Carson asked me to stay after school, and we talked for a while. I think she was trying to see if I was really messed up. She kept mentioning Mr. Griffith, the school guidance counselor. But I explained everything to her and told her about how everything is all right and how I'm really a pretty well-adjusted kid, I think. Mrs. Carson said she admired me, that I must be made of iron. I felt guilty hearing that, as if my family's life is all about me. Mom is the one who has been disappointed. Mrs. Carson says family is important and people get depressed over the holidays if they are alone. She makes a big point out of telling me this is not my responsibility — that Mom is the adult and I am the child. I ask her what she thinks Mom should do, and she says if she were my mom, she would plan all kinds of nice things to do together and make it really special.

So that's what I do. I plan out every minute from first thing in the morning on Christmas Eve to midnight on Christmas Day. But there are problems. For one thing, Mom had it in her mind that I was going to Daddy's Christmas Day, and we argued about that for a long time. Then she laughed when she saw my list of events. She vetoed half of them right off. Although I agree we can't build a snowman if it doesn't snow, I didn't see why she wouldn't go caroling with me. Also, she wouldn't agree to wake up at eight o'clock Christmas morning. That was already a compromise because I really wanted to get up at six o'clock. I finally got her to agree to ten o'clock if I was allowed to open two presents Christmas Eve. She agreed with all the food things, like baking Christmas cookies together and making lasagna and roasting Cornish game hens on Christmas Day. And she agreed that we'd watch her all-time favorite movie, *Auntie Mame*, on Christmas Eve and that we'd go out for Chinese food at that great restaurant down in Newark.

So far it's not going so well. Christmas Eve morning I come down to breakfast to find Mom sitting in front of the stove doing nothing except fiddling with the stove clock. I think she was about to set the timer for soft-boiled eggs, but now she's fixated on it and it looks as if the eggs have boiled over. She doesn't hear me at first, so I come up really quietly as I've learned to do.

"Mommy, are the eggs done?" I ask, realizing I am trying to sound innocent and wondering why.

She snaps to then and takes the eggs off the burner. "Wouldn't it be nice, Annie, if we could really turn back time?"

I don't think so, but I say, "Yeah, I guess that could come in handy," just to be agreeable. I hate it when she gets like this, all weird and everything. I hope it's not going to be one of those days. "Where would you like to go in time, Mom?" I ask, thinking maybe it's another century. Mom would have been stellar in the 1800s, when no one ever got divorced.

"I'd love to go back to 1965, the year I met your father and fell in love," she says. "I remember the night he asked me to marry him. It was like a dream. He brought me roses and took me out to dinner in a fancy New York restaurant, The Rainbow Room. It still exists. I'll take you there sometime. He had the waiter put the ring in the bottom of my champagne glass. And then we danced and danced."

I've heard this story before, about how they did the carriage ride thing through Central Park and it was the happiest night of her life and then it all went downhill fast almost as soon as the wedding was over. But she doesn't go on with it. She looks at me and says, "You used to love that story when you were a little girl, but you're all grown up now almost, aren't you?" And she gives me a great big Christmas Eve hug.

So we get off to a shaky start. Then I get my period, and by lunch I have the worst cramps that ever lived. I never used to get cramps, but lately every month I spend at least one day doubled up on the bed. Mom gives me a couple of aspirin and goes out for some last-minute shopping. She always waits till the last minute, but since I know it's for me, who can complain? It makes me nervous, though, because you never know with Mom. She could come back in an hour or two or a day or two. But she comes back around two o'clock and then of course she has to hole up in her bedroom wrapping presents for an hour. I think it's an excuse not to roast marshmallows over an open fire, activity number five on my list.

My present to Mom has been wrapped and ready for weeks. I got her a whole bunch of painting stuff. Mrs. Carson helped me figure out what to get and even donated a few things. There's an easel and a canvas, a set of acrylics, and two really cool brushes made out of sable. I think they're actually real fur. I even made her a painter's smock. It cost a mint, but I've been saving for a year out of my babysitting money. Mom used to paint all the time before I was born, but she stopped painting years ago. All her stuff is still down in the basement — dried-up brushes stiffened into funny shapes, used-up tubes of paint, half-done paintings all cracked and bruised looking. It's like an artist's graveyard. Daddy says leave it alone, she's through with painting. But I think if she were, she would have thrown all that stuff away.

We are supposed to be having pizza soon and watching *Auntie Mame*. So I'm waiting and waiting, and I'm starting to get real hungry. She's not wrapping anymore, I know that. I sneaked over to the door before and I couldn't hear anything. I wonder if I should order the pizza like we planned or what? So I knock on her door real soft, and there's no answer. If I go in, she might get mad, but what if something's wrong? So I get this idea. I call Aunt Billy, who is not really my aunt but is Mom's best friend. Aunt Billy has a big family and I can hear them all in the background having fun being with one another. I tell her Mom is feeling kind of low and a call from Aunt Billy would really make her feel good. Aunt Billy says what a thoughtful child I am and she'll call right away.

So I hang up and wait, and then a few minutes later, good as gold, the phone rings and I hope that's Aunt Billy because I'm not going to answer it. But the phone just rings and rings and then I think, Oh shit, Aunt Billy is going to think something is wrong. She'll probably get right in the car and drive over here and when Mom finds out I called, my hash will be cooked for sure. Please, God, I say, one more chance, please. And don't you know it, God must be listening because the phone rings again and this time Mom picks it up. I hope it's Aunt Billy trying again and not Nana calling to say how much she is losing.

It's Aunt Billy. How do I know? Because they always stay on the phone for a year, even though people are waiting for them to have Christmas Eve. I can hear Mom laughing, though, and that makes me feel really good. I get bold and knock on the door, and it swings open. Mom is on the bed surrounded by all my Christmas presents, which are wrapped, thank God. She's smoking a cigarette, which she's never supposed to do in bed, but it is Christmas, I guess — a dangerous time anyway. I lie down on the bed beside her in the middle of all my presents, and I put my head against her chest and my arms around her waist. I am really, really happy at this moment. Thank you, God, and thank you, Aunt Billy.

So it looks as if maybe we'll make it through Christmas Eve. The important thing is not to let her out of my sight again. Last Christmas Eve, she cried all night long and refused to come out of her room for days. That's because she was all alone. I wonder, though, what would it be like if I weren't here? I'll just have to make sure I always am, I guess.

Man Who Dreams Big Conquers All

If you want evidence that you are a loving person, you will only find it as your happiness. If you are happy, you are loving everyone.

The restaurant is crowded, but I see my father in the booth we like. He's already ordering for us, as always. Won ton soup. Egg rolls. Shrimp and lobster sauce. Our favorites. When I slide in to face him, he half rises up out of the seat and leans across the table to kiss me on the cheek, almost knocking over the soy sauce. We laugh, and I kiss him again on his cheek. "Hi, pumpkin," he says. "Hungry?"

"Sure, Dad, I'm starved," I say.

He asks me about school. I ask him about Michelle. His job.

They bring the food. He serves me himself. Even pours the tea, cooling it off with an ice cube from his water glass, like he's been doing since I was old enough to hold a teacup. It's our special ritual. I eat with chopsticks. He eats with a fork, his napkin tucked into his collar. Halfway through the meal, he says, "So when are you coming to live with us?"

I laugh. "Oh, Daddy."

"You can live anywhere you want, you know. Maybe a change of pace would be good."

"I'm still in school, Daddy," I say. "One thing at a time, right?"

"When you graduate, you can come live with us."

This is our conversation. It's lighthearted but it tugs at me. Someday

I would like to ask, "Daddy, why is it so important to you?" He would say, "I want my child near me. Is that so bad?" It's impossible to respond to that. Who can blame him? It's just that children are supposed to grow up and move away.

I say that. "Children are supposed to grow up and move away, at least live on their own."

"Sure, live on your own," he says, opening a fortune cookie. "Down the block. Across the street. Wouldn't that be nice?" He hands me the fortune. It says: Man who dreams big conquers all.

"Thanks, Confucius, you're a big help," I say.

I think it would be nice, but not for me. I'd like to tell him, "Daddy, I don't fit in with your family. I have to find my own family. In fact, I have my own family. Mom. What about Mom?" But I don't say that. It's not popular.

We finish, and he pays. He beams at me from across the table. I'm being adored and I know it. We hug goodbye outside the restaurant, and I take off down the street. A half block later I turn around and see him still standing there, watching me — his beautiful daughter, of whom he is so proud and who gives him so much pain.

The One Simple Truth

There is only one simple truth about unhappiness. When you believe you are wrong to be happy you will deny that you are and feel that you are not. That is all unhappiness is. Happiness is not believing that. Understand this. Your happiness depends on it. Unhappiness is believing that being happy is being not the way you should be. You are allowed to be any way you choose or happen to be. You are allowed to be any way.

*I*t's my job to wash the dishes. It used to be just putting them in the dishwasher and washing the pots and pans. But the dishwasher has been broken for months and everyone is waiting for Daddy to come over to fix it. Nobody cares if it takes me all night to wash the dishes. Nobody cares if I don't study for my geography test — if I grow up to be fifty and still don't know where Idaho is.

Why they think Daddy knows how to fix a dishwasher is beyond me. I never saw Daddy with anything like a wrench or a screwdriver in his hands. Other people's fathers fix things but not my father. My father is really good at calling up the plumber or the electrician and getting them to come that day even when they say they are booked for weeks. Mom and Nana won't even do that. They just call Daddy and then they blame him when he doesn't fix things. Eventually the doorbell will ring and there will be a repairman, and Mom and Nana will look at him as if he's the Boston Strangler or something. They used to send away all the repairmen that Daddy sent, but then I got big enough to answer the door and let the repairman in before Mom and Nana could do anything about it. I'm so sick of this nuthouse. Am I a bad person?

There are piles and piles of dishes from breakfast, lunch, and dinner. No one around here washes a dish now that the dishwasher is broken. They leave them all for me as if I'm the only one who knows how to wash a dish. So I wash the dishes every night before I do my homework, and that gives me plenty of time to think about how screwed up things are around here. What would it hurt if just once we could all eat a meal together like normal people? Mom is so busy with her activities that she barely has time to ask about my life. Does she even know that I'm a senior in high school now? She hasn't asked me once what I want to do with my life. If I said I wanted to be a drug dealer, she probably wouldn't blink. She would just say, "Whatever makes you happy." Okay, so that's probably an exaggeration, but the thing is, some people think I'm a smart kid. The teachers say I have a lot of potential. Mom wouldn't know that, and Nana is even more clueless. Neither of them has ever been to the school to speak to the teachers. Not even Daddy. As far as the school is concerned, I'm an orphan.

I hate washing the carrot grater worse than anything. When I have my own place, I won't even own a carrot grater. They're the worst contraptions in the universe. First you scrape your knuckles all off and then you have to pick out millions of carrot specks from these little tiny holes, just to have grated carrots. How insane is that?

So all the kids in my homeroom are always going on and on about what colleges they visited and will they get accepted. One kid and her father went to four different schools in four states last year. I can't believe her father spent all that time running around the country like that. I couldn't even ask Daddy to take me, and why would I? College is for other kids. If college were for me, wouldn't someone be suggesting it? But no one ever mentions anything. It's as if they believe I will be a high school kid forever, forever washing mountains of dishes. Maybe that's what I should do — find a job as a dishwasher. I can work down at the local Italian restaurant and maybe marry one of those guys with the rubber gloves and the long apron smeared with god knows what. I could have all the free lasagna I can eat and by the time I'm twenty, I'd be as big as a house. Would they even care?

Was that dish chipped before? Oh shit, I'll never hear the end of that from Nana. As if it's heirloom china or something instead of a bunch of mismatched dime-store stuff. Other families have those big china closets in the dining room with fancy china that has been in the family for generations. Maryanne's mother even keeps hers in these quilted bags with zippers that are exactly the right size to fit all the dinner plates in or the bread plates. I love to watch her take the plates out of those bags and set them out on the dining room table, as if each one were a priceless treasure. If she treats the dishes like that, imagine how she must treat Maryanne. It's mind-boggling.

Daddy says I should just relax. Real problems, he says, are like when someone has cancer. "You're just a kid," he says. "Kids don't have real problems." I know he thinks there's something wrong with me that I don't walk around grinning and happy all the time. "You have such a carefree life," he says. What does he know? I can be happy and I will be happy, as soon as I get a little older and have someone to love me. If I just had people who really care about me, I know that would make all the difference in the world.

What really scares me is, what if I'm just not the kind of person other people can really love? What if there's something wrong with me? What if you really have to be loved when you're a kid for other people to love you after you grow up? Like all the kids whose parents didn't love them are sort of in a class by themselves, like special ed or something. They have to be there because they can't keep up with the other kids — the ones who have experience in being loved. And what if the special ed kids can only love each other? That makes me start to cry, and here I am washing the butter dish and crying like a dumbass. There's no hope for me. Is there?

Bruce would think there's hope. He would say, *"When things are not the way you would prefer, that does not mean that certain things shouldn't be happening in your life. It doesn't mean your life is not what it should be. There is no way it should be and you do not need to make it be any way."* Bruce would say, *"People believe they 'need' things in order to be happy because they believe they will be caused to be unhappy without them. But unhappiness was merely believing in the first place that it would be wrong to be happy without those needed things. Continuing to be unhappy or fearing becoming unhappy is just denying that that belief 'caused' the way they felt."*

That's what Bruce would say. When I think about that, it takes the wind out of my sails. I have to sit down and just think for a few minutes. What if I was happy anyway? In spite of it all? I'm not sure I'm okay with that, but it doesn't matter. I feel better anyway, just by considering such a thing.

Cause and Effect

If you believe something is bad, you feel bad about it.
If you believe something is good, you feel good about it.
If you believe something is neither good nor bad,
  you feel nothing about it.

Saturday I go to the mall with my girlfriends as always. We take the bus right after breakfast, and we don't come home until seven or eight o'clock. As I pass the kitchen coming home, I see a place set at the table for me, and my heart sinks. I missed dinner. Forgot all about it. Mom and Nana are going to be mad. Sure enough, they both ignore me as I pass through the living room where they are playing Scrabble in front of the TV. I heat up my dinner and take it to my room and eat it while I talk on the phone with Matthew. Matthew is a freshman in college now. He's in the doghouse, too, for not calling home enough.

Why is it that grown ups are always getting mad at us? At least in Matthew's family, it only lasts a few hours. In my house, the mad goes on forever. It's as if they think being mad is really doing something, like painting a wall or baking a cake. In the end, they can look at the wall and admire it. They can eat the cake. But what can they do with the being mad, I wonder. Is it supposed to make me different? When they get mad at me for not doing something, I usually feel as if I never want to do that thing in this lifetime, even if I felt like it. When I have kids, I will never get mad at them for not doing stuff. In the meantime, when Mom and Nana get mad at me, I just feel terrible.

I secretly dream of the time when I can leave this place and have my own life. I've had this dream since I was very young, maybe even nine or ten. I would always say to myself that no matter what happens here in this house, it can't touch me, because some day I will be gone. My whole life up until now has been a temporary situation. They're the ones who are stuck with this. Or are they? The truth is, they are the ones who think they are stuck. I never want to forget that.

I'm not in any hurry, though. Next year most of my friends are going off to college, like Matthew. He promised he will be coming home a lot and I can go up there too. We'll see. It's hard to believe Matthew will still want to hang around with me when he has college friends. Matthew doesn't understand why I'm not going to college. He is the only one who seems to think about this. He says I have a good mind. "When you're ready," he says, "I'll help you if you want." I just say, "College is for other people."

Me, I'm going to work right after school lets out. I've been on six interviews in the City already. The City is awesome. Several of us took the train in together and got off at Penn Station, New York City. The school had set up interviews at these enormous companies, like ABC and The New York Times. They gave us these slips of paper with the address of the company and directions on how to get there. I blew the first two interviews because I was so nervous. I could see the lady in charge felt sorry for me. In real life I can type faster than anyone, but you were supposed to type this letter perfectly with no mistakes. She let me do it twice, but it still looked like a second grader had typed it.

That was at ABC. I was sorry about that. I had visions of starting in the typing pool and working my way up to be a producer or maybe even getting discovered. I could be the star of my own sitcom. But I have a feeling I'm going to end up at this big law firm. I could tell they liked me a lot and they didn't care about how many mistakes I made, as long as I corrected them all neatly.

I liked going to the City for the interviews. I loved getting my donut and coffee first thing in the morning — Chock Full o'Nuts chocolate honey dipped donuts are my favorite. I loved being on the train with packs of people going to work. There are a lot of young people on the train too, and they talk all the way in. My girlfriend, Brenda, who is a year ahead of me, already has a job at an advertising agency. She says there's no end to the fun. They go out every Friday after work, and everyone dances up a storm, and the guys buy the girls these fruity drinks with umbrellas sticking out of pieces of pineapple. At lunchtime they all eat in the park together, and some of the companies even have their own cafeterias, like school only with real food. I can't believe that this time next year, I'll be a working girl.

Nana already said that I'll be expected to give Mom my entire salary. As if that's going to happen. Daddy said I should keep the whole thing and save for my future. When I'm eighteen, Mom is going to have to go to work anyway, because that's the end of child support. Mom and I never talk about money and she never brings up my future. I think she wants to think that things will just go on the way they are forever.

What really does upset me, though, is when Matthew and I fight. It doesn't happen too often, but we have these certain subjects on which we can't seem to see eye to eye. College is becoming one of them. Matthew says I'm apathetic about my own future just because I'm not going away to school. As if I even have the money anyway. That's what makes me so mad. Matthew's father is this big important businessman with loads of money. Matthew is getting a free ride all the way. Me, I'll have to pay my own way in whatever I choose to do, most likely. All I've heard all my life is how much money Daddy has to shell out to support two families. Last year when I asked for money for tennis lessons, Daddy actually said, "What do you want me to do, get another job?" Like that's an answer. Did I ask him to have two families? And I can't help noticing that he and Michelle go on actual vacations, like to the Bahamas and Puerto Rico. When he was with Mom, they never went anywhere. I know it's really bad of me to notice that, but it's true. I feel funny asking for anything, so I try not to want things.

Tonight I can see that a big fight is about to happen. Matthew wants me to apply for a scholarship, but I don't see the point and it's too late anyway. I don't see a reason to go to college. Especially if it's going to cost money. When I say this, Matthew goes bonkers.

"Why are you always thinking about stuff nobody else ever thinks about?" he asks me. "Kids just go to college. That's what they do. They don't ask why. You find out why once you're there."

I honestly don't know what he's talking about. "You're starting to kind of sound like my father," I say, and then he gets really mad.

"You won't let anyone be a real friend to you," he says.

I can't respond to that, it hurts so much. I don't say anything but deep inside me, my mouth is hanging open and I am completely horrified. Why is he being so unfair? He wants me to want what I don't want just because he wants it. I know that sounds complicated, but that's the real truth. That's why everyone always seems to be mad at everyone. The conversation ends with my saying, "If that's the way you feel, maybe you want to take someone else to the prom." Why I thought the prom had anything to do with this is just bizarre. But when I get like this, you just never know what will come out of my big mouth.

"Fine, if that's the way you want it." He slams the phone down in my ear. I look at my prom dress hanging on the door of my closet. I babysat three months to pay for it. In the end Matthew calls back and apologizes, and we sort of make up. But things feel different now that I know that Matthew is disappointed in me. I always thought he was the only person who would never do that. And then I realize I'm doing that thing again, where I think I should be different and I understand something Bruce said that I never understood before.

Since we can believe about ourselves that we should be different, we can and will believe it about others. To believe that another needs to be, or should be, different is judging another, and simply an expression of our being unhappy.

I go to sleep happy.

We All Have Our Reasons

What happens or what we believe may happen can be desirable or undesirable or neither. It is never bad or silly or foolish or anything that can make us feel bad. It is simply desirable to us or not. It is never bad, silly or foolish to not enjoy something or to expect not to enjoy something or to want to change or avoid something.

I don't know why, but there's just something about graduation day that makes me sick to my stomach. It's two weeks away, and every morning I wake up feeling really happy and carefree for a second or two, and then I start to think about what I have to do that day. If it has anything to do with graduation, I start to sink back down into the bed until I'm practically part of the mattress. I can hardly make myself get up out of that bed and go to school. This morning I remember I have to give Mrs. Hodges the size for my cap and gown, and whoosh there I go, right down into the bedsprings. It's hopeless.

"Why are you so nervous about graduation?" they all ask, but what they really mean is, I shouldn't be. Everyone has his theory. Matthew says it's because I'm growing up and I don't want to. Maryanne says it's because I'm nervous about going to work in the Big City. Mom says it's just nerves, having to walk up in front of everyone on the big stage. I don't know why I'm so freaked out about graduation, but it's not any of those reasons. That would be stupid.

But I can tell you this. It's really ruining my fun. Last weekend we were bowling at Sunshine Lanes and I was having a good time. All my friends were there and no one was fighting and they all were playing really well or not caring how they played. And we were having those great curly French fries and hamburgers at the snack bar, and all of a sudden those French fries reminded me of something about graduation. Don't ask me what. But my face almost fell into my plate. After that I couldn't even get the ball to go all the way down the alley. It's like the ball gained about a hundred pounds when I wasn't looking. Everyone kept asking, "What's the matter? What's the matter?" As if I knew. And then Maryanne piped up, "She's depressed about graduation," and everyone said, "Oh yeah," and kind of slumped down into a big heap. So what, now everyone is depressed?

The truth is I'm excited about everything else, except *that day*. I can't wait to start my new job. I am so ready to be finished with school. I will finally have money to spend. I can wear what I want. I'll make new friends in the City. Maybe I can even get an apartment of my own. It's just *the day*. Getting through *the day*.

Mom is really trying to be nice. She takes me to Bloomingdale's to buy a dress for graduation day. We don't fight the way we usually do about clothes because I just don't care. I let her pick out this really boring navy blue kind of A-line thing with white trim. And I get new white shoes with the highest heels I've ever had and even new underwear. And this cute little leather purse. "You're all set," she says, looking at me in my graduation finery. I try to answer her, but I have this lump in my throat. Mom pats me on the head as if she understands, has been through it all before. Everyone thinks they know what's bothering me. How can they? I hardly know myself.

So finally the day rolls around. I spend so long in the bathtub that Mom has to knock on the door twice. I'm just lying there in the warm water trying to talk myself into having the good time I'm supposed to be having today. I finally just let the water roll down the drain around my body. I wish I could disintegrate and go down the drain with it.

So I get dressed up in my new dress and put on pantyhose and my new high heels. My hair is all done up in a French twist from Mom's beauty salon and I have these new pearl earnings that Nana gave me. I look in the mirror, and I almost scare myself. My face looks frozen, as if I'm stuck in the middle of a giant ice cube. I actually try to shake it off, but the feeling sticks to me like a giant Ace bandage. I seriously start to consider running away. I am plotting it out even as I walk down the stairs to the car where Mom and Nana are waiting. But they're not waiting in the car. Mom is on the phone and she's really mad. I can tell she's talking to my father because she's using THE VOICE.

I come into the kitchen in time to hear her say, "Well, you'll just have to tell her yourself," and she hands the phone to me. "It's your father," she says, as if we all didn't know that.

"I'm so sorry, honey," says my dad. "Michelle woke up really sick this morning and I just can't leave her. You understand, don't you?"

"Sure, Dad," I say, thinking, Thank you, God, and then almost smacking myself because I would never really want God to strike Michelle down, even temporarily.

Mom comes and puts her arm around me immediately, as if I had just lost my best friend. The plan had been that Nana, Mom, Dad, Michelle, and I would all go out to a Chinese restaurant after graduation. For the first time in my entire life, my mom and dad and Michelle would sit down to a meal together. In a way, you would think it was the most natural thing in the world, but the look of relief on my mom's face tells me how horrible the rest of the night would have been.

Now I think she really wants me to feel bad that Dad is not coming, even though she didn't really want him to come herself. So why did she let it happen, I wonder. Why agree to something that you don't like? I'm getting the feeling again that I'm too young to be thinking about this stuff. But at least I understand why I have been dreading graduation.

I feel as if a giant cloud just lifted up and blew away, except that Mom is intent on making a big deal out of Dad's not coming. She's going to be mad for hours. I guess she was going to be mad today, one way or another. As for me, I'm finally excited about Graduation Day. "Just a minute," I tell them. I run upstairs and for a minute I seriously consider pulling off this stupid navy blue dress and wearing that hot pink dress that I wore to the senior dinner. But I don't want to hurt Mom's feelings, so I just pull my hair out of the French twist which was already starting to hurt the back of my head and let my hair tumble down my back. Then I look at myself in the mirror again and smile. It's me again, and I'm really ready to graduate this time.

Working Girl

*What are we truly capable of? Only by being happy will
we find out, and we see our capabilities manifested.*

I guess I'm a working girl now. Every morning I get up at 7 a.m., get
dressed in my work clothes, and get on the train to New York with
the other commuters. I love going to New York, and I love my job. I
work for two lawyers, Mr. Frey and Mr. Collins. I type up their briefs
and motions. I make their travel reservations. I file their papers away
and help them set up for meetings with clients. I think I am good at
my job, and that makes me feel really good about myself. I am the
youngest person around by far. Mr. Frey and Mr. Collins are both
way over thirty, with wives and children. I see their pictures behind
them on their credenzas, smiling out at me from the beach or their
living rooms. Families. I can't imagine what it would be like to be in
a family like that.

There are a few other girls and guys who work at the firm. On
my first day, the office manager, Mrs. Melton, takes me around and
introduces me to every one of them. They have all been here a few
years and look like they know exactly what they are doing. I see them
going out to lunch together, and Friday nights they leave in a group.
They must be going out to a bar or a club. No one invites me, but
that's okay, I guess.

There is this one girl, Martina, whom I really like a lot. Martina
works for Mr. Larson, who is the head of the firm. Martina has this

gorgeous wavy chestnut hair and blue eyes. She's tall, much taller than I am, and even so, she wears the highest high heels I have ever seen. When Martina walks down the row of desks, everyone looks up. No one talks about it, but everyone does it. It's like, "Oh, the sun just came out, let's all look. Oh, there's a parade. Let's all look. Oh, Martina is passing by. Let's all look." We all do it. Then we get back to work. Martina is beautiful.

Eventually, after a few weeks or so, Alice, who works for Mrs. Melton, comes up to me and says, "Hey, Annie, we're all going to the park for lunch. Wanna come?" So I become part of the crowd who goes to lunch in the park. Martina is not part of that crowd. Martina is part of the crowd, which is really only Martina and three guys, who go to lunch at Small's Deli on the corner. This group also makes up the nucleus of the Friday night crowd that goes out to the Playboy Club every week. You can eat there for free between five and seven o'clock, I heard. Sometimes, I think, they even go dancing afterward. The park crowd and the deli crowd don't seem to mix.

I wonder how I can get to be Martina's friend. I want to say hello some time, but something always stops me. I was even with her in the ladies' room last week. We were standing right next to each other. Martina was going over every inch of her makeup in the mirror. I was pretending to have something in my eye. I don't wear makeup, so that was the only thing I had to do after I fixed my hair. It was fascinating to watch Martina freshen up her eyeliner and put on new lipstick. She has a way of putting on eyeliner without stretching her eye all over her face like I've seen other girls do. And she has this makeup bag that is bulging with cosmetics, not from the drugstore, but the kind you have to ask for at the department store. I was standing right next to her and she never looked at me once. I can't understand why I even want to be friends with her. She's just so cool, I can't stand it. She'd never want to be friends with me.

"So, are you making friends at work?" Mom asks me every weekend.

"Sure," I say. "I go out to lunch every day with a bunch of kids from all over the firm. They're nice."

The truth is those kids are kind of babyish, even though they are older than I am. They still talk about the kids they knew in school. They don't do anything interesting. They don't seem to read books. I think they still spend weekends hanging out in their friends' basements.

So I start going to Small's Deli on my own. I sit in a booth in the back and I bring my writing pad. Every afternoon I order a sandwich and a drink, and I work on a short story about the people in Small's Deli. Every day Martina and her friends come in all loud and gorgeous-looking and ignore me completely. So little by little I start to move where I sit closer and closer to where they go, the window table that looks out over the street. I can't believe I am doing this. They continue not to see me. The truth is that after watching Martina and her friends for weeks and weeks, I have actually lost interest in them, but I can't seem to let it go. I want them to see me. I can't stand it that they won't acknowledge my presence. So one day I sit at their table. The door opens and here comes Martina with her entourage — all men, by the way. She finally looks at me, and I can see that she does not recognize me. What kind of person sees someone every day for two months and never even notices them? "Hi," I say, like a dope. "I'm Annie. We work together."

"Oh," she says, tossing her hair, and turns her back on me. She goes to the next table and the whole entourage changes direction and goes with her. I can hear them talking about me. "Who is that weirdo?" Some of the men look over, and I can see in their eyes that they are sorry for the way Martina is acting, but no one says anything. And that's when I realize something. This is not the place for me. And I don't just mean Small's Deli. I mean this job, these people, and this way of life. I could do it. I could even be good at it, but it wouldn't really be me somehow. I don't know where I belong yet or what I should be doing, but it's not this. I get up and leave without ordering. I don't feel bad. I feel grateful to Martina. She was the only one at work I aspired to be like. What was I so attracted to, I wonder.

Growing Up

⌒*M*⌒

Real love is to be happy and to just want your loved ones to be happy. You make your choice: Do you want to be happy and love or be "loving" instead?

The last evening I spend at my father's house starts out like any other visit. I meet my father in the City and we take the train to his house together. On the way home, we talk about my job and Dad's job. Nothing special. Dad is encouraging me to think ahead to what I'd like to be doing in five years. It isn't that he has any particular aspirations for me. He just feels as if everyone should always be thinking ahead. I'm glad to hear him say that because I'd love to talk with him about my feeling that it's time to move on. I've begun to explore ideas with anyone who will listen to me. But Dad isn't a very good listener. Every time I try to say what I think I might want, he starts to lecture me on what it should be. By the time we get off the train he has figured out that I should learn some sort of trade. "Like a mechanic?" I ask. He doesn't get the joke.

"No, more like a dental technician or a court stenographer," he says, pointing to the placards in the train station. "See," he says, "they're everywhere." I can't believe that this is what he thinks I should do. Secretly I had been thinking about becoming a writer or a therapist like Bruce. I want to say something, but I'm afraid my father will laugh at me.

Over dinner, Michelle launches into her third degree about what guys I'm dating, what exciting things I'm doing. What are my plans? She is full of excitement and enthusiasm about my life, much more than I am myself. In fact, I wonder if I'm a disappointment to her. Even though I want to change things, I still like my life. I'm just not all that dramatic about it. I tend to take things in stride. I'll get excited when the time comes. It just hasn't come yet.

Somewhere between cleaning up and dessert, Michelle gives my father the look, and asks, "So did you tell her yet?" They both look at each other like it's some kind of life-changing moment or something, and then Dad says, "Your mother has been having a romance. We thought you should know."

"Well, how do you know?" is the first thing I can think of to say.

"Your father saw her several times with a man she is obviously involved with."

"That's just crazy," I say. "Mom doesn't have a boyfriend. She doesn't even go out that much."

"That's what she wants you to think, pumpkin, but that's really more for your benefit and your Nana's benefit," says Dad. "Believe me, she gets out. You know she does. Where do you think she goes all those times she disappears?"

"Wait a minute. Am I supposed to care about this?" I ask. "She *is* an adult. Why are you telling me this?"

They both look at me as if I have two heads or something. And then the old tape starts to roll. "Your mother is a severely disturbed woman. This could mean she may just disappear, maybe for good this time. We just want you to be prepared."

"Okay," I say, feeling like crap. Dad drives me home, and I don't say anything all the way.

"I'm sorry, honey," he says, when he lets me out of car. "I know it's a shock."

That night I lay in bed half the night thinking about the conversation. I can't sort out my feelings. I'm amazed that my mother could be so secretive, on the one hand. On the other hand, I couldn't care less. I don't tell her everything. And deep down I am actually pleased that she has found someone. Maybe she won't be so lonely and unhappy. I am completely confused by my father and Michelle. What do they expect me to do? Why do they care? Thinking about it, I get angrier and angrier. I start to imagine what I would have liked to say to them. It goes something like, "How dare you? This is my mom you are talking about. Why do you always want me to believe she's this crazy person who should be locked up? Leave her alone." I resolve that tomorrow I am going to tell my father what I think of him and Michelle.

Lots of tomorrows come, and I never get around to telling him. He calls to invite me to dinner and I pretend that I have a date. He calls me at the office to meet for lunch and I say I have to work. I get a cute little card in the mail with a basset hound on the front looking all lonely and dejected. "Don't be mad. We love you," Dad writes. Finally I get up the courage to write my father a letter. "Dear Dad," it says. "I'm sorry if I haven't been around lately, but the truth is I can't listen to you and Michelle talk about Mom the way you do anymore. It hurts me, Dad. I hope you can understand that. Love, Annie." I sleep with the card under my pillow for about a month, and finally one day I toss it in with the office mail, feeling as if I just tossed a grenade.

About a week later, I get a phone call from Michelle. "You broke your father's heart, you know," she says. "He doesn't understand why you are lashing out at him."

"I'm not lashing out," I say.

"I think you are," she says. "I think you know very well what you are doing."

I don't know what to say. I am no match for her. But the conversation leaves me so depressed I have a hard time getting up to go to work the next day. I start to get a headache every night that doesn't go away until the morning. I keep going over and over my last conversation with Michelle — what I wanted to say to her, what I should have said, for Mom's sake.

So I do what I always do when I'm stuck. I read Bruce's poem and what jumps right off the page and into my heart is this:

Confess that no one has to be unhappy . . .

And do whatever you want.

What do I feel like doing? I ask myself. I feel like loving my mom no matter what. I feel like hoping for the best for her. And I feel like forgiving Dad and Michelle. I also am not sure how involved I want to be with them, but I don't worry about that for now. I feel better instantly. I go to the florist and buy a dozen roses. It practically costs me all my mad money for the month. At the florist, I write out a card that says, "I'm sorry if you're mad at me and I wish you happiness today and every day."

I don't get a thank you. I should have sent the flowers to Mom instead.

The Door in the Maze

Fearing our motivation is fundamentally the fear of selfishness.
We can only have this fear because we have believed that it is wrong
*   to be selfish.*
The only sense that being selfish could be believably wrong is be-
*   cause it would somehow ultimately make us unhappy.*
The fear of mysterious punishment (guilt) would follow from this.
Secret terror is the fruit of this fear.

"So are you coming with us or not? We need to make our reservations by this Friday or all the rooms will be gone."

Four of us girls are having lunch in the park across from the office. Since January we've been talking about going down to Florida for spring break. It's going to be crazy at the beaches with all the kids coming down from school. The fact that we aren't college students and don't even get a spring break is not a factor.

I want to go, but I'm terrified that something bad will happen. I've been hearing stories. Last year a whole carload of kids were killed when their car stalled on the railroad tracks. What if we get halfway down there and get lost in the back hills of North Carolina? What if our car breaks down in the middle of the night? Last night I had a dream, a nightmare I guess. I was all packed and ready to go home. But I couldn't find anyone. Where did they all go? I was supposed to meet them by noon. They said if I wasn't there by noon, they'd have to leave without me. But I couldn't find them. I pushed myself out of my sleep and looked at the clock. It was only twelve thirty at night. I'd only been asleep a half hour, and I was already having nightmares.

"So, are you coming?"

"I think so," I say, thinking, Who am I kidding? I'll never go. "I have to make sure I have enough money."

"How much do you need?" they ask. "We'll lend it to you. It won't be the same without you. Please say you'll come. Please, please."

They are all begging and laughing. I laugh too, but I feel weird about it. Nobody notices except Susan. Susan is my new best friend since I started work. She lives in Queens with her parents, and she really wants to be a model. She's working as a secretary, saving her money up to pay for the photographer. When we're walking back to the office, she says, "You don't have to go if you don't want to. Maybe it's not your cup of tea." But I do want to go. I already bought a new bathing suit. I love the beach and I've never been to Florida. In fact, I've never been anywhere. I hear the sand is white as snow and the beaches go on forever. Of course, I want to go. Only, what if . . .?

"I don't know if I can get permission from my mom," I say. "She's really freaked out these days thinking I'm going to fly the coop any minute and never come back."

"Well, just ask and see what she says. You know you can always talk your mother into anything. Besides, why do you even need permission? Jeez, Annie, if you had gone away to school, you'd be doing all sorts of things she wouldn't know about. You're eighteen, you know."

So when I go home that night, I bring it up at dinner, and sure enough I get the exact reaction I expected. Mom looks at me and asks, "Why would you want to do that? Hordes of kids will be swarming down to those beaches. You hate crowds. And spring break is for college kids. You're going to feel awfully out of place there. Won't you?"

She's hitting a nerve there, but I don't want her to know it. "Why would I?" I say, digging into my baked potato.

"You know what I mean. Most of those kids, it's their first time away from home. They're going to go wild. You see it on the news every year."

"I know people that have gone before. It's really nice. You meet a lot of nice kids. Everyone has a lot of fun."

"Well, all I can say is, your Nana will be worrying about you every minute," Mom says, glancing over her shoulder at Nana, who is already washing her dishes at the sink. "And your father would never permit it."

"Daddy doesn't care," I say.

She looks at me with raised eyebrows. "You already spoke to him about it?"

"Yeah, I called him last night," I say, lying through my teeth. Mom doesn't know I haven't spoken to Dad in months. "He thinks I should definitely go. He even said it would be good for me."

"Well. Your father," comes Nana's voice, muffled by the running water.

"Well, if it would be good for *you*, far be it for me to interfere," says Mom. The words drip off her tongue and roll over to where I sit at the table. And that's the end of the conversation.

My heart feels as though it's taken up residence in my shoes, but I am determined not to be beaten down. Even when Mom says she has a headache and goes to bed early. Even when Nana gives me that look and makes a big show out of making Mom tea and bringing her the ice pack for her head.

That night I dream that I'm in a maze and I can't find the way out. For hours and hours I search and search, but every turn seems to be a wrong turn. I wake up in a sweat, and I remember the dream vividly. I decide right then and there I'm going to get out of the maze. I close my eyes and see myself back in the hedges between our house and Bruce's house. I can smell the bushes all around and hear the sound of other people finding their way out to the sunshine. I start to think about all the places I don't go and all the things I don't do because of that maze. There was the trip to Bermuda last winter and the shore house in the Hamptons last summer. I haven't been up to visit Matthew at school yet because Mom always seems to get sick when I plan to go. I'm tired of that maze. I'm determined to find a way out. And you know what I did? I just put a door right there in the middle of the hedges. I go up to that door, and I just open it up and step out like everybody else.

The next morning I tell the girls I'm going, and I hand over the money for my part of the expenses. I'll worry about how I'm going to eat down there later. I feel scared, though, and I can't explain it. I would feel so much better if Mom could just be happy for me. Maybe even help me shop for clothes for the trip or even stand still for a few minutes so I can tell her about it. But that's not the way it's going to be. I hear Nana's voice in my ear saying, "Selfish girl." Yeah, that's me, S.G. Why don't you just love me anyway?

Selfishness is believed to be wrong because it may lead to behaviors that are harmful (cause unhappiness) to others or to our greater good (mysteriously defined). This greater good is understood or inferred to be our greater happiness. This is simply the belief (fear) that we are somehow against our greater happiness.

I Tried to Love You

You only fail to love if you get unhappy.

I remember nights when I would open my eyes from some deep sleep to find my mother sitting in the chair beside my bed. I remember the feel of her warm hand rubbing my back under my shirt. I remember how she'd find just the right dress, the right shoes, the right winter coat. When we went out together, everyone looked at her, like she was some famous person whose face they knew but whose name they couldn't quite recall. She'd glide through the mall with me in tow, head held high, high heels clacking. Salesmen would fall over each other to help her. It made me feel special to be her daughter. Did it make her feel special to be my mom?

All my life, people would tell me that I had family problems. I came from a broken home. My father was neglectful. My mother was self-involved. My grandmother was psychotic. Everyone applauded me because I was so strong, because I did well in spite of them. Did anyone ever stop to think that nothing was *wrong*, that I didn't have to be negatively affected unless I wanted to be? With the exception of Bruce, everyone assumed I had to feel bad.

"I tried to love you," my mother cries. "I tried to be a good mother. The disease got in the way, that's all. You understand that, don't you?"

I don't want to talk about it. I'm packing my bag to go to Florida.

"This is just the first step," my mother says. "In a year, you'll be leaving for good. Won't you?"

I wish we didn't have to have this conversation. The conversation I want to have is the one where I say, "Mom, I'm going to go to school upstate. I'll be leaving in September," and Mom says to me, "I'm so thrilled. I'm so proud of you. What can I do to help?" I'm sure that conversation is taking place somewhere. Just not in my house.

"Why don't you just hold off for now? We can go somewhere together. Would you like that?"

"Sure, Mom, I would like that," I lie. "We can talk about it when I get back, okay?" I look at her hopefully, but I can see she hasn't heard me.

I pick up my bag and bring it down to the front door. The girls are picking me up in a half hour. I wish I had left last night when she was asleep. It would have been so much easier.

"How did you get to be so unfeeling?" Nana says. "Can't you see your mother needs you?"

My stomach twists into a pretzel knot, and I suddenly have to go to the bathroom. But I am leaving in that car when the girls get here. I could never live with myself if I don't go.

When I come out of the bathroom, Mom is doing her hand-wringing pacing dance. Talking to herself. Not making eye contact. I can't leave without talking to her. She knows that.

"Your mother never loved you," my father used to tell me. There is much evidence for this. He and Michelle would list them for me in case I should forget. "Remember the time she wandered away from the playground when you were three? Then she called me, frantically saying you had run away. We found you asleep underneath the sliding pond. It was almost dark."

I wonder, if my mother never loved me, then how come I love her so much? How come she owns my heart in a way Dad could never even understand?

The girls are honking outside. I run out to tell them, "I'll be out in just a minute. I have to talk to my mom." They give me that knowing look, and I shoot them my own look right back which says, "Don't *even* go there."

Back in the house, Mom paces and mutters. I put my bag outside the door and the muttering gets louder. Nana is yelling at me over it. It's a nuthouse. "If you leave," she tells me, "don't expect me to stay here and take care of her. You did this. You can clean it up."

I try to get Mom to look at me. I pace with her, talking to her in a soothing voice, telling her, "I love you. You'll always be my mom. But I'm going now. I know that's what you really want. I'll be home in six days." She ignores me. And I leave. Just like that. Going out the door, it's like my body has to defy gravity. I catapult myself down the front steps and into the car, breaking all ties with planet earth. We drive away hoping to have a wonderful time down in sunny Florida.

I have an overwhelming feeling that I must go home and take care of her. I need her to forgive me, to let me know it's okay. But I know that is impossible for her. Before we even get to the highway, we have to pull over so I can throw up my breakfast by the side of the road. The girls applaud me when I come back, which really makes me angry. I sulk for a few miles, and then I start to laugh. My saving grace. I always seem to be able to laugh eventually. And when I do, I start to let go of the certainty that I know how it all has to go. And I start to remember that Mom is just unhappy, not damaged or demented or condemned. In fact, if I really tell the truth, I have to say that I'm just unhappy, too, not damaged or demented or condemned by anything Mom is doing.

Epiphany in Florida

*We use our mistakes as "proof" that we are not on our own side.
We often say that we knew better, or ought to have known better, as
if we chose what we really believed would prevent us from having
the very thing we were making the choice for in the first place. We
always choose to do that which we believe will best get us what
we most want. It is self-defining.*

The trip down to Fort Lauderdale is probably the worst thing that
ever happened to me. I'm not going to say I'm sorry I went. Let's just
say, it was a learning experience. The first mistake was taking Susan
and her car. We hadn't even gotten to Washington, D.C., when I knew
it was a big mistake. Four girls in a Volkswagen is fine if you're going
to the mall, but after three hours, I knew we'd never make it past
Washington, D.C., without a serious blowup.

When Susan said she was allowed to borrow her mother's new
car, I imagined something shiny and smooth-riding, not this old junk
heap. There's actually a hole in the floorboard, and is there supposed
to be a grinding sound every time you turn the wheel to the right?
And the car has a name, Old Blue, because the car is old and blue. We
were all going to share the driving, but at every rest stop Susan finds
a reason why she should drive. It becomes clear very soon that she
doesn't trust any of us behind the wheel of Old Blue. When I finally
push my way into the driver's seat, she drives me so crazy with her

backseat driving that I give it up after only an hour. I guess no one can handle Old Blue like Susan.

Then we try to find a place to stop over in North Carolina. I told them we should make reservations, but no, they wouldn't hear of it, wanted to be spontaneous. Who do they think they are, Jack Kerouac? After the fifth motel, we decide to just keep on driving, but that falls apart because no one is comfortable with Susan, who keeps nodding off over dinner, doing all the driving. So we pull over in one of those rest stops and sack out in the car. It is the single worst night of my life, and I've had a few bad nights. The next morning, we're ready to roll around 3 a.m. because no one can sleep anyway, and then it happens. The car just stops in the middle of the highway. Lucky for us, it's right by the exit and it's just a stupid little Volkswagen. We push it off the road with Susan behind the wheel, crying. Will Old Blue have to be put out of his misery?

There's a gas station right by the exit, but of course no one is there. The sun hasn't even risen yet. So we sack out again, but no one can sleep because of Susan whining and crying. She blames me for not driving right in my single hour behind the wheel. "You drove too fast. That's what did this," she moans. Some people.

Finally, around 9 a.m. the owner shows up. He takes one look at Old Blue and shakes his head. "Don't see a lot of VWs round here," he says, pronouncing it B Dubya. "But don't you worry, pretty ladies," he tells us. "I know just who to call." We all trail after him into the office where he calls someone named Leroy, who must be deaf because B Dubya, as I've secretly begun to call him, has to yell into the phone. One hour, he tells us, and Leroy will be here to save the day. We wait for one hour, then two, and just as we are ready to push the car to the next gas station, a pickup truck painted bright orange swings into the station with the radio blaring country music. Leroy steps out. Leroy is about eighty years old. He looks at the four of us and smiles this big toothy smile and then ruins it by flinging a big wad of spit over his shoulder. You heard me. Over his shoulder. We all try it later but no one can do it.

He takes the keys to Old Blue from Susan and tries to start it. He sniffs around the engine for a few minutes like a bloodhound in overalls and gives us the verdict. "It's the alternator." Whatever that is. He can fix it but it will take a few hours. He suggests that he run us over to this motel where we can rest up while the work is being done. We huddle over it and everyone decides to take him up on his offer, except for me. I think it's a really strange and bad idea, but I am outvoted. The next thing I know I'm in the back of this old pickup that has brown clods of something or other all over the place. Leroy drives and drives, and I am starting to get visions of white slavery, but then he really does pull up to this motel, which is a sort of bungalow colony in the middle of the woods. Before we can say, "But, we thought . . . ," he fishtails out of there, leaving us in the dust.

We go into the office, which is really someone's home. The owner, Peggy, is Leroy's niece, it turns out. Talking to her, we all feel better, because we can see she is a regular person, only with a lot of kids. She's holding two of them. We can see two others playing in the yard and three more are chasing each other through the house. She doesn't look like she's too much over thirty. She gives us the keys to number nine and tells us she'll call us when she hears from Leroy. We all just stand there, shuffling our feet. "Don't worry girls, it'll be all right," she says, in this soft curling drawl. The baby pukes on her shoulder.

Number nine should have been called number two. The place is disgusting. The bungalow consists of one room with a double bed, a dresser, and one chair. I don't want to touch anything, let alone sit down or lie down. It smells, too, and I am sure I see bugs jumping up and down on the bed. Having a sleepover. After a few minutes in the room, I feel as if I have creepy crawly things in my hair. Susan and Jill plop right down on the bed and fall asleep. Alice and I just sit on the decayed front step telling each other the story of our lives. Every hour or so we go over to the office to see if Leroy has called. Peggy tells us, "No, ma'am. I'll be sure to let you know," like this is most natural thing in the world. By now, it's been three hours and we're really starting to get anxious. We get Peggy to call the garage, but there's no answer. I start to feel like we're going to spend the rest of our lives right here in this broken-down motel. There is no way in hell, I tell myself, that we are going to spend the night here.

No one seems to have any idea what to do. I promise myself that if I get out of this alive, I will never go anywhere in a car older than me. I ask Peggy to call us a cab. "I don't know," she says. "You-all should really stay put. We don't exactly have cabs out here. This is the country," she says, like we don't know that.

Now I am getting really mad and really scared. "Can I use the phone?" I ask. "I want to call my mother and let her know I'm okay." But I don't call my mother. I ask information to give me the local police station. The girls get all wide-eyed and start arguing with me, and Susan starts to cry again. "This is such a nightmare," she keeps saying over and over. I know she blames me. That's the worst part about this — her snively finger-pointing. Now she's blaming me for calling the police, like that means we're all criminals or something.

The sheriff comes and we all pile into his car and we get back to the garage, and guess what? It's closed. We can see Old Blue locked inside and there is not a soul around. It *is* a holiday weekend, the sheriff tells us. They must have closed up early. We can't believe it. What are we supposed to do? Where are we supposed to go? How could this happen? Everyone starts wailing, except for me, of course. Then I decide to get smart. I remember something I saw Matthew do once. I pull a $20 bill out of my wallet and ask the sheriff if he has change. He takes the money and holds it up to the light, as if to make sure I hadn't just manufactured it right on the spot, in the little printing press in my wallet. Then he stuffs it in his pocket and gets this really thoughtful look on his face. "You know," he tells me, "I just might could help you out here."

And you know what? He suddenly remembers that the gas station owner is a friend of his. So he calls old B Dubya, who appears twenty minutes later, with his overalls on backwards and his hair every which way. Apparently, the work has been done, he tells us, but nobody knew where we were. What a giant crock. Unfortunately, they were not able to fix the problem completely, but we should be able to get to Florida at least. It's dark already and I'm really getting nervous. If I have to spend another night in that car, I'll kill myself.

So we all pile back in, and if I tell you that not one word was exchanged until we rolled into Fort Lauderdale, Florida, I am not lying. It's so late that the office of the Flamingo Motor Lodge, where we are supposed to stay, is closed. So we sack out in the car again. In the morning, instead of taking my bags inside with everyone else, I take my bags and tell them all goodbye. I find out that there is a Greyhound bus station a mile away. I walk all the way there, dragging my bag along the pavement. I buy a ticket home for six o'clock that night, then I stash my bag in the terminal and start walking to the beach. There is no way I am leaving Florida without seeing the ocean.

In spite of it all, I can really say that this morning I am happy. Here I am in a strange place, separated from my friends, my plans completely turned upside down. Still, I am proud that I got us all out of that creepy situation even if no one wants to admit what I did. I am proud that I walked away from all of them. And I feel really good that I have finally gotten out on my own. I love thinking that all my terror about something bad happening evaporated when something bad did happen. All I want to do right now is feel the hot sun on my skin and see the Atlantic Ocean.

Before heading to the beach I call home. Nana answers the phone. "Mom is sleeping," she tells me. "When are you coming home?" She doesn't ask how was the trip, am I having a good time? She starts to tell me a long story about how Mom wouldn't come out of her room even when Nana made her favorite meal, chicken soup with matzo balls. "Tell Mom I love her," I say, and hang up the phone. I know I'll pay for that when I get home, but for now there's the beach and the sunshine and I'm free.

I don't have to worry about finding the beach. All I have to do is follow the line of cars. There is a parade of cars of every make, color, and age overflowing with kids.

I get a ride with a bunch of girls from Oneonta, New York. They make college life sound like one big party. "How come you didn't go?" they ask. I really have to think about that. The truth is, no one had even expected that I would go, except for Matthew. "I guess," I say, "I don't know what for." They all look at me. "You don't have to have a reason," they say. "You just go."

They invite me to hang out with them. They have a huge ice chest loaded with cold drinks, sandwiches, and fruit. They tell me to help myself. Then we all baste ourselves with suntan lotion and station ourselves on the blankets. There are an unbelievable number of people on the beach. By noon, there is not one square inch of burning sand available. There is nothing but bodies for miles in each direction. Every once in a while, a huge whoop goes up in the crowd as some girl whips off her bikini top or some guy moons the crowd.

The girls invite me to sleep on their motel room floor if I have a sleeping bag. I don't, but they decide I just have to stay with them and we will all go to the local army navy store and buy one dirt cheap. Then we'll swing by the bus station and pick up my bag. They can drop me off in New York City on their way back up north. So it's decided. I really like these girls. They actually have ideas. They solve problems. They like me.

Sitting in the midst of all these college kids, I really start to wonder, Why don't I go? They all seem to think I already am a college girl. They accept me just as if they had seen me on campus last week. One girl, Kim, is especially nice to me. She and I walk to the motel together, which is only a few blocks away. She tells me if I want to come to Oneonta she will recommend me for her sorority. I can't quite see myself in college, let alone a sorority.

"Why not?" she asks me. "Everyone does it. It's fun and you make friends you'll have forever."

I don't know how to tell her, I'm not like them. I'm not smart like they are. I don't come from a good family. "I don't think I'm the type," I finally blurt out.

"Sure, you are," she says. And then she tells me her story. She's been in foster homes since she was two years old, when her parents were killed in a car accident. She got left back twice because she changed schools so much, but by the ninth grade, she decided she needed to save herself. She decided she was going to be a teacher, and she buckled down and made sure she had great grades. She did so well that eventually she got a scholarship. She told me she felt really weird when the sororities starting showing interest in her. She didn't think she was the type either, but eventually she joined Kappa Delta. "It's a much better life," she said. "You get to live in the sorority house. Your sisters watch out for you."

I have to admit I am excited, but I still can't see myself going to college just to go. I would need to have reason. Nobody is going to give me a scholarship.

"Just go back to your high school and at least talk to your guidance counselor," Kim begs me. She is the most persuasive person I have ever seen. I can see I am becoming her little project. That night as we all get dressed to go out, she gives me the once-over and shakes her head no. I am wearing this cute little A-line number that I just bought at Loehmann's on sale. "How come you never wear anything revealing?" she asks. "You have the cutest figure I have ever seen. Much better than anyone else in this room. Show it off, girl. And tomorrow we're going shopping for a bikini."

"My mother won't let me wear a bikini," I say, and feel like a total fool before the words even hit the air. When they stop laughing, Kim tells me the rule. "Parents can only tell you what to wear when they buy it. When it's your own money, you wear what you want, go where you want. End of story. Now try this on." She tosses me a white minidress with blue trim which buttons up the front. It has a V-neck which ends up just above the bra line. It doesn't exactly cling but, let's say, you can really see my stuff. I have to admit, I look adorable.

"Now that we've freed your body, let's free your hair," says Kim, and she pulls the rubber band off my ponytail. My hair falls down to my shoulders and I start to smooth it down. "No, this way," she tells me and she bends forward, letting her hair fall free, and then flips it back the other way so it has this really wild earth mother look. When I do it, I think I look like the cowardly lion in the Wizard of Oz, but they all love it. Then they make up my eyes and lips, and trot me over to the mirror. Looking back at me is this really beautiful but very slutty-looking character. I could never go out like this, I want to say, but I bite my tongue. I look exactly like them.

You Just Go

We do not ever have to justify or explain our preferences or choices. We may wish privately to explore our motive or rationale. We may choose to explain to gain another's agreement, but we do not have to do so in order to be satisfied that we have the right to our choices.

I'm not the same after Florida. Kim's words keep ringing in my ears. "You just go," she had said, as if it could actually be possible. I can't stop thinking about it. It's as if I have a giant itch that won't go away — an I-want-to-go-somewhere itch, an I-want-to-do-something itch. Something big. Something completely different. I start to wonder seriously what I want to be in life. I guess you're supposed to have figured this all out in high school. That's how come most of the kids I went to school with are already in college somewhere studying to be somebody. But me, I didn't get it. When I was in school, I think I was just going through the motions. I always had other things on my mind. I would flip back and forth between Algebra and When Is Mom Coming Home? and Geography and Why Doesn't Nana Like Me? and English and What Can I Do to Get Dad and Michelle to Understand Mom?

Somehow I have to move on. All the adults in my life are too distracted with their own problems to help me with my future. I finally understand that it's all up to me to chart the course of my own life. No one is going to make it happen. And that's probably the way it should be. Once I get an idea in my head, I go completely nuts until I figure it all out. Matthew says it's the Virgo in me. I think I'm just determined.

So I start driving everyone insane about what I want to be in life. The girls at work think I am really off my rocker at first. We're eating our sandwiches in the park, talking about what we are going to do this weekend, and I say, "I really want to know what I'm cut out to be." They all look at me as if I just spoke Swahili. "Huh?" says Susan, who is finally talking to me again after the spring break fiasco. Then it turns out that really no one really knows what she wants to be, except Jill, who is just trying to find Mr. Right, settle down, and have a pack of kids. She even has her house picked out. This becomes the main topic of conversation from that moment on. Only for me, it's really different. I'm going to find out what I want to do, and I am going to do it. Period. Hell or high water. Take no prisoners.

It only takes a few weeks. The answer comes on a date with this really gawky guy I met on the train. He picks me up Saturday night to go to the movies. But we never make it to the movies, because I start yammering the minute he puts the car in gear. "I've been thinking that there is something I really want to do," I tell him, "but I don't know what it is and I really want to help people in some way and I know that being a secretary is really not the thing for me although there is nothing wrong with it, you understand, and I just don't know, but all my life I've been struggling with my family and my mom and dad and my grandmother and I wish I could really help people with stuff like that, you know?"

"Yeah," he says, "and what do you think you'd like to do?"

"Well, I don't know," I say, more from the shock of knowing he actually really heard me. And then I hear myself say, "I think I'd like to be a therapist. You know, there's this man who lives next door to me and he is the kindest and most genius person I have ever known and he told me he helps people all over the world get over problems they have had forever, and I once read an article he wrote which says people can actually really be happy no matter what, so maybe just maybe I could help people. What do you think?"

"I think you would be really great," he says. "I think you're really pretty too," and he kisses me. He's a good kisser, but I have to go home right away and plan out my life.

So I go back to my high school and talk to the guidance counselor I used to have, Mr. Griffith. He tells me you need to go to college to be a therapist. He tells me my best bet is to go to one of the schools right here in New Jersey, where I could commute if I wanted to. There's one in my own town. I can't even begin to explain how completely unappetizing that idea is. High school was tough enough with all the distractions of home. I need to be at least ten hours away, if not more. I have to have a reason to leave home; otherwise, I might never get out. I tell him that, and to his credit, he shifts gears immediately and takes out a map that shows all the colleges in the State University of New York system. "Show me," he says.

I see Oneonta, but it's closer than I would like. There's Matthew's school, in Ithaca. It would be nice to be close to Matthew, but he's going to graduate before me anyway, and I know he's planning to go to out to Colorado for graduate school. "What's the farthest away?" I ask.

He laughs and shakes his head and then his arm goes up and up and up almost all the way to Canada. "Potsdam," he tells me. "But get ready to freeze. It gets to be forty below."

"What do I have to do to apply?" I ask.

I used to have fantasies about going to college, but never in a million years did I think I would go. College is for smart people, and I am not smart. In all my high school years I never, never raised my hand once. In college, kids are yelling out the answers, jumping out of their chairs, bursting with inquisitiveness. They have debates and write papers and look down their noses at kids like me. In my fantasies, I am in the classroom where the professor is expounding on something and everyone is spellbound. The room is so quiet, you can hear a pin drop. Nobody wants to miss a word. My hand shoots up as soon as he stops talking, and I ask this really pithy kind of soulful question. Not just a clever question, but a question that comes from a quiet kind of intelligence. The teacher looks at me like, Wow, there she is, my future protégée. All the other kids look upon me with silent respect. I'm a college girl.

But first I have to get accepted and somehow find the money. Mr. Griffith sends them my transcript, and I get invited up for an interview. Mr. Griffith tells me not to get my heart set, that I might not get accepted right away. It is May, after all, and I am almost two years out of high school. He tries to get me interested in a community college, where I could go for two years and then matriculate to a four-year school. I'm not interested in that plan. In my mind, I am already sitting in the front row of some psychology class, asking questions that no one else has thought of. So I make reservations at some little motel up there, pack my overnight bag, and get on the Greyhound bus at Port Authority, New York City. This is my first time away from home except for the trip to Florida and the time I spent at Dad's house. I hope this works out better. When I tell Mom and Nana at dinner where I'm going, they just look at me as if I had said, "Tomorrow morning I am going to shave my head and join the Hare Krishnas."

"I thought you loved your job," Mom says.

"I do love it," I say, "but I have something else I want to do now."

"When I was your age . . . ," says Nana, but Mom stops her.

"Things are different now, Mother. Annie has to make her way in the world."

That sounds good to me, but I think I see Mom's lip trembling. Or maybe that's just the light. Or maybe she's going to sneeze. There's no talking for the rest of the meal. I can feel the deep dead weight of despair settle on my chest, but I just keep chewing and swallowing, and I do not look at either one of them. If I do, I'll be a dead duck. Mom offers to wash the dishes so I can finish packing. Not a good sign. Late that night I hear her leave the house. I wake up every hour, it seems, to see if she's come home yet. What if she's not home by morning? How can I leave? I decide I am going to leave no matter what. Mom is a big girl, I tell myself. She's probably out at the beach. I get up around five and go into her room. The bed hasn't even been slept in. She's been looking through photo albums of me age zero to five. There I am in her stomach. There I am in the bassinet. A tiny blur with an astonishing shock of dark hair. There's Mom and Dad, together, walking on the beach with me between them. I am looking up at them as if they were gods. What do toddlers know?

I fall asleep in her bed, breathing in her smells, skimming the surface of sleep until Mom wakes me up at 6 a.m. I sit bolt upright and look at her as if she had just come back from the dead. "Shhh," she tells me. "Let's not wake Nana. Get dressed. I made breakfast. I'll drive you to the station." I panic immediately. It's a trick, I tell myself. She's not really making breakfast. She's not really going to drive me to the station. I didn't think she was even paying attention when I said I was leaving by 7 a.m.

I get dressed, pack up the last few things, and go out to the kitchen. There is my favorite, French toast made with challah. With cinnamon. I look at it, and my eyes fill up with tears. I feel guilty as hell for thinking she would freak out. I feel like a crumb for expecting her to short-circuit. I'd like to be relieved, but I can't do it. I want to be ready just in case.

But there's nothing to be ready for. She has pulled herself together to do what needs to be done. At the bus station she amazes me further by giving me an envelope. "Just in case," she tells me, "for emergencies." I get that childish gigantic lump in my throat as we try to say goodbye as if a major life change isn't creeping up on us. "Remember," she says, "if you don't like it, you don't have to go there. You have options."

I can't imagine what those might be, but somehow I believe her. "Okay, Mom," I say. I pull my things from the trunk, and she drives slowly away, straining to look forward while watching me grow up in her rearview window.

To Love Is to Be Happy

To love is to be happy and do what you want, whatever you want. Be with. Don't be with. Smile; don't smile. Be loving; don't be loving. Give or say whatever you want; take or ask for whatever you want. Do your own thing. If the one you love gets unhappy, don't believe you are not loving them enough for them to be happy. Their happiness does not depend on you. If you find you want them to be happy, it is because you want it; not because you must be a "loving" person to prove to them or you that you can love. You are loving if you are happy.

Matthew looks at me across the table. He has come down from school to see me for my birthday and celebrate my acceptance to college. I will be starting next September, so that I can work for a year to cut down on school loans. We're at the Lobster Garden, my favorite restaurant. There are candles on the table and a dozen roses on my chair. Next to my napkin is a small blue velvet box.

"Open it," he says, pushing it towards me. I am instantly afraid. I laugh, and Matthew laughs too. He pushes it closer. "Open me. Open me now," it says in Matthew's voice, muffled behind his hand. I open the box and breathe a sign of relief. It's not exactly a diamond ring, but it is a gold ring with two hearts. He takes it out and puts it on my finger. He never asks me if I want it. He thinks he knows.

"I love you," he tells me for the first time ever.

I love you, too, I think. But I don't say it. It's as if we're speaking different languages. How can I say, "I love you, but not that way."

The waiter comes with the lobsters and bibs. We hold hands around the steaming plates and melted butter. I am in shock. I thought we were just friends.

"I love you," he says again. "Don't be freaked out. It's not an engagement ring. It's an I Love You ring."

I like hearing this, but the words float through the air between us, never really settling in the way I think they should.

"What's wrong?" he finally asks.

"I don't know. I didn't think we were going to do this."

"Do what?"

"You know, the ring thing. The love thing."

"Okay," he says, like he just changed his mind and decided to have chocolate ice cream instead of vanilla. "Give it back." He holds out his hand, palm up. He's not mad. He knows who he's dealing with.

I twirl the ring around on my finger. I can't seem to hand it over. "Is it okay if I'm confused?"

"Sure, as long as you love me."

I can't help but smile. "You are just so cute," I say.

"But not cute enough to bring home to Mama?"

"You've been there, remember?"

"Yeah, but as Matthew, the best friend, the pal, the chum, the lap dog. Not as Matthew, the stud, the man, the intended."

"I thought you liked being the lap dog."

"Sure, when we were ten and twelve. We're nineteen and twenty-one now. It's time to move on, no?"

"I don't know."

"Okay, you don't have to know now. Just tell me that you'll consider it."

"I'll consider it."

Later, in the car, when Matthew kisses me, I feel the pressure of his lips and not much else. We used to sit in the car for hours before he went away, talking about everything under the sun. I'm not sure why things have changed. I'd like to ask, but I feel I should already know. Is there something wrong with me that I don't feel differently? I love Matthew, have always loved him. But this doesn't feel right. This is not the way it's supposed to go, even if it's not an engagement ring.

I put the ring in my pocket before I go into the house.

How Can I Help You?

How can I help you is the most loving question you can ask
    someone when they are unhappy.
How can I help you see that you don't have to be unhappy?
How can I help you know that you are not bad for yourself?
How can I help you understand that there is nothing wrong
    with you?
How can I help you know that your desires are good?
How can I help you accept yourself?

This is what Bruce taught his students, but he knew it was not something that could be taught. It was something that had to be discovered. So many of his students struggled. They worried whether they would apply his Method correctly, whether they ask the right questions. He had a secret. It didn't matter much what you asked once you asked the first question, "How can I help you?" The only way to help was to let them realize that unhappiness is not necessary.

Tomorrow is a big day for Mom. She is thinking of selling the house and has an appointment with a real estate agent at one o'clock. She jumps up from the dinner table six times to call and cancel the appointment. "Why am I even thinking of selling?" she says. "I love this house. Look at these floors. Look at these wonderful big windows. How could I leave this?"

"You don't have to leave if you don't want to," I say.

"I know, I know. But with you going off to school, we don't need this big house. An apartment would be fine. Besides, I don't want to waste this man's time, do I?"

"Mom, that's what agents do. They look at real estate. You think everyone that thinks about selling, sells? I bet they have to go through ten people before they get to handle a sale. Maybe even twenty."

In the middle of the night, I can hear her pacing. She goes up and down the back stairs endlessly. I finally get up and go downstairs to see what's going on. The house is ablaze with light. She is rearranging the furniture in the living room. She shoves the couch across the room with a mighty thrust of her left hip. "I want the couch under the windows," she tells me breathlessly. "I always thought it would look good there."

"Mom, it's three o'clock in the morning," I say, sitting on the first step. "Can't this wait?"

"Just help me," she says, and I can see she is trying to stifle hysteria. So I help her move the couch. She sits down on it like a ton of bricks. "This works, don't you think?" she asks, blinking away tears.

"Mom," I say, "how can I help you, really?"

She looks at me as if I just offered her a million dollars. "You are helping," she says. "It's just . . ." But she doesn't continue.

"Just what, Mom? What can I do?"

Her shoulders sag and she starts to cry. "You can be a little girl again," she says, stroking my cheek. "Let's start all over again. Remember when you used to hide under the stairs? Remember how you used to sneak out of the house when I was playing cards?"

I pull away and look at her as if I've never seen her before. My eyes must be bugging out of my head. "You knew about that?"

"Of course I knew. I wasn't the best mother, but I knew where my child was."

I couldn't imagine how that could be possible, but in some strange way, I am relieved that at least she believes it. "I never said you weren't a good mom," I tell her.

"No," she says sadly. "You wouldn't. You were always an amazing kid."

She stands up and looks at the room. "You can help me by moving the couch back. It looks ridiculous."

So we move it again, together.

"I wish I could really help you," I say.

"Help me with what?" she asks.

"I wish I could help you be happy."

She smiles at me and touches my face. "That's the nicest thing that anyone has ever said to me."

Be Happy and Do What You Want

What would you be afraid would happen
if you were not unhappy about that?

"**I** know you're mad at me, but you don't have to be mad," Matthew tells me.

"What do you mean, I don't have to be?" I ask. "That would be convenient for you, wouldn't it? Then you could just do whatever you want." I can't believe I'm saying this, but I can't seem to stop myself.

"I'm not trying to make you unhappy," says Matthew. "I just can't come down this weekend. I would if I could."

I don't want to let him off the hook. "But you said you would." Even I can hear the whining in my voice. "I asked you six months ago. You said you would."

"I said I would if I could. But I have this psychology test. I couldn't study enough because I had the flu."

"Yeah, right." I make the words drip with venom.

Matthew laughs at me. "I have to know all about anxiety disorders by Monday."

"Why, so you can call people names?" I sneer, starting to cry.

"Annie, you're even funny when you're upset," he says.

The tone of his voice makes me fume even more. He's not upset and I can't stand it. "I don't care." I have this huge lump in my throat.

I really want to hang up because I'm getting embarrassed about how bad I feel. "I have to go," I say.

"Don't go," says Matthew. "I know you're mad at me. But I can't fail this test."

"You can study while you're here. I'll help you."

"You know that won't happen. There are two many distractions. Like your cute little tushy."

That starts to crack me up, but I stifle it. The last thing I want is to feel good right now. "I hate you."

"I don't hate you," Matthews says. "You're still my little bubala."

"Don't joke. What am I supposed to do now? I have to go to this stupid wedding all by myself? Why do I even have a boyfriend?"

Matthews laughs. "Oh, now I'm the boyfriend! You never let me be the boyfriend until you don't get what you want. Why don't you ask someone else? What about your cousin, what's his name? Davie?"

"Don't even try to go there, Matthead. There's this guy at work that keeps asking me out. Maybe I'll invite him."

"Matthead! Ooh, now you're really getting nasty. Now you're trying to make me feel bad."

"I know you don't feel bad. You never get mad. What's wrong with you?"

"I don't get mad at you because you are the love of my life, and I will never be mad at you."

"You don't mean that."

"I do mean it. There's no question about it."

"You're such a worm."

"Annie, my sweetie. When will you learn?"

"Oh, now you're so wise. Go take a flying leap," I say. He's scaring me now. I'm starting to feel like my mother.

"I wish you wouldn't feel bad. You don't have to take it so hard, you know?"

"Who says? That would get you off the hook, wouldn't it?"

"I said I'm sorry. What more can I say? I can still be on the hook, you know. Just don't feel so bad, huh?"

"You can get your ass down here Friday night like you said you would."

"Well, now that you've brought my ass into it, I may reconsider. All right, I'll come and I'll fail my test. Would that make you happy?"

I hate it when he does that. Such a martyr. "I don't even like this whole conversation," I say.

"That's because you're not getting what you want exactly the way you want it. You're a spoiled brat, you know."

"Screw you, Matthew." And I slam down the phone. I can feel the rage boil up inside me, mixed with a sick feeling of fear. I want to smash something. So I stomp down the stairs and smash out the back door. I stomp around the neighborhood and finally I come back around to my house and sit in the backyard crying. In the dark.

The nerve of him to tell me I don't have to feel bad. Who the hell does he think he is? And there I am, nineteen almost twenty years old, sitting in my backyard with my arms crossed tight against my chest, my jaw clenched shut, fighting back the tears. Just like when I was six. I have a right to be unhappy, I think. Who is he to tell me I don't?

I look over at Bruce's house. What would he say? Probably tell me I didn't have to be unhappy, too. But it would be different coming from him. He wouldn't be saying it just to shut me up. He wouldn't be saying it just to get off the hook.

What kind of a schmuck feels good when they don't get what they want? I stew about that for a while. And then I go to my room and fling myself on my bed. My hand goes under the pillow and draws out the paper Bruce gave me when I was twelve.

To be the channel and expression of knowing and doing,
To enter into miraculous union
To live in habitual joy (simply)
Confess that no one has to be unhappy . . .

And do whatever you want.

Confess that no one has to unhappy.

Even when you don't get what you want? Even when you have to go to your best friend's wedding all alone like some misfit?

Confess that no one has to be unhappy.

In spite of myself, just saying the words calms me down, fills me with peace.

And do whatever you want.

What if I wasn't unhappy? I turn over on my back and take a deep breath. Okay, if I wasn't unhappy, it would be like I didn't care. But I do care.

And do whatever you want.

I pick up the phone and call Matthew back. "Matthew," I say, "it's okay if you can't come, but I really want you to. I know you have to study, but I'm sure we can find a way. I promise. We'll spend all night Friday night and all day Sunday studying. With me as your coach, you'll be a regular Einstein."

"You mean Freud, right?"

"Whatever. Anyway, deal?"

I hear him take a deep breath.

"Matty, I miss you," I say, and my eyes well up. I want to say "I love you," but I can't quite get the words out. I'm not ready yet.

"Deal," he says.

"Really? Because it's okay, you know?"

"Really. But we study on Sunday. No ifs, ands, or buts."

"Thanks, Matthew."

"Oh, it's Matthew again, huh? What's the matter? Did you find yourself loving me for a minute, my little turtle?"

"Go to hell, okay?"

"No problem, as long as I can meet you there."

Mom's Turn

The absolute truth is simple.
There is no such thing as unhappiness.
People have believed there was.
You have been one of those people.

"What if you no longer believed in unhappiness?" Bruce asked.

Eve looked excited for a moment, but then gripped the arms of her chair as if bracing herself against the possibilities. "I guess all my life I have just been an unhappy person," she said. "Even when I was a child, I worried all the time that something bad would happen to my parents. Every little cut was going to turn into a flesh-eating disease. Every little cough was tuberculosis. I think I was a magnet for unhappiness. In my crowd of girlfriends, I was the one worried about Communism. I was the one who agonized every time we saw a homeless person. They all just laughed at me, thinking I was joking. I wasn't. There is just so much in the world to be unhappy about. I wish I knew how other people can be happy when the whole world is going to hell."

"What if that were possible?" he asked her.

It wasn't a question she was ready to answer. They both knew it. "If things had been different," she said, "I think I could have been happy. I didn't have a chance. My mother and father were always fighting. My mother blamed me. No matter what the fight was about, she somehow was able to prove that I instigated it. That's what she called me, The Instigator. If it hadn't been for me, they would have had the perfect marriage. That's because once I was born, Mother never wanted to have sex with Father again. I'm not supposed to know this, but I heard them arguing about it. I could have been happy if I didn't have to deal with all their problems all the time. I never had time just to be a child."

"Why does the fact that they had problems mean that you have to be unhappy?" Bruce asked.

He had asked her this question and questions like this for the five years she had been coming to see him. She loved the questions. She loved that there was someone who would ask her these questions, someone who was willing to believe she didn't have to be unhappy, someone who didn't treat her like a basket case. She knew it had kept her from jumping out a window, but she also knew that she hadn't let the questions change her on a fundamental level. She had been arguing with Bruce since the day she found her way to his door, on a day when she had awakened with that terrible sinking feeling and just couldn't take it another day. She sighed. "The truth is I don't believe in happiness. I think happy people are deluding themselves. They are only happy because they are sticking their heads in the sand. That's not me. I'm not the happy-go-lucky type."

"And what about now," Bruce asked her. "What are you unhappy about now?"

"I don't even know anymore. I just get this awful feeling and when I get it, I have to run somewhere. I can't think about it. My head just spins."

"What would you be afraid would happen if you did think about it?"

She thought about this for a while, not saying anything, studying her hands. She was quiet so long, he wondered if she had gone off somewhere even now, sitting across from him during her session. Finally she looked up at him, searching his kind face for any sign of judgment. "I would be lost," she said.

"What do you mean, Eve?" he asked.

"I mean, I guess, that I would be so unhappy, that I would sink down into the deepest, darkest hole of despair that I could imagine, and I wouldn't be able to find a way out."

He noticed how she seemed to sink deeper into her body, into the chair, even as she said this. "Why do you believe you wouldn't be able to find a way out?" he asked her.

She started to cry. "I don't know. I'm afraid I can go to a place where no one can find me, where I can't find myself."

"Where would that place be?"

"I don't know. It's a place of no reason, no will, no movement." She looked at him, then, eyes wide open. "Oh my God, I'm talking about being dead, actually being dead. I'd be dead and miserably unhappy. Is that even possible?"

"I don't know. Is it?"

She thought about it. "No, it isn't possible, but why do I think that it might happen anyway?"

"What do you believe would have to happen for you to go to that place?"

"I would have to do it myself, somehow. I would have to go into the hole and cover myself up."

"Why would you do that?"

"Because I can't stand what's going on around me?"

"Is that a question?"

"No, it's the truth. When I can't stand what is going on around me, I start to dig a hole, to try to disappear."

"What would you be afraid would happen if you didn't do that?"

"If I didn't do that. If I didn't do that," she said, studying her hands again, "if I didn't do that, what would happen? Nothing. I think nothing would happen."

"What do you mean by nothing?"

"That I would be okay."

"When you think about being okay if you don't run away, how do you feel about that?"

"Afraid."

"Why do you believe if you were okay, that you would be afraid?"

"I can't answer that. That question is totally confusing."

"What is confusing about it?"

"That I would be okay and afraid at the same time. Now, that doesn't seem possible. It's like what I just said about being dead and being unhappy — is it possible to be in both places at the same time?"

"Is it?"

"I don't think so, but yet, I am doing it, aren't I?"

"Would you like to stop?"

"Yes, but I'm not sure I can."

"What's preventing you?"

She didn't want to say. She realized she was deeply ashamed. "I can't say it," she said. "I'm sorry. I just can't say the word."

"It doesn't matter. Can you say the word to yourself?"

"Yes, I can."

"Then say it to yourself."

She closed her eyes and thought: Crazy. I'm not afraid. I'm just crazy.

"And without telling me the word, tell me, why do you believe that about yourself?"

"I've just always believed that."

"Always?"

"Well, ever since I can remember."

"And what does it mean about you that you are that way?"

"That something is wrong with me that I can't help."

"And if that were true, why would you feel bad?"

"I don't know," she said, and she stood up. "Our time is up, anyway, isn't it?"

He looked at his watch. "Actually, we have plenty of time."

But she had had enough that day. "I have to go," she said. She wanted the serenity of her bedroom, the darkness beneath the covers, the familiar smells, the lack of thinking.

"That's fine, dear, see you next time."

She made her way downstairs, through Bruce's house, across the driveway, to the house next door, to her room, which was just as she left it. Except for one thing. She had this question, now, which didn't seem to want to go away. She had brought it into the room with her. She didn't burrow under the covers as usual. She opened a window and sat in a chair looking out at the trees.

"Even if I am crazy, why would I feel bad?" It's a question that made no sense to her. It seemed to define itself. Of course, if I am crazy, by definition, I have to feel bad. If I didn't have to feel bad, wouldn't that mean it's not bad to be crazy? How could it not be bad? I don't want it, do I? Or do I? Is there something about being crazy that I do like? How could that be? What could that be? If I didn't feel bad about being crazy, maybe I wouldn't even be crazy. Because then it would be okay and somehow that feels more like I have a choice about it. Crazy by choice? That doesn't even feel like crazy now. And if I weren't crazy, I would be in charge, wouldn't I? I'd have to be responsible for my behavior. What if I were responsible? That thought was the single most terrifying thought. She fell asleep hoping to wake up and be free of it.

Let the Bedspread Do the Talking

There is nothing, absolutely nothing, to cause unhappiness.
Since there is no unhappiness, and never can be, no one has
    to be afraid of anything.
There is nothing to be afraid of or angry about.
Nothing that happens can bring about unhappiness.
Once you know the truth that all is happiness,
You will have reminders.
All that is can be the cause of your awareness of the truth.

On my twentieth birthday, Mom and I fight so much that she ends up throwing my presents into the street. Then she picks up my cake with the twenty pink-and-white candles ablaze and smashes it into the side of the house. We stop screaming at each other long enough to watch the greasy still-flaming icing slide in chunks and smears down the house into the flower beds. I would laugh if I weren't so mad.

"You are an ungrateful child," Nana reminds me as I march back into the house after my mother.

Mom bursts into tears and flies into her room, slamming the door.

"Who's the child here?" I rage. It seems so unfair that she is playing my role. Where did that leave me? Ever since graduation, and especially since the announcement that I would be going away to college, we had begun to fight over everything — if I stay out too late, if I don't do my chores, if I'm sassy or sullen or too loud or too quiet, if I don't call when I am going to be late for dinner, if I do call and say I'm not coming home for dinner. Inevitably she ends up crying in her room and I have to apologize because I can't live with myself if she is mad at me. I am guilty of "no compassion." That seems to be what every fight is really about. I don't care. Don't understand. Didn't do whatever it was that she needed me to do. Now that the day of my departure draws near, things have escalated to the point of no return, I think.

This time I'm not going to apologize, I tell myself. I gather up my bag and jacket, and head out the door. I grab Mom's car keys defiantly and get into her car. Screeching out of the driveway, I don't even know where I am going. I just want to drive away, drive her away. I will drive until I reach Timbuktu, wherever that is. Or better yet, I will drive up to see Matthew at school. I will pour out my heart, and he will put his arms around me and rock me and then hold me at arm's length and say, "Repeat after me. I am a good little girl whom everyone loves." Who am I kidding? Matthew would never say that. He would tell me to think about what I am doing. I hate that. It strikes me that I am not good at being good, not good at loving. What's wrong with me?

In the end, I drive to the end of the block like a lame-o and just sit there unable to decide whether to turn right or left or go straight. The longer I sit there, the more frustrated I get and the more I blame her. Finally I just pull the car over and shut off the engine. Then grogginess comes over me like a fog and before I know it, I nod off with my head on the steering wheel. I wake up feeling cottonmouthed and confused, and all I want is to be home in my bed.

As I roll into the driveway, I almost run over my presents. The sight of them in a heap makes me so sad, I start sobbing right there in the car. All I can think of is my mother buying the presents, wrapping them up, and having me reject them. That was what had started the fight. She had bought me the kind of presents you would buy a twelve-year-old. There was a paint-by-number set and some really cheesy makeup (I now wear Lancôme) and a really cute but strangely inappropriate stuffed lamb. And a copy of *The Secret Garden*, which

I actually do love, but I don't want her thinking that. When I opened the first present, I thought it was a joke and I laughed. She was just sitting there looking at me with the strangest expression on her face, which I realized later was no expression at all. She was waiting for my reaction before she would let anything register on her face. When I opened the second present, the stuffed lamb, I started to get a very strange feeling that something weird was about to happen.

"Do you like it?" she asked me.

I didn't even think. I just blurted out, "Well, I might if I were six."

She shoved the last present at me, which was the book.

"Isn't this for children?" I asked her. "I don't get it, Mom. How come you're giving me all children's gifts?"

"Well, if you don't like them," she said through clenched teeth, "let's just toss them out." And she swooped them up and marched right out of the house to the curb and dumped them. Then she stomped back in and lit the candles on the cake, which I had already blown out. God only knows why she had to light them again, but it did add to the drama. So she lit that damn cake all up, and Nana and I followed her out in the dark like moths to the flame, and with a mighty "Oomph!" she nailed the side of the house with my double-dutch chocolate torpedo. Happy birthday to me.

I don't go into her room that night, and the next morning is Friday. It's my last day at work. They have a surprise party for me at lunch and I get all kinds of presents for school, things I wish Mom could have thought to give me. I go over to Maryanne's and sleep at her house. The next day is Saturday and I have to go home because I promised to do Mom's hair. I am the only one she trusts to color it. If I don't go home, it will be like declaring war. So I go home, and I'm relieved to see the dye all set out with the towels and rubber gloves. She sits like a statue while I section her hair and apply the dye. I set the timer and sit with her while the dye sets, and then I wash her hair at the kitchen sink. We don't say a word the whole time. The silence is healing in a way I hadn't expected.

When I go to my room, I see that there is a new bedspread on my bed, one that I had admired at Macy's last week. When I see it, my heart falls right down into my boots. I know I'm doomed. I go back into the kitchen. "Thanks, Mom." I give her a little hug. My heart goes out to her. She is a person who can never say "I'm sorry," and I've been blaming her for that all my life. I finally realize what a terrible deprivation that must be for her. Thank God she has the bedspread to do her talking.

I leave the next day for college. I go to say goodbye, but she is so sound asleep, I can't bear to wake her. I give her a light kiss on the cheek. I actually wonder if I will ever see her again. I can't say why.

Letting Go

There is no greater kindness nor a more loving vocation than to question unhappiness. Why are you unhappy about that? This question really means, "Why do you believe that you have to be unhappy about that?" This question asks the person to realize he has his own very personal reason for being unhappy about whatever it is.

I'm like a fish out of water up at school, but a very, very happy fish. I float around from class to class back to the dorm to the dining hall to my job at the library feeling as if it's Christmas every single day. My roommates are strange, though. They never smile, and they don't speak to me much. We never go to the dining hall together like the other roommates do. They both have boyfriends, and they seem to spend every available minute with them. I see them walking all over campus holding hands.

Every night at six o'clock I call home. Mom never answers the phone. Nana always sounds surprised to hear my voice, as if she forgot I'm not down the hall in my room. "How is Mom?" I ask. "Mother is sleeping," is all she will say. Or, "Mother has gone out." Or, "Mother is in the bathtub." It's like trying to talk to a rock star. You would think Mom would want to talk to me, to find out how I am doing. Nana asks, "When are you coming home?"

"It's college, Nana," I say. "I come home for Thanksgiving."

Because I am a freshman, I am supposed to do silly things, like wear my underwear outside my clothes or sing the school song whenever some upperclassman asks me to. I refuse. There's an announcement that at midnight all the freshmen are supposed to sneak down to the field behind the school where we will have a bonfire and sing songs until sunrise. It's a tradition. I don't go. Some of the kids try to pressure me into joining in, but I ignore them. I'm a serious student. I am here to learn.

It doesn't take too long to figure out I may be the only one. The kids copy each other's papers and cheat off each other's tests. They ask a lot of questions in class, trying to distract the professor from the day's lesson. My fantasies of college where everyone sits around late into the night discussing Nietzsche fly out the window. Instead, I stay up all night memorizing the bones of the body for a biology exam. I never stayed up all night before. At the exam, we walk around the room where skeletons swing from hooks, their numbered bones shimmering before my glazed eyeballs. In my mind, I can turn to the page in the textbook and read the name of the bone from the picture. It feels like cheating, but I can't help it. I just can't remember my own name. Leave it blank, I tell myself. It will come to you.

Matthew calls me every other night to remind me of his existence at a school farther downstate. I had re-established that we weren't boyfriend and girlfriend before I left, telling him that I wanted a fresh start. As usual, he completely ignores me. He drives me crazy. I've never really had a boyfriend except for Matthew, and I'd like to see what that would be like. But all the boys just seem to want to get laid. A really good-looking boy asks me to his frat party. I like him a lot, and we have a good time dancing and talking. After an hour he invites me to his room. "No thanks," I say, and the next day, it's all over school that I am frigid. I'm too young to be frigid, I think. I haven't even had real sex yet for all my gropings with Matthew over the past few years. Apparently, I'm in the minority. All the girls seem to be on birth control.

Thoughts of Mom are never far from my mind. One night in the middle of the night, the wall phone rings. One of my roommates answers. I know before she even tells me that it's Mom. I take the phone out into the hall. The cord goes under the door and it isn't that long, so I have to practically lie on the floor outside my room to talk to her.

"Hi, Mom." It's been three months since we talked.

"I thought we'd plan dinner," she says.

At first I don't understand what she means, until I realize Thanksgiving is in a week. I'll be coming home. "You want to know that now, Mom? It's two o'clock in the morning."

"Really? Oh, honey, I am so sorry. I didn't even notice the time."

I hear the drugs talking. She must be medicated to the max. "It's okay, Mom," I say. I'm glad to hear her voice, but I can hear that something is wrong. "Are you okay, Mom?"

There's no sound coming from her side. I think I can hear her crying.

"Don't cry, Mom," I say. "What's wrong?"

"I miss my daughter," she says. The way she says it, I wonder if she has another daughter I don't know about. "Everyone I love leaves me."

"Mom, I haven't left you. I'm just at school. I'll be home next week, you know?"

"Yes, I know," she says, "but I wonder if you should come home."

Alarm bells go off in my head and my heart sinks. It's going to be a long night. "Why shouldn't I come home?" I ask.

"I haven't made a very good home for you, have I? You are probably better off staying up at school."

This makes me mad. I hate it when she talks this way, making everything be just about her, twisting things around, ignoring the truth. But I'm a good girl; I don't say any of that. "Don't say that, Mom. I love my home. I love you, and I love Nana. My home is the only home I have ever known. I want to come home." (Because I will never rest until I see you with my own eyes and know that you are okay, I tell myself.)

"Do you really?" she asks. "Because I would understand if you wanted to go off to some friends for Thanksgiving. I'm sure you have all kinds of invitations."

Is she trying to get rid of me? I wonder, What gives? Where does she get these ideas? "Let's plan the menu," I say, even though we have the exact same thing every year.

She ticks off each thing. "Do you want turkey or goose?"

We have never in our entire lives had a goose for Thanksgiving or any other holiday. We wouldn't even know how to cook or eat a goose. We would all just sit there looking at it. "Turkey, of course," I say, and before she can start to dissect whether we should have a whole turkey, or just the drumsticks, or the breast, or stuffed or not — I spell it all out, right down to the brand name. "Butterball, okay, Mom? We'll go shopping together." And yes, I will make my special Libby's pumpkin pie, and Nana will make her famous ladyfingers, and we will have real whipped cream and a chocolate seven-layer cake and a napoleon for Nana.

She says she feels much better with all the planning and she's very excited, and we hang up two hours later with me feeling deeply disturbed. Something is about to happen. I can feel it. I consider packing my things right now and going home. Tomorrow I'll call Matthew and we'll figure it out. But right now I have to go to sleep so I can wake up early and take my exams. Of course, I don't sleep. I stay up all night worrying and finally just get up and study some more.

I get even more nervous when Daddy sends me a plane ticket to come home for Thanksgiving break. I was planning on taking the Greyhound bus with the money I saved from my library job. He picks me up at the airport and the first thing out of his mouth is, "Kitten, how would you like to spend Thanksgiving with us?"

"What's wrong, Dad," I ask. "Where's Mom? How come you sent me the plane ticket?"

"She's gone again," he tells me. "No note, said nothing to Nana. We have the police looking for her."

I stare at him in disbelief. "And you're just telling me now? When did she leave? I just spoke to her last week. We planned the menu together."

"Honey, we didn't want to upset you. You know your mother. She's unpredictable. Every now and then she has to go off. She'll be back."

I start to cry, and then I get really angry. "I want to go home. I have to see Mom's room for myself. There might be clues there. I want to see my room. No offense, Dad, but I'd just as soon you dropped me off at the house."

"We can't let you stay by yourself, honey. It's not right. You all alone in that big house."

"But where's Nana?"

"Nana went down to Florida to visit friends. She told you, right?"

I'm aghast. "How could Nana leave when Mom is missing? What's the matter with her?"

"Your Nana is too old for this stuff, honey. Your mother has been doing her disappearing act since way before you were born. Nana knows she will show up. She wanted to stay and make Thanksgiving for you, but I talked her into going. It's better for everyone."

"How is this better for anyone? I just want to look for Mom, Dad. That's all I care about."

"Honey, you always look for her and you never find her. You know she always comes home when she's ready."

I don't say anything. I'm a child again with no rights, no voice. This time I don't even have a bike. Maybe they don't need to look for her, but I do. It's just the way it is.

So I end up back in the basement at Daddy's house. I'm so depressed I can barely participate in the holidays. All I want to do is look for Mom. The day after Thanksgiving, Matthew comes and gets me and we go down to the shore and check out every beach, every beach guesthouse and motel, every restaurant. We show her picture, but no one remembers having seen her lately. I am sick at heart.

"Sweetie, she's doing what she wants to do," says Matthew. "You shouldn't worry so much. She always comes home, doesn't she?"

"I can't bear it," I say. I feel as if my heart is collapsing. I can feel what it feels like to be Mom. It's terrifying and lonely. I can't stand it that she has to go to that place. "She's not at some resort having fun, Matthew. She's roaming, like some homeless person looking for God knows what. As if she didn't have a home or a family. She's just roaming through nothingness. That's not okay."

"It has to be okay," he tells me, trying to take me in his arms. I don't let him. I'm angry with him now. I know it's not his fault, but I can't help it.

He takes me home, and I check every inch of her room, breathing the air deep into my lungs, trying to inhale what she was thinking when she left. All I think of is the night we went to the beach. How she loves to go to the beach at night. Even though it's getting dark, we go back there, to the same beach where Mom and I went when I was just a little kid. In the middle of the night, in the darkness, I had been afraid, but she was more at peace than I had ever seen her before. It's very cold on the beach. The sky is threatening snow. I sit there shivering and Matthew marches around me, trying to keep warm. I start to scare myself, I feel her presence so strongly on the beach. I wonder, was she here? Is she around somewhere? Or, I can't help thinking, did she just walk out into that inky darkness that she seemed to love? Did she just walk out and die? I say that to Matthew.

I think I hear a kind of snort coming from him. "Your mom," he says, crouching down to look at me. "Your mom did not walk out into the ocean, sweetie. Your mom is off somewhere warm, doing her thing, while you are here, waiting and freezing. Sweetie," he says again, lifting my face to meet his eyes. "Sweetie, it's time to stop waiting."

Matthew tries to pull me up into a standing position, but I won't budge. I am a rock on the shore. I am the shore, waiting for the ocean to come up to meet me. I am ready to spend the rest of my life here. When I think about what Matthew has just said, I think my heart is going to break. It is almost easier to think that she has become part of the sea. At least I will always know where to find her.

"Just take me home," I say.

"You mean your dad's, right?"

"No, Matthew. I am going home to my own home, to my own room. It's the only place I know where I belong."

He takes me but insists on sleeping on the couch. I sneak down the stairs and watch him watching television, but I don't go to him. It would be so easy just to curl up beside him, put my head on his lap, snuggle like we used to when we were kids. But I won't allow myself. Instead I go into Mom's room and get into her bed. It still smells like her. I feel like a little kid again, but it's not a nice feeling. I'm an adult, remembering what it was like to be a bewildered child.

Matthew has this idea that he is going to drive me back up to school. "It's on the way," he says the next morning. We're eating breakfast in the kitchen, which already seems deserted.

"It's a hundred miles out of the way," I say. "That's crazy."

"All the same," he says, "I will pick you up at 8 a.m. tomorrow." He kisses me goodbye and ruffles my hair. Matthew, you are so wonderful, I think. Why am I not in love with you?

In the morning when he comes to get me, I am still in the kitchen, still in my pajamas. The way he looks at me, I know he half expected this. "Don't tell me," he says. "Don't tell me you are not going because of her."

"You don't understand," is all I can say. He goes upstairs and packs my things. He brings the suitcase down. He is ready, I swear he is ready, to carry me out to the car in my pajamas. We go through all the cycles. He yells. I cry. He pleads. I cry. He tries to scare me into believing that I am throwing my life away. I get mad at him. He leaves, slamming the door so hard, the glass cracks. He is back in ten minutes. We hold each other. "I don't know what to do for you," he says.

"There is nothing you can do. Just go. I have to do what I am doing. It's okay, Matthew. I promise it's okay." I just want to be alone. I want to hide in my bed and cry. I can't explain it. I know I am grown, a woman. Somewhere in my mind I know my mother is okay, but I can't shake the deep-down trembling grief of her leaving me. Again.

I take a bath and get dressed. I sit at my mother's vanity table. I sit there and look into my own eyes and tell myself to leave, but I feel as if I must wait here. As if I would be abandoning her if I left. I suspect I am driving myself crazy, that I should not be alone. I wish Matthew had not left. I wish he would have waited with me. The next day the lights go out. In the sunlight, I look through the mail. She has not paid the utility bill. There is the notice saying the date service will be cut off if the bill is not paid. The date is today, the first day of the new semester.

So I go there. To the little room beside the basement in Bruce's house. It's cold there, but I bring my alpine sleeping bag. I sit in the orange beanbag chair and try to lose myself in it. I go to sleep, and when I wake up, I can hear the freezing rain coming down. It feels the way it has always felt here. As if time has stopped and I am safe. I have stopped the world. I think about going home to see if Mom is there. Maybe she called. I am hungry, and I have to go the bathroom. It occurs to me that depression is not my thing. If I were Mom, I could sit here forever, going hungry and dehydrated if I had to. I can't stop thinking about Mallomars and cold milk, a hot bath, but then I think about her leaving and I am immobilized again. I sit for another hour. I realize I may have to sit here forever, and I am getting so stiff and sore that when I get up to stretch, it takes a while before I can stand up straight. It's time to go.

Bruce catches me leaving. I don't know where he came from. I thought they were all away. The last I heard he was in the hospital. He's in and out of the hospital a lot now. He is standing by the back door watching the rain. He looks different. He is smaller, I think. He looks older and thinner. I can see then he is leaning on a cane. I have to pass by him to get to my house, and I can't do it. I just stand there looking at him, and he looks at me. Not surprised, just accepting that I am here. Smiling. He opens the door and I go in. In the living room, he sits in an armchair next to an oxygen tank and motions for me to sit down. His wife comes in and puts his legs up. I can see they are swollen. She brings him a huge glass of water, and he takes a handful of pills.

"You grew up," he says.

I shrug. "I don't feel so grown up," I say. I tell him about Mom.

"I know," he says. "She came to see me before she left."

I look at him. I remember the time she disappeared when I was twelve. He knew where she was then. Maybe he knows now.

"Did she tell you where she was going?"

"She told me she was taking a trip out west, but she didn't say where. She was afraid everyone would try to talk her out of it."

My mouth drops open, and I just stare at him. "So she said goodbye to you and not me. That's so unfair."

"She told me so that you would know that she is safe, in a place she wants to be, but she doesn't want you to look for her or go after her. She knew you would come here, eventually. She doesn't want you to worry."

"I didn't know you and my mom ever talked. Do you think she's coming back?"

"I don't know if she's coming back. She may not know herself right now."

"So was she a client?"

"Yes, in a way, but she was a friend, too."

"How could this be going on right under my nose?"

"I guess she didn't want anyone to know. That's her right, don't you think?"

"I guess," I say, but I feel cheated somehow, tricked. I always thought Bruce was my special secret. "I can't believe she's gone."

"How do you feel about it?" he asks.

"I don't know. I shouldn't be feeling like this at all. She does this all the time, you know."

"I know, but what's different about this time?"

"This time? She always came back! But now that I know she talked to you before she left, I know it means she's not coming back, at least not for a very long time. Maybe she wanted to go and she waited for me to leave so she could go."

"Do you think that's what happened?"

"Yes," I tell him. "I do know that. She left when my back was turned."

"How do you feel about that?"

"Angry. How sneaky is that? Why couldn't she just talk to me?"

"What is there about her leaving this way that you're unhappy about?"

"I just wish our relationship were more important to her. I wish she cared."

"What do you mean?"

"I wished she cared enough to talk to me, not just run away."

"What is there about her not caring about the relationship enough to talk to you that you're unhappy about?"

"These are dumb questions," I say.

"What's dumb about them?"

"The answers are obvious. And you keep asking the same things."

"Are you answering?"

"I thought I was."

"These are the questions I know to ask," he said.

"Did you ask my mom these questions?"

"Sometimes."

"Did she answer?"

"Sometimes."

"I know — and sometimes they helped her. Are you sure you're any good at this?"

He laughed. "I only ask the questions," he tells me. "The answers are up to you."

"You're trying to tell me that I shouldn't be unhappy, aren't you?"

"You can be unhappy if you want to be. There's no right and wrong. It's your life. Those are your feelings."

"But you want me to stop being unhappy, right?"

"Don't you?" he asks.

"Yes," I say.

"What?"

"Yes, I do want to stop." It feels good to say that. A huge weight lifts from my chest. We smile at each other. I know that this is a very special moment. "Can you help me stop?"

"I can try," he says.

"More questions, right?"

"Is that all right?"

"I just feel so bad that she left."

"What is there about her leaving that you feel bad about?"

"I love being around her so much. Sounds nutty, huh? She's supposed to be so messed up, but I never minded that. How come she doesn't feel that way about me?"

"You want her to be with you, but if she doesn't why is that something you have to be unhappy about?"

I'm having a hard time answering. I just keep going back to "I want her." Like a little baby. I want her and I am unhappy that I don't have her.

"Let me ask you this," he says. "What would you be afraid would happen if you were not unhappy about her leaving?"

"That's a good one. That's full of possibilities. You've been saving this one, haven't you?"

He laughs out loud and then coughs for about a minute. I almost forgot that he was sick.

"Are you okay?" I ask.

"Sure, are you?" He smiles at me when he says this.

I don't know what to say to that. "Shouldn't you go to bed or something?"

"I am perfectly happy here," he says.

And I know that he is.

"Answer the question," he says, and repeats it.

"I know this sounds stupid," I say. "But if I weren't unhappy, it would be as if I would be letting her get away with something."

"What would you be letting her get away with?"

"Well, that she left me."

"Is that a bad thing?"

"Yes, it's a bad thing." I wonder about him. "How come you didn't know that? What kind of mother leaves her child like this? We were just discussing turkey, for God's sake."

"I don't know. You tell me."

"A bad mother," I say. The words hang in the air. "I didn't mean that," I say. "She's not bad. She's my mom and I love her." I start to cry again, but the crying is not so painful, not so pitiful. "I love her," I say.

"Can you just love her and not feel you have to teach her to be a good mom by feeling bad?"

"What?"

He smiles. "What would you be afraid would happen if you just loved her and didn't feel bad?"

"That she wouldn't change."

"Why does she have to change?"

I can't answer.

"Why does she have to change, Annie?"

"So I can get what I want."

We don't say anything.

"So this is just about my getting what I want?" I ask. I don't like that it's about that. All of a sudden, the burden seems to have shifted over to me, instead of her. I'm not sure I like that.

"Is that what you think?"

"Yeah, that is what I think. I'm a selfish little pig." But I am laughing. The hurt is almost gone. But it's not completely gone. It's as if he can see the hurt.

"What's going on?" he asks.

And I am crying again. What's wrong with me? And I am back in it again, back to being the little girl whose mother left her.

"What's wrong with you?" he asks.

I look at him, wide-eyed. "How did you know?"

"I don't know. It's really a question. I'm asking."

"I don't like thinking there is anything wrong with me."

"What if you didn't think that?"

"Am I allowed? Am I allowed to think that when I don't get what I want, there is nothing wrong with me?"

"What do you think?"

"Don't you ever answer any questions?"

"Sure, what question would you really like me to answer?"

"You're tricky," I say, getting his point. "I really need to answer the questions, not you, right?"

"Right," he says, and we laugh.

He puts the oxygen thingy under his nose, saying, "So answer the question."

I try not to think about the fact that I am using up his precious time, sapping his strength. "I'm not sure it's okay not to feel wrong when I don't get what I want. If I don't feel wrong, how will I learn?"

"How do you think you learn? Does feeling wrong do it?"

"No, just learning what there is to learn does it. Wanting to learn."

"So what if you left it at that? Just want to learn. Could you do that?"

"I would like to. I really would love to know how to get what I want from her."

"And if you can't learn that? What if it isn't something that you can do?"

"I guess I'd be okay with that. I'd have to be, wouldn't I?"

"Well, you wouldn't have to, but you could and that's all that counts, right?"

I nod my head, give a little shrug, wondering if it could really be this simple.

"So how do you feel now?"

"I feel better," I say. I actually feel happy and lighthearted, but I am too embarrassed to admit it. And hungry. "Do you have any Mallomars?" (I know full well that he does and exactly where they are.)

"Let's see what's in the pantry."

We don't walk to the pantry together that day. The pantry is too far for him to go because of the excruciating pain in his feet and legs. Instead, I go to the pantry and find the cookies, pour us each a glass of milk, and bring it all back into the living room on a tray. He smiles at me and falls asleep. I kiss him on the cheek and leave. It dawns on me that he is in pretty bad shape, and I'm surprised that I hadn't realized it before. It isn't quite that he hides it well. His spirit seems to exist independently of his body. In spite of the pain and what must be the knowledge that he may not have long to live, he's not afraid to show the world that he is happy and okay. I love that about him and I love that I can be that way as well. The next day I return to school.

Waiting

Any future I hope to have can only come from who I am.

Sometimes at night, right before I go to sleep, in the darkness behind my eyes, I see my mother dancing. She is wearing a long white cotton dress, something she could have made herself. Her hair is long again, and she has let it go curly. She is dancing barefoot on a moonlit beach, twirling and twirling at the inky shore, leaving tiny sandstorms in her wake. There is no music and no partner, but she looks completely happy and completely at peace. She stops and looks at me, reaching out her lovely long arms to me to come and join her. It has been five years, and we still have not heard from her.

In the house that used to be our home, I stand at the kitchen door looking over at Bruce's house. Our house is empty now, having just been vacated by the family we've been renting it to for the past five years. I had convinced Daddy to let me rent the house when I left to go to school, instead of selling it like he wanted to. He reluctantly agreed, willing to do just about anything to try to mend our relationship. He doesn't understand why I don't come to visit anymore. He keeps asking me what he did wrong. I can't answer. I love him but I don't want to be part of the story he and Michelle have written about my mother and me. In their story, she's the self-centered, manipulative, damaged parent and I am the unwitting accomplice. The two of us are caught up in an endless circle of defeat. When she left, they told me it was the best thing that ever happened to me. Now I was free to take care of myself and attend to my own life instead of always being drawn into her hopelessness.

It's a story that is supposed to make me feel good about myself because I am the innocent victim. The truth is the only time I felt like a victim was when they told that story and I believed it. The real story, the real truth, is that she did what she did, and I always loved her. The only circle the two of us were caught up in was unconditional love. I always will love her. And if she returned tomorrow, I would try to worm my way under her skin the way I always had. They would ask me, But did she love you? Meaning she never loved you. And to that I say, Of course she did. And they would say: She never acted like it. She never did this and she never did that. And to that I say, Then why do I love her so much? I trust myself that much. I know when love is love, pure and simple. When I go to their house, they serve this story along with the pot roast and mashed potatoes. If I go there, I have to betray her with every bite. Instead, I choose to eat alone and know that the love in my heart is a direct response to her love, her supposedly invisible and damaging love that still holds me to her simply because I am her child and I felt loved by her. I am the one who looked for her love. I am the one who expected it.

So when it became clear that she wasn't coming back, at least to everyone but me, it was decided that the house would be sold. I could come home and stay with Daddy and Michelle on my vacations. They presented me with no choice. So I divorced them. I told them I would never come home if they did that. Michelle was ready to dig in, but Daddy was too afraid of losing me for good. So they agreed to let me rent the house to a family from North Carolina. The husband worked at Daddy's firm and was being relocated up north. So I went away to school, but I didn't keep my part of the bargain. I always found some reason not to come home. I worked through the summers or I visited Matthew at his parent's summerhouse in the mountains.

In our old house, a little girl from North Carolina grew up in my room while I completed my BA in psychology with a minor in English literature and went on to complete my master's. I often wondered if she noticed the man next door, always writing and writing on slips of paper, yellow pads, notebooks of all shapes and sizes. Did she see him on his porch or under the trees in the summertime? Did she overhear the kitchen conversations or maybe even just see his kind eyes looking at her as they passed each other coming and going? I'll never know. They're gone now and as I walk around my house for the first time in five years, I feel the emptiness. Everyone who lived here has gone except for me. It's time to make a decision. Until last night, I secretly believed Mom might come back some day. I wanted the house to be here for her. Now I believe differently. Somewhere in the misty world that she inhabits, a shift has occurred. Or maybe the shift has occurred in me. Somehow a door that was once open has been gently closed, not slammed or emphatically closed, just ever so gently eased shut. It's time to open a new door.

Matthew is waiting for me in Colorado. He is teaching at the University of Colorado. I'm supposed to be starting work as an administrative assistant at the university. Matthew can't understand why I would do that after I spent all that time in school. I don't understand it either, but I know when the time is right, I will see what there is to do.

Matthew still likes to fantasize that someday I will see the light and fall in love with him. "I do love you," I tell him. "Just not like that."

"So what?" he tells me. "No one will ever love you the way I do."

"I know that, Matthew, but why does that mean we should be lovers? Can't we just love each other? I can't help it; you're like a brother to me." And we go on and on like we have been doing for the last ten years.

I have my tickets for Denver for next week, but I can't really be sure I will get on the plane. Somehow I'm still rooted here. Matthew thinks I'm stalling, but like him, I'm also waiting. I'm just not sure what I am waiting for.

God's Prayer to Man

Let go. Let me have my way with you. My power is in your heart, your mind and in every cell of you. All that you do, you do for happiness. That is why you exist — to have happiness.

Sister Mary Sylvester and Sister Thomas Marie tended the sick and dying at St. Michael's Hospital. This day, they made their way through the ICU hoping to lift the burden of death, to release the despair of terminal illness. The two had been at it for nearly four hours, and Sister Mary Sylvester was starting to feel the strain. As she sat by the bedside of a thirty-year-old cancer patient, she felt the unwelcome hollowness of exhaustion in her chest. She had thought the tiredness was just part of getting older. Until last Tuesday.

The young man in the bed wants to know why God has let cancer happen to him. Before last Tuesday, she could answer that question, but now, it's as if the answer was lost somewhere between her heart and her throat. Last Tuesday in this very hospital she heard the news that she has breast cancer. She knew what she was supposed to say to the patient but had simply lost the will to say it. She heard Sister Thomas Marie talking about God's divine will and the blessing of submission. For the past thirty years, these words had always brought her peace, but now they confused her. Is she really such a hypocrite that she would believe that God's will only applied to others? Where was the faith that had been her rock these many years?

All that is, is the will of God. Period.

In the last bed was a familiar face, someone she was always glad to see, yet so sorry to see at the same time. A fifty-three-year-old man. One of the unlucky ones who did not benefit from a quadruple bypass done a few years ago. One of the unlucky ones who did not respond to treatment for diabetes. The disease had run rampant through his body, compromising his vascular system, starving his heart, stripping his nerve endings. He was in constant searing pain. He could no longer stand on his feet for the pain and swelling.

She knew that over the past few years, most of the pleasures of life had been lost to him. Common smells made him extremely nauseous. A turkey roasting in the oven at Thanksgiving would have him retching all day long. The perfumes he used to love made him sick to his stomach. His diet was so heavily restricted because of heart disease, diabetes, and gout that there was very little he could eat anyway. And music, his greatest love. He used to spend hours at the piano most days but had to give it up because of the paralyzing neuropathy in his hands. His passionate response to opera caused torrential nosebleeds. She had watched his condition steadily worsen over the past few years, reducing the quality of life to a shadow of what it once was. She had heard he was back again, having suffered some kind of stroke the night before.

And yet he smiled at them as they approached. He smiled. Not a brave smile. Not a tentative smile. A huge beaming smile lit from within. And his eyes, unlike the turned-inward eyes of the dying, still seemed to send sparks through the air. He was sitting up in bed with his wife and friends nearby. They never left him alone. She had never seen such devoted people. He has aged a lot since last they met. The disease was having its way with him. Yet she knew that even with the drugs and the pain he had delivered a brilliant lecture not two weeks before at the home of friends. She had been invited to attend, and she was glad she had. Looking at him now, her hands spontaneously reached toward him as if to try to pull him back. He was dying.

At the lecture in a cozy living room in New Jersey, a group of twenty or so people had waited patiently as he made his way into the room. He should have used a wheelchair, but he wouldn't have it. With the use of a cane and the help of friends, he made his way to the chair reserved for him and welcomed them all with a warm smile, not unlike the way he was looking at her now. He had talked for almost two hours about happiness and unhappiness, never once referring to his own suffering.

"All people in all societies," he told them, "have always believed it is necessary to be unhappy, even the most brilliant among us. Even Jesus."

She had had a physical reaction to that remark and he had noticed, she thought. She didn't like to hear lay people talk about what Jesus thought. But she was intrigued. He spoke so comfortably, so knowingly, and with such confidence. As if he had just spoken to Jesus about this question yesterday. Where did he get such confidence about things that could not be proven?

"The problem with calling things bad and evil," he said, "is that they tend to be moral judgments. Perhaps the only evil in the devil is that we believe the devil has the power to make us unhappy against our will. The only evil in cancer is that it supposedly has the power to make people unhappy against their will. You can go all the way down from the greatest to the least of evils. By definition, these are all things that make you feel bad against your will."

She had not remembered his saying that until just this moment. She had not known about her cancer then — the cancer that was going to eat her up inside, ruin her chances to achieve her dreams. Cancer and feeling bad seemed to be two sides of the same coin, impossible to separate.

A young woman in the group had asked, "You talk about feeling bad against our will. You mean, we choose to feel bad? We choose to feel good? I'm not aware of making those choices."

"No," he had said, "I'm not about to jump into your lives and say: Guess what? Nothing made you feel bad without your consent. You wanted it, you loved it, you asked for it. You wanted to be unhappy. But that's not true. Nobody wakes up in the morning and says, 'I think I'll be unhappy about six things today,' and starts choosing them as the day goes on. People don't choose to be unhappy. People don't choose to be happy."

He paused and took a long drink, which gave her time to realize that even though he was presenting them with an apparent contradiction — we don't choose our feelings, yet we have the will to feel bad or not — she was not confused. She knew exactly what he meant. If unhappiness didn't happen to you, you had to choose it on some level. It was just like belief in God. God couldn't make you believe in him. You had to choose it, although it was so natural, it didn't feel like a choice at all.

"People don't choose to be happy," he told them, "yet it is not true that it's not chosen. Meaning, unhappiness doesn't happen to you. It's a feeling in your own body that only you can create. I am using the word 'choose' in a way that it has never been used before, because I can't really think of a better way to say it. I don't want to have to say that people want to be unhappy. People universally describe unhappiness as a feeling they don't want. If they call themselves unhappy, they are feeling as if it is happening to them, like they're a victim."

Sister Mary Sylvester wondered, was there some way she was choosing this overwhelming sadness that was always with her now? Was she making a judgment about her cancer — calling it bad? But it was bad, wasn't it. It would make her suffer greatly, perhaps even kill her. But she was not afraid to die. Of that she was certain. What was it, then? All her adult life she had been telling people to trust God. Why was it so hard for her to do that now?

"How are you, Sister?" he was asking her now. "It's good to see you again."

"I'm doing well, Bruce," she lied, "and how are you doing?"

"Well, they say I've had a stroke. They're still trying to find out how much damage was done. I'm somewhat paralyzed on my right side. The good thing about that is that the pain is a lot less than it was."

"You've had so much pain. Are you coping well?" she asked. She knew he was coping well. What she really wanted to ask was, How do you do it? How can you still smile? How can you point out the bright side of a stroke?

He was silent for a while and so was she. For a brief moment it was almost as if they were praying together. Then she noticed his hands resting in his lap, and as she did they seemed to come alive, floating up and opening palms up like a beautiful strong flower responding to the light of the sun. Out of his hands seemed to rise all the stress and strain of the need to explain. Out of his hands seemed to rise all the fear of physical pain and death. It was the most beautiful gesture she had ever seen. She didn't need to hear him say, "His will be done," to understand the power of his complete and total acceptance.

The will of God is that all men enjoy his presence as their happiness, which is their desire also.

His will be done. She had said that phrase so many times, but she had never heard it like this. Something in the way he said it — or was it the way he looked when he said it? — caused her to remember something she had forgotten long ago, something that she had not even known until now that she had forgotten: that moment so many years ago when God had come into her heart for the first time. And the moment so many years ago when she had closed part of herself off from God.

She had been very young, perhaps six or seven years old. Her mother had taken her to live with an aging aunt for the summer months. The two of them had spent many long afternoons walking on the beach and down the long wooden boardwalk. One crowded afternoon over the 4th of July weekend, as they were walking a crowd of young boys on roller skates came careening down the boardwalk. There must have been twenty or thirty boys in wave after wave having fun zigzagging through the crowd. Somehow in all the commotion, she was pulled away from her aunt and carried down the boardwalk with the crowd going in the opposite direction. She could actually see her aunt, looking for her and hear her calling her name, but she was powerless to do anything about it. There was so much commotion on the boardwalk caused by the skaters that no one noticed a little girl being pulled through the crowd. The further she was pulled away from her aunt, the more frightened she became, until finally she was so panic-stricken that she couldn't even catch her breath.

And then, it was as if something told her just to stop. "I can't," she said. "I'm afraid."

But the voice was persistent. "Stop moving your legs. Stop keeping up with the crowd. Just stand still and be a little statue."

"I'm afraid," she said again. "I'm little. I'll get trampled."

But the voice kept saying, "Just stop where you are and raise your arms way up high over your head and look at every single person who comes your way. You'll be all right."

"I can't," she cried. "I'm afraid."

And then the voice was silent. She tried to hear the voice again but it did not come. And all in a moment, she yearned for the voice and reached out to the voice to hear it again. And when she did not hear the voice, she yelled, "Stop!" in the biggest voice she could find inside her. She stamped her feet as hard as she could and planted them on the boardwalk. She threw her arms up into the air and looked at every single face coming her way. And the crowd parted around her. No one touched a hair on her head. No one brushed against her. No one knocked her down. Some people looked at her and smiled. They thought she was playing a game. Others thought she was a precocious child having a tantrum. Many people didn't see her at all. But all steered clear. Over ice cream, her aunt asked her, "What made you think to do that?" And when her aunt heard the story of the voice, she leaned close with knitted eyebrows, put her index finger to her lips, and shook her head ever so slightly, saying "Let that be our little secret."

How many decades had it been then? That she had made the voice something outside of herself? She hadn't stopped listening, but not until this very moment had she listened with the innocence of a child again.

Happiness is feeling however you choose to feel or experience your-self, and not believing that anything makes that wrong. Knowing (or not denying) that nothing can make you feel other than how you really do or will, is happiness.

She nodded to the man in the bed and said as much to him as to herself, "His will be done." And then she rose and went on her way, leaving her burden behind and carrying her blessing to everyone she touched.

Bruce: Happier Than Happy

Could it be as he remembered it? He remembered being at peace, consenting to be at one with the separate being, choosing to be alive. It felt like waking up from a sleep he hadn't slept, almost like waking up from nothing. He was content, blissful, self-contained. He remembered a change. There was a whiteness, brightness, and he was in awe, amazed, shocked, fascinated, surprised — really surprised and really glad to meet it.

He couldn't hear anything, he remembered. In fact, whatever he had been hearing up till then seemed to stop, almost as if he had been full of sound and then there was an empty sound, or no sound at all. It was as if he could trade his sound for that different sound outside of him, any time he wanted. He remembered the curiosity. He saw and saw, and he was delighted. He was not unhappy in any way. Not about hunger, diapers, thirst, or pain.

He remembered when the unhappiness started. He was older then, small but not very young — an older, experienced child perhaps. He remembered sitting on the floor and, all of a sudden, seeing a big person. He was a man of around twenty-five years, average height, broad-shouldered, but not muscular, strong-looking, solid-looking. He wasn't fat, but he was slightly heavier than average, and he had yellow hair. His fair-skinned face was a little pink or red, almost Germanic. He was wearing a flannel shirt with large red squares. Bruce remembered it all so well.

And what he remembered most vividly was that the man's sound filled him, along with the most extraordinary overwhelming feeling of love. This is the most beautiful sight I have ever seen, he remembered thinking. I *know him more intimately than anything I ever knew. I love him more than anything. And then the most amazing thing happened. He was struck with the realization: You are who I am going to be. You are the Big Me. I will be you when I am big. And he remembered the question that rose up within him, When? When can I be you? He knew he could never see him again until that day. When? he asked. The answer came, "Not yet. Not now."*

Then what? He remembered crying inside and yearning deeply. He felt undone, unraveled. Perhaps he even started to die a little. He knew that was the day he started to believe in unhappiness.

From that distant memory, from that distant passion, a vow formed —*I will stop believing in unhappiness and be the happy child again, but this time, this time, I will be happier than happy. It will be more than picking up where I left off.* And now, the pain that filled every muscle, bone, and nerve in his body is gone. The struggling, suffocated heart and lungs are kept alive through drugs and respirators, but he is gone. For all his suffering, his body still reflects the strong, but not muscular, average-height, stocky, broad-shouldered man he was, fair of skin and hair, all his life a generator of unconditional love, an untiring crusader in the war against unhappiness.

I had been calling the hospital those last few days before I was supposed to leave for Colorado. Like that night so many years ago, I had seen the ambulance come for him, but this time I did not see them bring him home. Somehow I knew this had to be the end. I heard about the massive heart attack, and they told me he was in a coma. It was only a matter of time. I would see his wife and friends coming home all hours of the night from the hospital, going back a few hours later. I longed to go with them, but I couldn't quite get up the nerve to face what was happening. I even found out where the hospital was and spent a day or two parked in the lot, too hesitant to make a move inside. Then one day, his wife spotted me there. She simply stopped in front of the car and held out her hand. We walked into the hospital together.

That was the day he died. She and I were talking in the waiting room when a priest appeared. We chatted for a while, and then he asked, "Wouldn't you like to go see him now?" The question was so subtle, we almost missed its meaning. Then we both realized in an instant what was happening. Bruce had been in a coma for a week. His kidneys were failing, and the family had declined dialysis and other extraordinary measures the night before. He was dying.

We walked into the ICU together, past the nurses, doctors, and orderlies. No one would look at us. At Bruce's bedside, the doctor indicated the rapidly failing vital signs and left us alone with him. It was almost over. His wife stepped over to the nurses' station to call his mother and closest friends. She had been his main caregiver for almost ten years, seeing him through every crisis, administering his medications, sleeping with one eye open, turning their lives inside out to try to find him any comfort to ease the unending pain, to keep him alive a little longer. But the moment of his death was something she hadn't known how she would deal with. My presence there gave her the distance she needed to cope and still be there for him. I had the distinct feeling that I was there for her, for all of them, who loved him with such devotion. I put my hand over his heart as the last few beats registered. It felt like a tiny bird, so fragile yet somehow still infused with the tiniest breath of life. And then it flew away.

Could it be as I seemed to remember it? I was peaceful and I happily consented to be one with this separate being. When will I be him? When will I see him again? I know that I will. I'll be happier than happy. I will be picking up where I left off.

Once There Was a Man Who Was Happy.

Raymond's eulogy, December 8, 1995

As the service grew to a close, I knew that the last speaker was about to begin, the last in a long stream of people who had been there at various times in his life. It dawned on me that I, among a few others, had actually been there consistently for close to twenty years. Even at the very end. I was so used to living on the outskirts of Bruce's life that I had taken my place quite willingly in the overflow room, away from the people who were closest to Bruce. I wondered if by separating myself so much over the years I kept myself from truly embracing everything that he had taught me. I was holding on to a vision of myself in the past as if I had never known him. As if the unhappiness I felt as a child had more power than the knowledge that I didn't have to be unhappy. That knowledge was my legacy, and I wanted to accept it wholeheartedly. I stood up and made my way out of the overflow room. In the main room, Raymond was standing up to take the mike. At that moment, Bruce's wife turned around and looked my way, beckoning me to come and sit beside her.

Raymond began:

"There were times when Bruce would ask me to tell him a story . . . which I would do with great relish . . . for, as many of you know, Bruce was a superb and skillful listener. A long time ago in China there were two friends, one who played the harp skillfully and one who listened skillfully. When one played or sang about a mountain, the other would

251

say: 'I can see the mountain before us!' When the one played about the water, the listener would exclaim: 'Here is the running stream!' But the listener fell sick and died. The first friend cut the strings of his harp and never played again. Since that time the cutting of harp strings has always been a sign of intimate friendship. And so it was.

"In the Hasidic tradition of Judaism, a teaching regarding death says, 'There are three ascending levels of how one mourns the death of a loved one: With tears . . . that is the lowest. With silence . . . that is the higher. And with song . . . that is the highest.' So, then, with what sign will we mark the passing of this most remarkable and uniquely compassionate man, Bruce Di Marsico? With tears? No, too low. So, no tears for Bruce, today. As for silence . . . Well, 'Bruce' and 'silence' just don't compute, so I'll not be cutting any harp strings . . . silence is not the way. That leaves song, and today, my sign of our friendship will be 'song,' but the kind of song Bruce sang, as no other man I have ever met, the song-music of words. Bruce was a master of words; but always working, polishing, perfecting words so as to accurately describe feelings, sensation, attitude. But what words can you use to talk about Bruce and his recent change of venue that Bruce could not have said better . . . and did! Listen! Listen! Listen to Bruce, from his 'Option Theology.'

"*To be able to rest in the breast of The One Who Knows and Loves You . . . The One Who You Know and Cannot But Love is the joy of life. To live by letting God live as you is the true self-abandonment of all fear and care, which self-abandonment is the goal of true selfishness and the highest fulfillment of self. To act in any and all your actions enveloped and suffused with the total protection of the Author of all acts, to be truly invulnerable to any fear of doubt, punishment or mistake is the gift of the Option mystic.*

"Words . . . Bruce's words . . . For me, there are two words I will never again say, see, or hear that will not remind me of Bruce. In truth, which of us will ever again hear the word 'happy' and not remember Bruce Di Marsico? If ever a man made a word, it was Bruce for happiness.

"The second word is 'free' — freeing, freedom. Bruce's greatest gift to me was freedom . . . or, rather, his insight, guidance, and patience as he led me, prodded me, to uncover the Truth of Truths: I always was, I am now, and I always will be free. I have absolutely nothing to be afraid of. And with that, of course, comes the flood of happiness; or is it vice versa? Bruce?

"Up to now, I could always resolve my confusion over this kind of question by asking Bruce, for Bruce always had the answer. In coming to him with some such question, I would joke, saying, 'I'm asking you this because I don't know everything about everything, just most things about most things.' And without missing a beat, Bruce would quip, 'Speak for yourself.' And for the kind of problems I brought to him, it seemed Bruce did know everything about everything. Bruce always came up with the 'dawning light' perspective, and I found myself in a constant state of A-HA! You remember that one, don't you? We've all been there . . . it goes like this: 'A-HA! Yes! Now I see! Wow! I never thought of it that way!' And you know the feeling, too . . . it's called happiness!

"Happiness . . . what a word. Many have used it in many ways. The Dalai Lama once said, 'The very purpose of our life is happiness . . . The secret to my own happiness is within my own hand. I must not miss the opportunity.' Every society, in every time, from every corner and point of view, has held happiness as the goal. We have all been told 'what' in ten times ten thousand ways, but Bruce showed us, showed me, 'how.' And if I was told in other times, in other ways, I never heard it till there was Bruce. If that sounds like a song, you're right . . . it's Bruce's song. Old Brucie one note, but oh, what a note it is! 'You're already happy, you merely believe you're not . . .'

"These words, given this circumstance, would be called a eulogy. Do you know the meaning of the word 'eulogy'? Webster defines it as '. . . praise in fine language . . .' and, originally, '. . . to bless,' from the

Greek eulogia, which means to speak well of in blessing. And did you know that the Aramaic word usually translated as 'blessed' was their common word for 'happy'! A 'blessing' means 'to restore happiness.' So, this very act of eulogizing Bruce means we have been dispensing and restoring happiness, which is the only thing . . . but I mean THE ONLY thing Bruce ever wanted for any of us! What an awesome gift to the world is Bruce Di Marsico's Option Method! Let those who have eyes to see and ears to hear . . . Stop! Look! Listen!

"Now, then: If I were to tell the story of my friend, Bruce Di Marsico, a story that would capture the essence and ground of his being, a story that would capture, in words, everything Bruce would want us to know and remember . . . it would be this story . . .

"'Once upon a time, there lived a man . . . who was happy!

"'. . . and so it was . . . *Amen.*'"

Epilogue

After the service, I stood in Bruce's living room amongst all those people I had seen come and go over the years. I felt as if I'd been invited backstage after some long-running production for the final cast party. There was the music room where I watched him play the piano so many years ago, the chair he sat on when we had so many of our wonderful earth-shattering conversations. I went into the kitchen, and there were his wife and several others sitting at the oversized kitchen table, talking. I imagined them having so many conversations while I crouched in the wine cellar all those years ago.

I was not really quite sure what to do with myself and I started to wander, into the backyard, where all those fantastic lawn parties had taken place, down the steps into the cellar where the blackboard still hung on the wall. It's older than I am. I went up the stairs to the second floor library. It was a comfortable room with wing-backed chairs, floor-to-ceiling bookcases, a small love seat. And boxes upon boxes piled upon each other in one corner. They were marked by the years 1965–1975, 1976–1986, 1987–present. I sat on the love seat and looked at the boxes for a while. And then I got up and opened the one on top: 1965–1975. There were folders inside labeled Creation of the Option Method, Spirituality, Love, Fear, Children. Inside each folder were writings on lined yellow sheets, small pads, spiral notebooks, even a few napkins. His writings.

The boxes took my breath away. I felt connected to them in a way that surprised me but somehow seemed very natural. I had been connected to Bruce's words my whole life, and now here they were in boxes. Boxes.

I took out the folder labeled Creation of the Option Method, opened it, and read:

I created the Option Method for happiness.

It was dated 1970, the year I was born. And —

If you believed that at this time tomorrow you were going to be un-happy, what would you feel now?

If you were to believe now that at this time tomorrow you were going to become very happy, what would you feel now?

There was a folder filled with his handwriting on scraps of paper of all shapes and sizes. One piece was dated September 9, 1975. It read:

Becoming aware that things may not be perfect, or that you may be unhappy, or God isn't taking care of you, or that something is wrong, or you can think bad things — are all merely thoughts. Since you don't like those thoughts, don't believe that they reflect reality or truth. What they really mean is that you would love to be more aware that nothing is wrong. You are always happy. God is all.

I opened the folder labeled Love. There was a paper entitled "To Love is to be Happy."

To love is to be happy and do what you want, whatever you want.

Such a simple statement. It could change my life if I let it.

"That's not even everything," said a voice from the door. Bruce's wife. She came in and sat down, and we both looked at the boxes. "What do you see?" she asked me.

I laughed because I was just thinking of a fire. What if a fire de-stroyed all of this? It could all be lost. But I didn't say that. I said, "I see possibilities. What do you see?"

"I see books," she said. "I'm not sure what the books will be, but I see them. I see all these writings in books." She looked at me. "Aren't you going to be a writer?" she asked.

"A writer? Why would you think that?"

"Well, let's see," she said. She went over to the tower of boxes, moved some out of the way until she came to one that said Miscellaneous. She pulled out a file and handed it to me. It was labeled Annie. A chill ran up my back all the way to the top of my head. I opened the folder and there were all my silly stories from school, from the writer's club, and even one I had written for Bruce but never gave him called "The Diamond Field." It was a story about a man who finds a diamond in a field and is so grateful and happy, until he notices another diamond and another and another. With each new discovery, instead of feeling richer, he feels poorer, as if his multitude of riches renders each diamond worthless. That story had poured out of me and I had never truly understood what it meant.

"Where did these come from?" I couldn't believe these were in there, with his writings. My mind was spinning like a top, trying to grasp the meaning of all of this. My writing had always been kind of a secret thing. I rarely showed them to anyone and kept them filed in a box under my bed with my high school yearbook and assorted pictures and old birthday cards. Me, a writer? I thought I was an administrative assistant. There was a job waiting for me in Colorado right now. It's as though some giant gear just clicked into place, moving me forward on a whole new track.

"Where do you think these came from? Your mom."

"My mom? I don't understand why she would do that? She never even showed that much interest in my writing."

"Your mom was very proud of you. When she came to see Bruce, she always brought something you wrote, I think as a kind of gift. She noticed things in your writing that reminded her of Bruce, actually. Like 'The Diamond Field.' When you wrote that story, Bruce was actually talking to his students about casting pearls before swine. He was noticing that he was teaching them all the same thing, but some were joyous and some were blasé. Your story kind of said it all. He read it to his class."

"He didn't! He couldn't have."

She laughed. "Annie," she said. "I know Bruce had a huge effect on you from the time you were a little thing. Did it ever occur to you that you affected him as well?"

I couldn't help it. My eyes welled up with tears. It felt as if Bruce were standing right here in the room with us. "I loved him so much," I said. "What can I do to help with all this?"

"He always used to say that you were his best student. Maybe it's time for you to be the teacher."

I nodded, remembering his words: *There is no more loving vocation than to question unhappiness.*

She smiled and handed me a box. "Get to work," she told me.

And I did.

Credits

This book is based on the life and teachings of Bruce M. Di Marisco. I gratefully acknowledge his wife, Deborah Mendel, who has given me permission to reproduce his published and unpublished writings, as well as recorded material. I have used this material in three ways:

First, most chapters begin with italicized portions taken directly from Bruce's writings. Portions of his writings also appear within chapters in italics. Bruce's writings are also available in a book edited by Deborah Mendel, entitled *The Option Method: Unlock Your Happiness with Five Simple Questions*, available at *www.choosehappiness.net*.

Second, portions of taped lectures have been included in two chapters: "Consider the Possibilities," on page 19, contains portions of a lecture given at the Ethical Cultural Society, April 1, 1973. This chapter is not meant to recreate the entire lecture, which is available in its entirety under the title, *The Key To A Happy Life*. Bruce Di Marsico presents the Option Method, available at *www.choosehappiness .net*. The chapter entitled "God's Prayer to Man," page 241, contains portions of a lecture taped in New Jersey, November 1995. This lecture is available in its entirety under the title, *The Happiness Secret: Is Happiness a Choice? The Option Method Philosophy*, available at *www.choosehappiness.net*.

Third, several chapters include Option Method sessions, as follows:

"What If the Answer to Your Problems Is Already Within You?" page 63

"The Opposite of Wrong," page 110

"Happiness Is for Other People," page 118

"Mom's Turn," page 215

"Letting Go," page 224

The sessions are fiction and are based on my extensive experience with Bruce Di Marsico over more than two decades, through Option Method training, including my own sessions with him, as well as extensive observations of his sessions with clients.

All other chapters that include Bruce's thoughts, words and actions have been constructed by me based on my longstanding personal relationship with him as a student and friend, as well as his extensive writings.

Next, I am grateful to Raymond Gombach for permission to use his wonderful eulogy, partially included in "Once There Was a Man Who Was Happy," page 251.

About the Author

Wendy Dolber has been involved in Option Method training and consultation since the early 1970s. She met Bruce Di Marsico, the creator of the Option Method, in 1971 at a private institute devoted to training group psychotherapists and lay counselors. She was associated with Bruce for over twenty-five years as his student, associate, and close friend.

Following Bruce's death in 1995, Wendy began working to create a platform to expand the dissemination of his teachings and writings. *The Guru Next Door: A Teacher's Legacy* is the first of three books to be published. Option Method is the cornerstone of Wendy's life and worldview. She has spent the last three decades immersed in the practice of the Method for her own personal growth and happiness. Additionally, she has worked with clients all over the world.

In her primary occupation as a leading affordable housing bond analyst, she uses Option Method principles to successfully navigate the challenging and ever-changing corporate environment. As a managing director for a major financial services company, Wendy has authored many articles on affordable housing finance. Through the years, she has written as well about the Option Method, most recently at *www. OptionMethodNetwork.com*. She also contributed to *The Option Method: Unlock Your Happiness With Five Simple Questions*, by Bruce Di Marsico, a posthumous publication edited by Deborah Mendel, Bruce's widow.

Wendy has received ongoing recognition for her work in the affordable housing industry and also for her fiction writing by The New Jersey State Council on the Arts. She makes her home in northern New Jersey.

Index of Option Method Concepts

Order Form

Give the gift of *The Guru Next Door: A Teacher's Legacy* to your loved ones, friends, and colleagues.

Place orders at *www.TheGuruNextDoor.com*, check your favorite bookstore, or order here!

❑ YES, I want ____ copies of *The Guru Next Door: A Teacher's Legacy* at $12.95 each, plus $4.95 shipping per book. New Jersey residents, please add 7% sales tax.

My check or money order for $_____ is enclosed.

Please charge my ❑ Visa ❑ MasterCard ❑ Discover

Name _____

Organization _____

Address _____

City/State/Zip _____

Country _____

Phone _____ Email _____

Card# _____

Card Verification # (three-digit code on back of card)_____

Expiration Date _____

Signature _____

Please return form to:
   Pathway Book Service
   P.O. Box 89
   Gilsum, New Hampshire 03448

Call to place your credit card order: 1-800-345-6665

Email: *pbs@pathwaybook.com*

Fax: 1-603-357-2073